MATT WHYMAN

The Overlook Press
New York, NY

This edition first published in hardcover in the United States in 2014 by
The Overlook Press, Peter Mayer Publishers, Inc.

141 Wooster Street
New York, NY 10012
www.overlookpress.com

For bulk and special sales, please contact sales@overlookny.com,
or write us at the above address

Cataloging-in-Publication Data is available from the Library of Congress.

Printed in the United States of America
ISBN 978-1-4683-0856-3
1 3 5 7 9 8 6 4 2

*This book is dedicated to my children,
who put up with my cooking on a daily basis.*

APERITIF

At the table, Titus Savage spotted his son picking his teeth with one finger.

'Manners,' he reminded the boy quietly. 'We're not animals.'

As he spoke, the rest of the family continued with their dessert. Everyone seemed subdued and even exhausted, which was in complete contrast to when they sat down to eat. It was the boy, Ivan, who had been first to finish. Like any twelve-year-old with nothing left on his plate, he began to fidget and sigh to himself.

'Can I get up now?' he asked hopefully. 'My computer's waiting for me to make the next move at chess. I *will* beat it this time.'

His father responded by inviting him to look around.

'When everyone is ready,' he said. 'This is a special occasion, after all.'

At the opposite end of the table from Titus sat an angel. At least that's how Titus viewed his wife, Angelica. Without her, family life would fall apart. She kept the house immaculate, and her cooking today had been simply divine. Titus caught her eye as she spooned the last of the dessert into her mouth. It was a trifle she had prepared, using a home-made recipe for the jello. Like every course of the meal they had enjoyed, the taste was unusual but compelling. For a moment, Angelica looked embarrassed. It was as if she felt she should not have been caught losing herself to the taste quite so openly. Still, Titus seemed to relish her expression. He sat back, clasped his hands across a surprisingly lean stomach given the amount of food he'd just consumed, and considered his children. While Ivan had already finished, his sister continued to take small, almost reluctant mouthfuls. Titus recognized that the family had put away a feast. Even so, he was surprised to see her looking quite so indifferent to clearing her plate.

'Something on your mind, Sasha?' Titus reached for his water glass to freshen his palate. 'This is your favorite, isn't it?'

'I'm good,' she said, without looking up.

Both kids had inherited his crow-black hair. Sasha kept her locks pinned neatly with a series of clips, while Ivan's high hairline suggested it would one day whiten, thin and recede just as Titus had experienced as a younger man. Nowadays, he shaved his dome on a daily basis. Titus found it commanded respect, especially in the workplace. Right now, however, his attention was locked on his eldest child. Sasha ran her spoon around the inside of the bowl but was clearly just toying with it. He glanced at his wife, seeking some explanation for their daughter's behavior. Angelica just shrugged as if to suggest that she was none the wiser.

'Are you feeling sick, honey?' Angelica had spent much of the day preparing this meal. As ever, it had all been planned meticulously, from sourcing the ingredients to the cooking and the ceremonial serving. For Titus to see their firstborn show such a lack of enthusiasm was frankly a little insulting. 'There's nothing wrong with it, is there?'

Sasha set her spoon down in the bowl.

'I'm fine. The food is great. I'm just not that hungry right now.'

For a moment, Titus and Angelica shared the same puzzled and concerned expression. It was an awkward moment that was also felt by Ivan.

'Hey, I have a joke,' he announced, and waited until everyone was looking at him. 'OK, why didn't the chicken make it across the road?'

Titus turned to his son.

'Go on. Why not?'

'Because it was crushed under the wheels of a bus!'

The silence that greeted the punchline seemed to come as a surprise to the boy.

'That's really terrible,' said Sasha, shaking her head. 'Pretty sick, actually.'

'So, now you're an expert in comedy?' Ivan glared at his sister, stung by the criticism. 'There's not one funny bone in your body.'

'Nobody's laughing,' she said, and gestured at the others.

'But it's a great joke!'

'More like a cry for help.'

'That's enough.' Titus showed them both his palms. 'This is no place for an argument. Ivan, perhaps you should keep your jokes to yourself. Sasha, it's unlike you to be so harsh. What's the matter?'

'Dad, really. Just leave it.'

Ivan narrowed his gaze at his sister. A thin smile crossed his lips.

'Sasha's got a boyfriend,' he said, and sat back to watch her squirm. 'She's in love. It's killed her appetite.'

'He's not exactly a boyfriend,' Sasha said quickly, before scowling at her brother. 'Jack and I are just good friends.'

'Friends who hold hands at break time! And he's in the year above, which is basically cradle-robbing.'

'Ivan, maybe you shouldn't keep your computer waiting.'

The way their father said this, so calmly and measured, left Sasha thinking she might be in for an interrogation. Her parents weren't overly strict, but they were very, very protective.

'Could you look in on Grandpa on the way?' Angelica placed a hand on Ivan's wrist as he rose to leave. 'I put his main course through the blender, so he shouldn't have had a problem with it. Just go quietly. The baby is sleeping.'

Ivan sighed to himself, nodded once and then shot a victorious look at his sister. Sasha chose not to clash with him again. Their mother might have just tried to defuse the situation by changing the subject, but it was clear that wasn't going to work with her dad. Even a mention of the youngest family member had failed to draw his attention. Titus adored his little daughter, Kat, who at fifteen months wasn't exactly a baby any more, but that was just how they liked to treat her. Kat looked totally different from her siblings, with blonde ringlets and an expression of pure innocence. If Sasha was about to disappoint her father, as she feared might be the case, no doubt Kat would live up to his expectations in due course.

'Jack is really nice,' she said eventually. 'It's nothing serious.'

'Well, that's good to hear,' said Angelica. 'Isn't it, Titus?'

The prompt served to soften his frown. To hear that Sasha had a boyfriend was a new experience for Titus. It only seemed like yesterday that she was dressing up as a fairy princess just as so many little girls liked to do. This was a whole new challenge to him as a parent, but then it wouldn't defeat him. Family came first, no matter what.

'Maybe you'd like to invite . . .' Titus trailed off and looked to his wife for a prompt.

'Jack,' Angelica reminded him. 'She said his name was Jack.'

Titus nodded, clearly struggling with it all.

'It would be great if Jack could join us for dinner one day.'

'Dad!' Sasha looked aghast. 'Too soon?'

'She's right,' said Angelica. 'I'm sure we'll meet him when the time is right.'

'Maybe,' Sasha mumbled, staring at the napkin in her lap.

Angelica glanced at Titus, and then switched her gaze right back to their daughter.

'But, you know, when you're ready,' she told her, 'Jack would be welcome to come for a bite to eat.'

Sasha began to wring her napkin through her fingers.

'Is that too much as well?' her father inquired. 'Help us out here, honey?'

A moment passed before Sasha replied. When she did, knowing what kind of response would follow, it clearly took her a great deal of courage.

'You might as well know now. Jack is . . . well, not like us.'

'In what way?' asked Titus.

Sasha faced each parent in turn.

'He's vegetarian.'

For a second, it looked as if both Titus and Angelica Savage had frozen in time. Sasha reminded herself to breathe, and then decided it might be best for everyone if she too left the table.

FIRST COURSE

1

When bad things come to light about someone, it's easy to overlook what was good about them.

For Sasha Savage, only her close friends can remember what she was really like. They could tell you everything from the name of her first crush (some carefully constructed, badly chosen boy band bassist currently serving jail time for sexual misdemeanors), to what she told them was her guiltiest secret (the fact that she still dreamed her first time would be with him). She could laugh at herself, looked out for others, and was even ranked as 'trustworthy' in the last online quiz they ever took together, entitled *Friend or Faux?*

Before the story broke, Sasha was all set to turn sixteen with only her exams standing in the way of the best summer of her life. Then the truth emerged. Overnight, as if a spell had been cast from above, she and her family became monsters.

The investigation closed some time ago. The media feeding frenzy has moved on, while the controversial movie was just too soon, uncomfortably sensational and went straight to DVD. Despite everything, it is perhaps a measure of Sasha's character that her friends still claim they would like to carry on where they left off. Should she ever resurface, which is considered close to unthinkable, they wouldn't shut the door on her. Nor would they contact the Detective Inspector on the number he told them to call if there was ever a development. Not right away, at least. They might keep their distance from her, of course, which is understandable under the circumstances. More strikingly, nobody would push her for any kind of explanation. Sasha never breathed a word to them in all those years they'd known her, so why would she offer one now? Instead, they'd try to see through the portrait that'd been painted to find the girl who had shared so much of their lives. Besides, with every last scrap of evidence out in the open, from phone records to witness statements and even the grisly report from the drainage experts, it only takes a little imagination to get under the skin of the Savage family, and come close to the truth about what really happened.

Take her mother, Angelica. She headed into the garden the morning after Sasha overshadowed the family meal with news that she was dating. At times of stress, she always reached for her pruning shears in a bid to keep a sense of control.

'I know,' she said, with her cell phone propped between her shoulder and ear. Angelica paused to pinch another rose by the stem before snipping through it with the blades. 'Titus isn't happy at all about the situation. First she drops a grade in Spanish, and now this. A boyfriend.'

As ever, Angelica Savage looked as immaculate as her surroundings. She was an elegant woman with fine features and a dark bob tapered at the neck. A smile, which was rare, would shatter her cut-glass air, though she could be thoroughly charming where necessary. As a dinner hostess, for example, she was much admired by friends and neighbors. Her dishes were always adventurous, but cooked to perfection and served with fine wine and easy conversation. Things were different if you chose to just drop by unannounced. Then, just for a fleeting moment, Angelica would summon a look so cold it left you feeling as if you had invaded her time and space.

'I doubt very much this little love affair will last,' she continued. 'From what Sasha has told us he doesn't sound as if the young man has much backbone. I should imagine it'll be over before the next booking.'

The moment her phone had begun to ring, Angelica knew that it would be the agency. She had set up a ring tone for that number so she could choose whether or not to answer. This depended on her mood as much as her credit card bill, which was why Angelica had reluctantly signed up some years before in a bid to pay it off. The agency specialized in renting out domestic locations for commercial shoots. It wasn't something she relished, but opening up the doors to their home every now and then kept her bank at bay.

For all the wrong reasons, everyone remembers the advertisement for the furniture polish. It was running when the family dominated the news. Not that it'll ever be aired again. Even so, despite the reason it was pulled, nobody can deny that the Savages had good taste. They lived on the hill overlooking the park and the city beyond, in an elegant Georgian house with tall sashed windows and a gravel drive. The place is boarded up now. It's destined for demolition because no buyer can be found, and a far cry from how it used to be. Were you to pay a visit before the former owners made headlines, perhaps to guess what kind of family might live there, you'd be forgiven for thinking it had been professionally styled. Everything from the careful lighting to the antique wallpaper worked perfectly together. The large and airy living room was a highlight, while the equally splendid kitchen-diner suggested a household with a passion for good food. From the table in front of the French windows, you could look out across the garden, always heady with the scent of culinary herbs, and admire the color and life. In particular, the roses were a treat. They always bloomed like no other, even out of season, which Angelica Savage modestly linked to the home-cooked compost she used to nourish the soil.

'Very well,' she told Marsha from the agency, the woman who had called to check the house was available that Friday. 'Just be sure this time the client signs the insurance clause *before* filming begins.'

Despite her tone, Angelica got along well with Marsha. She admired the agent's steel grip on arrangements from start to finish. Angelica always chose not to be present during a shoot. She and any family members would head upstairs for the duration and stay out of the way. It was an upheaval, but she knew they were in safe hands. By the time her husband returned from work, the crew would be gone and everything back in place as if nobody had been there at all. Even if redecoration was needed, the agency wouldn't sign off the job until everything appeared as it had been found. Angelica couldn't afford to let such standards slip because Titus loathed the whole arrangement. He could've paid off her debt straight away. That's if he weren't married to such a fiercely independent woman. Just one more year, she had promised him the last time they clashed over the issue, and then the front door would be closed for good. As it turned out, Angelica was true to her word. It just wasn't in a way that anyone could've believed at the time.

With roses for the table grasped in one hand, Angelica headed back inside. Titus wouldn't be pleased about the booking, but he needed to know. Every now and then a little extra housework was required before they allowed any strangers into the home. Having arranged the roses in a vase, Angelica rang her husband. Eventually, when the call went to voicemail, she figured he was busy in a meeting.

Titus Savage cursed silently when the phone in his pocket began to ring. He had meant to put it on silent, and simply forgotten. There wasn't much he could do about it at the time. He was lying back with his hands clasped across his chest and his mouth wide open.

'Do you want to answer that?' asked the dental hygienist. At the same time she teased a sickle-shaped scaling instrument between his back molars, which made it impossible for Titus to reply. By the time she removed the scaler from his mouth, the hook impaled with a fine shred of meat, his phone had stopped ringing. The hygienist appeared not to notice. Instead, she held the instrument under the lamp for inspection. Her mouth and nose were covered by a mask, but the gleam in her eyes made it clear she was elated by her catch. 'You're a red meat fan, Mr. Savage, am I right?'

Titus plucked a tissue from the box on the steel-topped cart beside him.

'I eat well,' he said, dabbing at his mouth. 'Better than most, in fact.'

The hygienist wiped the scaler on the back of her glove. Titus eyed the shred, which had probably been there for no more than twenty-four hours, and wished he had flossed that morning. He had a meeting to attend in the next ten minutes, only now he risked having to endure a lecture.

'Can I ask about your brushing routine, Mr. Savage?

'Trust me,' he said, and balled the tissue in his fist. 'I appreciate how important it is to do a thorough job.'

Titus Savage enjoyed a formidable reputation in the city's financial district. The investment company he founded many years earlier sought to assist struggling businesses by restructuring them. It was only recently, following the investigation, that the true nature of the operation became clear. Back then, had anyone accused him of 'predatory working practices', chances are they would've been sued. Titus was a familiar figure in the district, with his bald dome, penetrating blue eyes and the signature silk scarf which he folded around his neck on leaving the dental surgery. He glanced at his watch next. Satisfied that he was still in time for his meeting, Titus began to walk briskly in the direction of the office, buttoning his coat as he went.

*   *   *

It was a bright morning, but with so many towering buildings the sun rarely made it to ground level. Unusually, for a man of Russian stock, Titus always felt the chill. He sometimes joked that this was because he'd never visited the motherland. He certainly looked on the Slavic side, but had been born and raised in England. London was his home, and the financial district his stalking ground. Titus Savage knew every restaurant, coffee shop and cut-through, which at first explained why he ducked unexpectedly into a back street within yards of the office doors.

Instead of heading for a side entrance to the building, however, Titus took to the gloom under a fire escape. There, he stood with his back to the wall and explored his freshly cleaned teeth with his tongue.

Three minutes later, a man in a suit hurried off the main street. He looked nervous, as if far from his natural environment. Seeing Titus Savage step out of the shadows did little for his manner.

'You're late,' said Titus. 'And I'm busy.'

'I'm sorry.' The man raised his palms. Perspiration needled his forehead. He wore rounded glasses that began to steam now he had stopped. 'This isn't easy for me, Mr. Savage. I'm toast if anyone from the firm knows I'm talking to you.'

'Your firm is toast if you *don't* talk to me.' Titus produced an envelope from the inside pocket of his coat. He offered it to the man, and then tipped it away from his grasp when he reached for it. 'The flash drive?' he said, as if to remind him why they had arranged to meet.

Hurriedly, the man found the drive in his pocket and completed the exchange.

'It's all there,' he assured Titus. 'The balance sheet for

the last quarter and the minutes from this week's meeting with the bank.'

'I hear they're playing hardball.'

'We're being hammered,' the man said. 'On their terms, we just can't meet the interest payment.'

'As I predicted several months ago,' said Titus. 'You've allowed yourself to become too bloated as a business. It needs carving up if you're going to survive.'

'Which is why I want to help you,' the man cut in. He looked around one more time. 'I know in your hands the firm is finished in its current form, and I'm grateful for the cash you've just paid for the flash drive. But what I need more than anything, Titus, is a promise that I'll still have a job once you've cut out all the fat. I have a family that relies on my income. Without it, we're finished.'

Titus Savage smiled and clapped the man on the shoulder.

'How are the kids?' he asked.

The man seemed uncomfortable about answering the question for a moment.

'Good,' he said eventually. 'Yours?'

'The same,' Titus answered. 'Sasha has some issues which I plan to work on, but my boy is really beginning to shine.'

For the second time that week, Ivan Savage took a seat in the principal's office. She sat across from him with both hands flat on the table, one on top of the other, and her mouth pressed tight. She had said nothing beyond summoning him into her office. Ivan looked up at her, well aware that she was awaiting some explanation.

'It was meant to be funny,' he reasoned. 'Those girls just have no sense of humor.'

The principal was a fair-skinned woman with shoulder-length red hair she tied back in a band. At home and weekends, when she let it fall in ringlets, she was known as Gemma. In school, to staff and pupils, Ms. Turner was not someone who thrived on having her patience tested.

'What is funny,' she asked eventually, 'about finding thumb tacks in your school lunch?'

The boy shrugged, like she just didn't get it.

'I wanted to liven up lunch break. That's all.'

'Ivan, you could've seriously harmed three of my students. There's nothing amusing about pain and suffering. You should consider yourself very lucky that one of the lunch ladies saw what you were doing.'

Ivan sat on his hands and stared at the floor. With his skewed tie and one shirt tail hanging free, he didn't look like a student capable of getting all A's in the sciences and mathematics. Still, that's what he was achieving. So long as the subject contained logic at its core, the boy would thrive. At the same time, Ivan was seriously struggling with the arts. Ms. Turner had his report card in front of her, in fact. It concluded that while Ivan was an enthusiastic student, his critical, creative and interpretive skills were often deemed inappropriate. Ms. Turner had an example right in front of her. It was taken from a short story Ivan had written about the day in the life of an animal. While most of his classmates picked playful pets, the boy had opted to write five hundred words from the point of view of a mouse being swallowed alive by an anaconda. The piece was capably written, but had left his English teacher so disturbed that she reported it to Ivan's homeroom teacher.

'Are you going to tell my dad?' Ivan looked up. He seemed troubled at the thought. It was something Ms. Turner spotted straight away.

'What do you think might happen if I did inform your father, Ivan? What would he do?'

'To me?' Ivan said with some surprise. 'Oh, nothing. I was worried about you.'

Ms. Turner blinked and tipped her head to one side. She drew breath to question just what the boy had meant by that, but then thought better of it. The kid was just weird.

'Ivan, I've consulted with your teacher. We've agreed that it would be good for you to have a session with Mrs. Risbie.'

'But she's the school counselor,' complained Ivan. 'I don't need to see a shrink. Everyone will make fun of me and I'll just get upset with them.'

'Then what would happen?' asked Ms. Turner.

'Nothing.' Ivan shrugged and looked to the table. 'Not right away,' he added under his breath.

'The session with Mrs. Risbie would be an informal arrangement,' Ms. Turner stressed. 'A one-off.'

'Why?'

Ms. Turner closed the report in front of her.

'School is an opportunity, Ivan. A chance for you to make the most of what we can offer in order to bring out the best in yourself. If you want any incentive, just look at what your sister has achieved.'

* * *

Two minutes after the lunch-break bell sounded, Sasha

Savage had still to peel herself away from an intense and passionate kiss with her new boyfriend. Jack Greenway had a lot to offer. To celebrate passing his driving test, and the beginning of his new life as a high school junior, the young man's father had gifted him a second-hand hybrid car. The vehicle ran on a combination of diesel and battery. Its low carbon emissions were in tune with Jack's commitment to the environment. When parked behind the school, it also proved to be the perfect place to make out with someone as hot as Sasha.

'You're so beautiful,' murmured Jack, who took a breath before going in again.

'I really should be going.' Sasha placed two fingers on his lips. 'It's chemistry next.'

She watched his mouth stretch into a lazy smile and then moved her fingers away.

'*This* is chemistry,' he told her, before finding her lips once more.

Nobody was surprised when Jack and Sasha started dating. If anything, it should've been something that happened earlier. Instead, Jack went out with a string of older girls, most of whom had now left for college, while in her year Sasha was just one of those types that tended to intimidate boys. She didn't do so on purpose. In a way, her striking looks could work against her. Sasha was willow-tall with long, slender limbs and carried herself like a ghost in human form. You could tell she had Russian blood in her by that heart-shaped face, delicate nose and high cheek-bones. Complete with the clearest blue eyes in school, she was out of this world in every way. Not that she recognized this in herself. Sasha wasn't shy. Just cautious. Unfortunately all those boys who gave it a shot found the power of speech failed them. That is until everyone returned for the start of the new school year and Jack looked around to see what was on offer.

Unlike Sasha, Jack knew that he had been blessed with good looks. Every girl in school placed him at the top of their list. Even from behind, his broad shoulders and tight hips told you this one was worth checking out when he turned. But it wasn't so much Jack's dramatically shaggy cut and easy smile that charmed as much as his manner. It was something he hoped Sasha was about to discover for herself, by his climbing into her orbit with such passion that anything else of importance in her life just fell away. In such a spin, her world would surely come to revolve around him. For now, however, Sasha was officially late for class.

'OK. Time out. I don't want to get into trouble.'

'Another minute, eh?' Jack breathed out with a faint moan and dipped down to nuzzle her throat.

'Oh, this isn't fair!' Sasha protested weakly. She half closed her eyes for a moment, only to snap them wide open on feeling his teeth find her neck. 'Uh, what are you doing?'

'Tasting you,' he said, before drawing her skin between his lips.

'Jack!' This time Sasha pulled away. She pressed a hand to her neck, looking both shocked and surprised. 'A love bite? Really?'

'Just a little gesture.' Jack grinned and pushed a hand through his hair. 'I want everyone to know you're mine.'

'What are you, like twelve years old? Nobody does love bites anymore.' Sasha examined her fingertips as if to check he hadn't drawn blood. Then she glanced back at Jack, and grinned despite herself. 'Promise me you'll never do that again,' she said. 'It wouldn't go down well at home.'

Jack stretched an arm across the back of Sasha's seat.

'Relax. We've been dating for what? Three weeks?'

'Four,' said Sasha, and flipped the visor down so she could check her reflection in the mirror. She lifted her head, just to be sure Jack hadn't left a mark, and then examined her lips. As she did so, Jack leaned across to kiss her on the cheek.

'Then we should celebrate our one-month anniversary,' he suggested. 'How about I cook for you on Saturday night? My parents are away. We'd have the house to ourselves and I can make you my signature dish. A pinto bean chili with eggplant and red pepper.'

By now, Sasha was beginning to feel deeply anxious about being late. Her chemistry teacher would only ask her where she'd been, and *everyone* would know before she'd even summoned an excuse.

'Dinner sounds great,' she said, and reached for the car door handle.

'I'll pick you up at seven thirty.'

'Don't worry. I'll walk over.' Sasha grabbed her school bag and pushed open the door. 'I have legs.'

'It's no problem,' insisted Jack. 'I'm beginning to think you're ashamed of introducing me to the folks!'

Standing now, Sasha hoisted her bag strap onto her

shoulder. 'Had I let you get away with that love bite,' she warned him, smiling warmly at the same time, 'my dad would've eaten you alive.'

2

'Ribs. *Ribs!*'

The baby on the kitchen floorboards gurgled happily when her mother turned to face her. At first, Angelica Savage looked unsure if she had heard her youngest child correctly. When the little one repeated the word for a third time, she shrieked with delight, set down the knife on the chopping board, and scooped her into her arms.

'You clever girl,' she said, and spun around with her in sheer delight.

Katya was late to the family, and a surprise to her parents. With two older siblings, her father sometimes said that Kat needed a big personality as a matter of survival. She displayed this in the form of an easy smile and tendency to babble and coo as a means of communication. As Kat had yet to show any interest in climbing onto her feet, Angelica regarded this moment as a milestone in her development. Just then, on hearing the front door open, she was ready to share the news with her husband.

'Something smells good,' said Titus, and parked his leather briefcase against the dresser. 'I had to skip lunch today, so I'm famished.'

'Guess what?' Angelica stood before him, a late sun pouring in through the French windows behind her, which cast both mother and child in silhouette. 'Go on, guess!'

After such a long day, including an afternoon spent poring over documents and spreadsheets from a flash drive that shouldn't have been in his possession, Titus was in no mood for games.

'I give up,' he said, as Angelica moved out of the glaring sun to soften him with a kiss. She knew Titus could be a little grumpy on his return from work, but it didn't last long once he was back in the family fold. 'Is it good news or bad?' Titus asked. 'If it's bad, it can wait until after dinner. I can't digest bad news on an empty stomach.'

Beaming still, Angelica gestured at the child in her arms. Katya was gnawing at her fist, a mark of her latest teething troubles. Titus watched her drooling all over her little knuckles and sensed his mood lifting. She was a sweetheart, spun from sugar and wide-eyed innocence. He was looking forward to seeing her incisors come through.

'It isn't bad news,' said Angelica. 'It's not even good news. It's *amazing* news!'

'Go on.' Titus touched his palm to the little girl's cheek. Katya beamed and giggled. 'What have I missed?'

'Listen.' Angelica turned her attention to the child in her arms. 'Do it again, Kitty Kat. Do it for Daddy.'

Katya continued to suck at her fingers, so that when she made a noise it was muffled. Gently, Angelica removed her fingers from her mouth.

'*Ribs!*'

24

Angelica switched her attention back to Titus, who stood rapt.

'Kat's first word!' she declared.

'Ribs! *Ribs!*'

'Ribs?' Slowly, a smile eased across his face. 'Oh, Kat, that's beautiful! What a proud moment this is!'

Sharing in his delight, Angelica handed their child across. Titus squeezed her to his chest and then raised the chuckling toddler over his head.

'*Ribs!*'

'I'm not even cooking ribs,' said Angelica.

'Maybe it's her favorite.' Titus returned the child to the floor, where several toys lay waiting for her. 'So, what's for dinner?'

'Leftovers,' she said. 'Nothing special, I'm afraid.'

For a moment, Titus appeared disappointed. Still, he managed a smile for his wife. He understood that nothing could go to waste, even if it lacked the taste and intensity from the first time round.

'In your hands,' he said anyway, 'I'm sure it'll be delicious. Now, what's everyone else doing?'

'Ivan and Grandpa are in their rooms.' Angelica returned to the stove before she finished. 'We're expecting Sasha any time now.'

'Where is she?'

'Oh, just out,' she said, with her back to Titus. 'I'm not sure where.'

Titus considered this news in silence. Out without knowing where didn't sound good in his books. Yes, Sasha was a growing girl, but somehow it was all just going a bit too fast for his liking. He didn't want to keep her under lock and key. Far from it. But if she was out there taking risks, he wanted to make sure she kept those risks to a minimum, or even eradicated them completely. He had been raised to believe in this approach to life, and that's what he strived to pass on to the next generation.

'Sasha really needs to let us know where she's going,' he grumbled. 'Have you texted her?'

Angelica faced her husband.

'She promised to be home in time for dinner,' she said, with some tension in her voice. 'We have to give her a chance.'

Titus held her gaze for a moment, and then his shoulders sagged. He returned his attention to his youngest daughter, who was shuffling across the floorboards. Slowly, his expression brightened.

'You know it won't be long before Katya eats with us. She's shaping up to be quite the Savage.'

Angelica smiled adoringly.

'All in good time,' she said. 'Let the last of her teeth come through first.'

Titus nodded to himself and then lifted his daughter into his arms.

'Well, let's hope that day comes soon. It'll be such an honor to have all my family around the table!'

Ninety minutes later, with the baby monitor beside the toaster indicating that Katya was asleep in her crib, Sasha returned home to find herself late for dinner.

'Hi,' she said breezily, well aware that her dad had that face on him again. There he was with one elbow on the table, gazing across at her with the fork poised like a spear fisherman.

'Dinner is in the wok,' he told her. 'Your mother had it ready some time ago.'

Angelica had served up a stir fry from the remains of yesterday's meal. Ivan was close to finishing. He made a lot of noise sucking in the last noodles before picking up the bowl to drink down the broth. It was only when he set it back on the table that he found everyone looking at him.

'Oh, Ivan,' said Angelica. 'How many times?'

At first, it looked as if Titus would also turn his displeasure on his son. Instead, leaving the boy with a stern look, Ivan waited for Sasha to take her place at the table. She was hungry, having skipped lunch to spend time with Jack, and had heaped her bowl with food. Any hope she might have had about getting away without being questioned stopped at her first mouthful.

'So.' Titus paused and cleared his throat. 'Been on a date?'

Sasha traded glances between her parents, chewing at the same time.

'No,' she said eventually. 'I was at a friend's house finishing a project for school.'

Titus didn't look as if he believed a word she'd just said. Even though it was the truth, he continued to look at her as if awaiting a confession. Sensing the atmosphere thicken, it was Angelica who changed the subject.

'Marsha called this morning,' she announced. 'We have a booking for the weekend.'

Her news was met with a brief silence.

'What's wrong with the week?' asked Titus, and scraped his fork around the bowl. 'When I'm out at work.'

'It's a magazine shoot paying double rate.' Angelica bristled in her seat. 'And they'll be here until late on Saturday.'

It was Ivan who groaned, though his dad made the very same face.

'That means we'll be stuck upstairs all day!' the boy protested. 'It's so boring with people in the house!'

'Why don't you spend time with friends?' asked Sasha quietly, and then smiled to herself because that wasn't an option for her kid brother. 'Oh yeah,' she said, as if to answer her own question. 'You don't have any.'

Titus balled his napkin and deposited it in his bowl. Then he drew Angelica's attention to the kitchen surfaces.

'After last night's feast we're going to have to work *very* hard to get this place ready,' he told her. 'I wish you'd run this past me first.'

Angelica listened to each complaint in turn looking increasingly tense.

'Actually, I'll be out that evening,' said Sasha. 'You should all do the same thing.'

'Where are you going?' asked Titus. 'Shouldn't you check with us first?'

Even though Sasha expected this kind of response from her father, it didn't stop her feeling a little suffocated.

'OK, well, I'm going on a date, actually. Jack is cooking.'

'A veggie meal?' Ivan sneered at her sister. 'That's not a date. It's just disappointing.'

Sitting opposite her brother, Sasha just stared at her brother as if to offer him a chance to face his own reflection in her eyes.

'Don't you have a chess game waiting?' she asked. 'Those pawns won't move themselves.'

'Well, I think it's a lovely gesture!' Angelica attempted to sound bright in a bid to support her daughter. 'Though you should make sure you eat properly at lunchtime just in case.'

'Now hold on!' Titus raised a hand to command their attention. 'Sasha, we really ought to meet this young man. It's called responsible parenting. We can't have our daughter going off with just anyone. We need to know he has your best interests at heart. Until then, I'm going to have to say no to an evening out.'

'Dad!' Sasha pushed back her chair to stand, which made an unpleasant scraping noise across the tiles. 'You're being so unreasonable about this. I'm old enough to make my own decisions.'

'Sit down and eat,' said Titus.

'I'm not hungry any more,' Sasha told him. 'Sorry, Mom.'

Angelica gestured for her to leave the room. Under the circumstances, it was better that both father and daughter cooled off at that moment.

'We'll discuss this later!' Titus called after her, raising his voice this time.

'There's nothing more to say.' Sasha left him with a withering look, and then closed the door behind her.

'Now just a minute, young lady! No daughter of mine has the last word in this house!'

A moment later, under the gaze of his wife and son, Titus Savage paid the price for disturbing the peace when the baby monitor popped and crackled.

'Ribs!'

3

Oleg Fedor Savadski, a former officer in the Russian Red Army, took a pinch of fish food and sprinkled it into the bowl. This was how Sasha found him when she reached his open door.

'Hey, Grandpa. What's happening?'

'Do you know what goldfish thrive on more than anything else?' he asked, peering through the glass as the two inhabitants rose to nibble at the flakes.

'Is it their short-term memory?' Sasha closed the door behind her. 'I'd imagine forgetting your past and starting afresh must be quite appealing sometimes.'

Oleg glanced at his granddaughter for a moment, before returning his attention to the bowl.

'The answer is fish meal and fish oil,' he told her, and turned to show her the tub in his hand. 'It's central to their diet. Feasting on their own kind is what brings out the very best in them. Yes, you can offer them a vegetable substitute but they quickly lose their zest, and I only want the best for my babies.'

Oleg, known simply to his family as Grandpa, was exactly one year away from celebrating a century in this world. Like his son, Titus, he sported a bald dome and thick eyebrows. His long gray beard was the most striking aspect of a man who had shrunken and withered over the years. It made him appear immensely wise, like someone who had produced several tomes of epic Russian novels. It was a look that fell away when food became trapped in the strands, however. Then he would appear more like the kind of lost soul you might find shouting at trash cans in a back alley. Since the last of his teeth had lost their moorings, Grandpa preferred his food in liquidized form. Whatever was on the menu, Angelica just passed it through the blender and he would literally lap it up. Like the rest of the family, Grandpa had enjoyed a stir fry made up of the leftovers from the day before. His bowl sat on a tray at the table under the skylight, along with the straw he had used to ingest it.

'I can take that down for you,' said Sasha, who had noticed the bowl.

'It can wait,' Grandpa told her. 'You're welcome to stay here for a while. I heard all the shouting downstairs just now.'

Grandpa occupied the loft space in the family home. It had been converted into simple, clean and bright quarters by Titus when Grandpa came to live with them following the passing of his wife. Both Sasha and Ivan had grown up sharing the house with him. Not that he left his room very often. Still, his door was always open for anyone who wished to spend time with him. Sasha considered herself lucky. Oleg wasn't the kind of grandfather who would sit there with one hand cupped to his ear and mumble incomprehensibly. Above all, he liked to listen as much as talk, which is why Sasha had headed upstairs having fallen out with her father.

'Why does he have to be so controlling?' she asked, taking the chair where Grandpa had just finished his stir fry smoothie. 'Sometimes it feels as if he'd like me to come with an off switch when I don't live up to his expectations.'

'Is this about Jack?' he asked, and placed the tub beside the fish bowl. 'I've heard all about him from Ivan.'

Sasha rolled her eyes.

'So, you know he's a vegetarian.'

Grandpa shuffled across the room. He peered through the skylight. There were no windows in his attic space. Just several points that offered him a clear view of the heavens above, as well as pictures on the wall of family and places from his past.

'There are worse things in this world,' he said. 'And your father is only being protective.'

'Has he always been like this?' asked Sasha, as Grandpa took a seat opposite her. He nodded and regarded his granddaughter.

'Since he was a little boy. But you have to understand why family is so important to him. He knows his roots, Sasha. I come from nothing. *Nechevo.* When I arrived in this country with your grandmother, we had only the rags on our backs. We'd been through hell to get here. The experience changed us both as human beings, and left him with a very strong sense that to survive this life no matter what, you stick together. It's what we did,' he said to finish, and looked at the table. 'During the Siege.'

* * *

33

THE SAVAGES

Sasha had no need to press her grandfather for an explanation. It wasn't because she feared it would lead to an hour-long look back through several chapters of history. The first time he had accounted for his experience during World War II, she and Ivan had sat throughout and barely breathed. Once he'd finished, it became clear to both grandchildren that what he had just shared could never be repeated outside the house. It was only later, during the course of the investigation, that Oleg's background became central to the Savage saga.

Without doubt, Grandpa's wartime experience went some way towards understanding what shaped them as a family. For Oleg Fedor Savadski endured unimaginable hardship and misery, alongside the citizens in Leningrad, when the city was surrounded and cut off from the world by enemy forces. For more than two years, including cruel, harsh and bitter winters, nobody could get out and nearly all supply routes were blocked. With no food available, the people suffered terribly. Up to one and a half million starved to death. Those who lived through it were forced to test the limits of resourcefulness. As the famine grew, people foraged for berries in parkland before going on to hunt birds and rats. Then, with the wildlife consumed, the desperate turned to boiling down belt straps into soup and licking the glue from the back of wallpaper. Oleg was among that number. Stationed in his home city, with a new bride to protect, he pledged to do whatever it took to endure the growing horror.

The city had come under an onslaught. Buildings lay in ruins and bodies sprawled in the streets. As the weeks turned to months, people grew familiar with death. It became a part of everyday life, and for some a means of survival.

At first, the surviving citizens of Leningrad believed that street dogs must be coming out at night to strip some corpses of organs and flesh. An alternative explanation was unthinkable, despite the fact that such dogs had already become food for the table. When word began to spread that gangs were roaming the city, picking off victims to ease their appalling hunger, fear and panic set in. At such an inhumane time, could some desperate souls really be driven to turn on each other? Towards the end of the Siege, the police even set up a special unit to investigate the claims. Oleg was among a small band of soldiers appointed as an army escort to accompany the unit. Unlike so many others, he was in relatively good shape and strong enough to help ensure their safety across the more forbidding quarters of the stricken city. According to reports, just as the investigation began to find substance to the awful rumors, so news filtered through that most had lost all hope of hearing. Thanks to advances by the Allies, the enemy had been forced to pull back from their positions. At last, the blockade that had lasted almost nine hundred days, and turned the city into a living hell, was over. Exhausted but overjoyed, the citizens were free to leave. Oleg and his wife were among that number. In fact, they chose to get out at the earliest opportunity, before the police unit's investigation was complete, and even departed the country just as soon as the war came to an end.

Some years after they arrived in England, with Oleg working quietly as a porter at Smithfield Meat Market, a son was born to the couple. By then, Oleg had changed the family surname to Savage. It sounded more comfortable to an English-speaking ear, and created some distance from their former life. Still, Oleg never forgot his origins. In particular, he and his wife continued to pursue the taste they had acquired during the Siege, and even passed it on to their young son. The food was carefully sourced, of course, and then effectively spirited away to be prepared for the table. With access to herbs, spices and other ingredients, and in the privacy of their kitchen, the couple embarked upon a culinary adventure like no other. They were careful not to overindulge, of course, by turning it into a rare and occasional treat. As a growing boy, it was something Titus came to relish. No other meal came close to stirring such a deep-seated craving in him. Like his parents, the boy found that every mouthful left him feeling blissfully alive. By the time Oleg decided to reveal the main ingredient, there was no going back for his son.

'It feeds the heart and soul,' was how Titus would go on to sell it to Angelica. This was two decades later, shortly before their engagement, after the couple had spent many date nights at his flat simply eating in. 'You feel it in your bones and in your blood,' he went on, before tapping the side of his head. 'Most of all, you feel it in your mind. Am I right?'

Angelica had also reacted with some questions, of course, once she'd come around from her faint and stopped screaming. Yes, it was a shock for her to learn what he had been serving her all this time. It was only human nature, after all. By then, however, Angelica had come to crave the sense of sheer satisfaction delivered by such a feast. Bonded by a shared secret, and deeply in love with this food pioneer, it seemed there was only one thing she could say when Titus dropped down on one knee and asked for her hand in marriage. From that moment on, as the couple set out to build a family, it was clear to Titus that the Savages were a breed apart when it came to good taste. No matter what challenges they faced, he swore to his new bride and then later to Sasha and Ivan, that's exactly how it would stay.

'But Daddy, eating people is wrong.'

It was Sasha who had spoken up. Barely five years old at the time, she sat at the table with her feet swinging under the chair while her father explained where they had obtained the meat on their plates.

'Honey,' he had said with a sigh. 'People are in plentiful supply. Most are free range for much of their lives, and enjoy a happy existence. We don't just eat *anyone*!'

Unlike his sister, Ivan responded to the revelation by asking for second helpings. He seemed completely unconcerned, which Titus put down to his tender age. The boy had only just turned three at the time, after all. As for Sasha, once she'd gotten down from the table she simply headed off to play with her doll's house. Titus wasn't worried, despite her protest. He knew from experience that once someone had tasted the ultimate in flesh, it became a part of who they were.

'So,' said Sasha, in a bid to rouse her grandfather from his thoughts. 'What am I going to do about Dad? I'm dating someone who chooses not to eat dead animal products. That doesn't put him in the same category as a drug addict.'

Oleg blinked as if in surprise at her presence in the room, and then squeezed his beard with one hand.

'Oh, my son is all bark and no bite,' he assured her. 'I'm sure if he meets this young man then his fears will ease. Why not invite him round?'

Sasha sighed to herself.

'Why does everyone in this family want to meet Jack?' she asked.

'Because everyone cares for you,' he said. 'We Savages look out for each other. If we didn't, God alone knows what would happen to us.'

4

The signature at the foot of the letter was convincing. Ivan had been practicing for some time. So, when the boy handed the letter across to Mrs. Risbie, the school counselor, he was confident she would believe the session that was about to take place had parental consent. In Ivan's view, it was in both their interests that his father wasn't involved.

'How are you feeling today?' she asked.

They were sitting across from one another on cheap and worn sofas. Mrs. Risbie wore her bangs like a badly closed pair of curtains. She curled one side behind her ear, which proved unsuccessful when she reached for a cup of tea on the low table between them. Ivan ignored the glass of weak orange juice that she had made for him.

'I feel fine,' he replied with a shrug. 'What do you want to talk about?'

As a psychologist working part time in a school environment, Mrs. Risbie did her best to make her room look as informal as possible. She made no notes, preferring to maintain eye contact with anyone who came to see her.

'Actually, I thought we'd start with an exercise,' she said. 'Would you like to do an exercise, Ivan?'

'Do *you* want to do an exercise?' he asked.

39

'I'd like that.' Mrs. Risbie had already stashed the pack of square cards down the side of the sofa in readiness for the moment. She plucked out the pack and quickly thumbed through to find one to begin. 'It's very simple,' she said, and selected a card to show the boy. 'Each picture features the face of a child. I want you to look at them in turn and tell me what her expression says about how she's feeling.'

'Is that it?' asked Ivan, who was already beginning to sound bored. 'Well, seeing that she's smiling in that one I'd say she's happy.'

'Very good.' Mrs. Risbie brought the next card to the front.

'Perplexed,' he said after a moment.

'Excellent!'

Ivan studied the next card, and then sat back in his seat. 'Thoughtful. Reflective, perhaps?'

Mrs. Risbie smiled and nodded. The kid didn't seem to have an issue relating to other people. Given his vocabulary, it was simply revealing a higher than average intelligence.

'How about this one?' she asked, and flipped around the picture of the girl with the sad face. It showed her looking down, with tear-stained cheeks and her lower lip jutting out.

Ivan sat forward again. He studied the picture for a while, tipping his head one way and then the other.

'It's a tough one,' he said, before looking back at Mrs. Risbie again. 'She looks like someone who can't take a joke.'

'Right.' At times like this, Mrs. Risbie wished she could put the student on pause while she rushed to write down some observations. Instead, she nodded sagely and placed the cards flat on the table. 'Ivan, has there ever been a time when you've felt sad?'

The boy sat on his hands while he thought about this. He looked to the floor, pressing his lips together. Mrs. Risbie couldn't help noticing how focused he seemed. Just waiting for him to answer left her feeling tense.

'When people don't understand me,' he said eventually, and looked directly into her eyes. 'That's when I feel angry . . . sorry, I mean sad.'

'I see.' Mrs. Risbie shifted in position. Ivan wasn't unpleasant company. He was polite. He listened. He considered every question. Even so, there was something about him she found unsettling, though she reminded herself not to entertain such unprofessional thoughts.

'How is home life?' she asked next, hoping to build a bigger picture. 'Tell me about your family.'

This time, Ivan didn't hesitate in his answer. Much to the surprise of Mrs. Risbie, he sat back in his seat and provided a full and detailed description of a seemingly content, stable and supportive domestic environment. By the time he had finished, stopped by the lunch-break bell, she had drawn her own conclusions. Often kids from damaged backgrounds felt the need to protect their parents by making out that everything was fine. Ivan didn't seem to fit into this category. It really hadn't sounded forced or tailored, as if he had just told her what she wanted to hear. Nor were there any holes or inconsistencies in the picture he had painted. Instead, the boy had spoken in detail about each family member with heartfelt love and admiration.

That had extended to Ivan's grandfather and siblings, and though it was clear that he and Sasha liked to wind each other up, it was her considered opinion that he came from a very close unit indeed.

'Can I go now?' he asked, having stopped abruptly when the bell rang for break time. Mrs. Risbie was surprised that Ivan didn't want to continue, given how enthusiastically he had just been talking about their best ever vacation.

'Well, I was enjoying your account of the safari,' she said, keen for him to continue. 'Looking out for all those wildebeest must've been fun. Animal conservation is an admirable cause.'

Ivan looked confused for a moment, as if perhaps she had misunderstood something, but nodded all the same.

'I really should go,' he said, and gathered his schoolbag from the floor. 'Do I need to come back again?'

Mrs. Risbie considered this for a moment. There was nothing in Ivan's life that needed unpicking, she decided. Yes, he had some difficulties empathizing with people, especially those in need of help or sympathy, but that clearly didn't apply when it came to his life at home. The kid was just a little odd. That didn't make him a bad apple.

'Shall we see how it goes?' she suggested as Ivan Savage rose to leave. 'My door is always open to you.'

Just seconds after leaving the school counselor's office, Ivan had completely forgotten about his conversation with Mrs. Risbie. He'd even switched off the light on his way out, despite the fact that she was still on the sofa behind him. Swinging his bag from one shoulder to the other, he made his way along the hallway with just one thing in mind. After the reception his last practical joke had earned him, the boy had something new up his sleeve. He'd ordered the device online and made some small adjustments to the way it worked. What he planned now was a public performance before class that would be sure to make him the center of attention.

As he headed for the classroom, Ivan spotted his sister approaching. The pair made eye contact, which was about as friendly as they could be at school. It was only as he passed that Sasha glanced over her shoulder with some concern.

'What's he up to?' she muttered to her friends. 'I know that look.'

By the time the bell rang again, Ivan was waiting for his classmates to file in. They found him standing at the teacher's desk, as if preparing to teach the lesson. With his schoolbag open at his feet, he was holding an object in his hands that some of them had seen at magic shows.

'It's a finger guillotine,' he announced, as people took to their seats. 'With a difference.'

'Here we go,' whispered one girl to her friend.

Nobody thought that Ivan was dangerous. They just considered him to be a bit different. He wasn't a popular boy, but nor did he easily attract enemies. If anything, most people just kept a little distance from him. On this occasion, however, Ivan had a captive audience. When no one accepted his invitation to volunteer, he shrugged and announced that he would perform the stunt himself.

'Now, this could be bloody,' he said, ignoring the groans and the sound of notebooks being opened in readiness for the teacher. Ivan was disappointed to see that only a few of his classmates were paying any attention at all. Most were pretending not to notice. With the guillotine placed on the desk, he stood behind it and slipped his index finger through the hole. 'Observe closely,' he announced, and raised the handle that lifted the blade. With one final glance at the class, where he was pleased to see a few more eyes on him, he squeezed his eyes shut and prepared to slam down the blade. He held his breath, counted to three in his mind, and then opened his eyes with a start when a voice commanded him to stop what he was doing right away.

'Ivan, this is no time for tricks!' his teacher barked, a man with a mouth that everyone said looked too large for his face. 'Sit down right away!'

The boy glanced across at the rest of the class. Now everyone was looking at him.

'But it isn't a trick,' he grumbled, and reluctantly withdrew his finger from the guillotine.

The device was to make a second appearance later that day, at the back of the school bus home. According to those who witnessed the episode, Ivan was asked to move from his seat. It wasn't a threat, by all accounts. It's just that's where the sophomore boys liked to gather. Most kids in the seventh grade would've moved without question. Instead, Ivan showed some reluctance, and that's when things turned nasty.

'Am I going to have to make you move?' growled a

redheaded boy called Thomas, who had come to accept being called Ginger Tom by everyone, including his teachers.

'You can try,' said Ivan, matter-of-factly, 'but you'll regret it.'

Ginger Tom looked back at his friends. He wasn't a bad kid at all. It's just that he'd gotten himself into a position where he couldn't back down. Turning back to Ivan, he saw a way that might persuade the boy to shift that didn't involve physical force.

'Let me help you.' Snatching Ivan's bag, before he could be stopped, Tom opened it up and peered inside. 'What's this?' he asked, on spotting the little guillotine in among the school books.

'Don't play with that!' Ivan lunged at it, but Ginger Tom was too quick for him. He jerked it away and then held it aloft, grinning.

'There's only one magic trick you need to perform,' he said. 'And that's a disappearing act. Now give me the seat and you can have it back.'

Ivan held his gaze for a moment.

'It isn't a magic trick,' he said.

'Oh right,' said Ginger Tom. 'It's for real, is it?

'Yep.'

By now, Ginger Tom's friends were pressing around him for a closer look.

'Stick your finger in it,' someone suggested. 'Give it a go, Tom.'

Grinning, Tom rested the guillotine on top of the seat rest in front of Ivan and inserted a digit.

'I wouldn't do that,' said Ivan, who watched with interest nonetheless.

'Or what? You'll look like a liar?'

Returning his attention to the guillotine, Tom lifted the blade. A phone camera appeared over his shoulder, fired up to film the event.

Do it, Ginger Tom. Do it!'

He glanced at Ivan one more time, but didn't look so gleeful any more. Tom's attention moved back to the guillotine, with calls of encouragement still filling in his ears. One last look at the Savage boy was enough to change his mind. It was the gleam in his eye, coupled with the faint trace of a smile, that told Ginger Tom this wasn't a good idea at all. Snatching his finger from the guillotine, much to the disappointment of the crowd, he quickly reached inside his school jacket and produced a pencil. Without a word, he jabbed it into the slot and slammed the handle down.

The blade cut through the pencil as if it was made from butter. In the brief moment it took for the sharp end to drop to the floor of the bus, every single witness had fallen silent.

5

When his face went on to make the newspapers, Vernon English didn't seem like the kind of person a company would hire as a private investigator. With his soft leather cap, worn at an angle, his flattened nose and stubbly, hangdog chops, he looked more like a boxing trainer ready to throw in the towel.

'Could passengers move along the aisle, please? We can't close the doors if people are pressing against them.'

Vernon was cheap, however, which made him attractive to a struggling organization at the mercy of a hostile take-over. Just then, the man responsible for moving in on the company was traveling to work by subway. Vernon could just about see him across the crowded train. When the company's boss had first called Vernon's office, which wasn't an office at all but the phone in his pocket, the man sounded desperate. Titus Savage is set to pounce on us, is what he told the private investigator. Everyone knows he's unconventional in the way he does business. We need to prove he's actually breaking laws if we stand any chance of survival. Get the dirt, Mr. English. Do whatever it takes so we can persuade the man to prey elsewhere.

'The gentleman in the cap and quilted bodywarmer. Will

you please find some space or step off and wait for the next train. There's one right behind.'

It took a moment for Vernon to realize that the conductor on the Tannoy was addressing him directly. He glanced around. Everyone was looking in his direction. Much to their annoyance, he used his considerable weight to push himself further into the car.

'Sorry,' he grumbled, as the doors finally closed. 'Sorry, is that your foot?'

There was no way that Vernon was going to lose sight of Titus Savage. He'd been on the case for just a short time, but already there had been a suspect exchange in a back alley. Vernon had noted it all from his favorite observation post, which was on a high stool facing out of a coffee shop with a grande latte in one hand and crumbs from an almond croissant all down his front. Now he had chosen to follow Savage home. It was important that he built a complete picture of the man, not just at work but also at play. As the train pulled away, Vernon reached up from the throng to grab the rail. Beside him, level with his armpit, a young woman closed her eyes, crinkled her nose and evidently tried to picture herself in her happy place. Vernon pretended not to notice her. He did the very same with the bald man in the silk scarf further down the car. Titus was standing over a couple in matching anoraks who were consulting a map of London. He too was holding onto the rail, and seemed totally lost in thought. The private investigator paid him no more than a cursory glance. Titus lived some way out from the city, and would be traveling eight more stops. Until then,

Vernon assured himself, while gazing at an ad for laxatives, his target wasn't going anywhere.

There was a point just behind the ear that Titus considered a guilty pleasure. Towards the end of a warm day, it was possible to detect a slight but telling odor. This was due to a sweat produced by the eccrine gland. The fold in the skin behind the lobe interested Titus because it formed a trap where a particularly oily film of the stuff would mature. Even though the smell was undetectable to most people, it revealed a great deal to experienced nostrils.

Leaning over the couple with the map, Titus breathed in and savored the intermingling odor of two specimens. Like a wine connoisseur, he was able to break down the components and make a quality assessment. In this case, the couple were in good health, well exercised and enjoyed a balanced diet. In terms of appeal, however, they were both a little too mature for his liking. What put Titus off completely was the top note of trimethylamine he detected. This natural chemical was released in times of stress, and could make the flesh a little fishy. Given that these guys were clearly tourists in a strange city and quite possibly a long way from home, it was no surprise that they were feeling tense. As the train pulled into the next station, the pair appeared to be torn as to whether or not they should get off. They looked at one another, and then back at the map, before bickering in their mother tongue.

Titus stood back and smiled to himself. It was an amusing exercise. Something he often enjoyed during rush hour to make the journey go that much quicker. The Savages didn't just go around slaying people day after day to feed their appetite for human flesh. It was a delicacy. A treat they enjoyed on an occasional basis. Sometimes they would prepare a feast to mark a special moment in their lives. At other times, consuming someone would be necessary because they had come too close to the truth for comfort.

'Excuse me, sir,' the male tourist said in broken English, and turned to face him. 'Which way to the Palace?'

As visitors to this country, the couple would've been mightily impressed by the time and courtesy Titus went on to display. He showed them their destination on the map, explained that they were traveling in the wrong direction, and then stood at the open door and pointed out the correct platform. As the couple stepped off, thanking him profusely, Titus bowed his head and wished them a good day. At the same time, in the furthest recess of his mind, he was debating whether salt curing might draw out the stress taint, particularly from a nice cut like the thigh or ribcage. If that worked out, he thought to himself, it could just leave the meat ripe for a mouth-wateringly tender, slow-cooked Stroganov.

Titus was just calculating the likely oven time when a young man rushed between the closing doors of the train. It was a dramatic entry and Titus was alone in ignoring it. He continued to enjoy preparing the imaginary dish, gazing at the roof panelling as the train pulled off once more. Then, as a distinctive smell reached his senses, he lowered his gaze and blinked just once. The young man across from him was wearing a suit, open at the throat. He was eating a cheeseburger, which was what now commanded the attention of the bald man opposite. Titus watched him take a bite, and then another in a desperate bid to stop the ketchup from slopping on his shoes. Judging by his outfit, and sharp, angular haircut, he was either a real estate agent on an early rung of the career ladder, or in direct sales of some description. Either way, he wasn't much older than Sasha, and looked both ambitious and hungry to make his mark on the world.

What was his daughter doing, Titus thought to himself, going out with a *vegetarian*? Those vitamin-deficient sissies really couldn't be trusted. It just wasn't right, in his view. It went against man's early instincts as a hunter. OK, so someone had to stay back and tend to the potatoes and the cress or whatever, but Titus doubted very much that anyone who was fit and strong enough to stalk elk and bison would volunteer. Meat dodgers just made him nervous. That was all. Watching the young man cram the last of the cheeseburger into his mouth, Titus hoped that Sasha would see sense soon. Even if this new boy in her life had a good soul, he'd still lack heart and guts. Ultimately, she could do so much better than that.

Titus had just decided that he would help his daughter reach this conclusion sooner rather than later when the train pulled into the next stop. Having licked the grease from his fingers, the young man turned for the doors and waited for them to open. With several more stops before he reached home, Titus sighed to himself and looked around. Quite a few passengers remained in the car. A couple more suits, both too depressed for his liking, a man in his sixties in full jogging gear and some bulky guy in a jazz hat and sleeveless body warmer. Titus was just wondering to himself whether the hat was leather or synthetic when the guy glanced around and caught his eye. In a blink, he pulled the brim of his cap low, switched his attention to the floor and then did his level best not to look back. Titus smiled to himself, and wondered what his dear wife had prepared for dinner.

6

Angelica Savage wasn't just a unique cook. Nor was she simply an accomplished homemaker. One look at her credit card statements revealed that she was also a formidable shopper. She kept them in a shoebox at the back of her walk-in closet, which also contained the reason why she had racked up so much debt.

When it came to fashion, Angelica was cutting edge. Her style was simple and elegant, but it came at a sky-high price. She would shop in boutiques where the staff dropped everything knowing what she could spend. Sometimes she went directly to the internationally admired dress designer, Gerado Figari. It was an association that would later come close to ruining the man's reputation, of course. Back then, whenever his cell phone rang and her name appeared on the screen, he would always be quick to pick up. His dresses from across the seasons hung from every rail in Angelica's wardrobe, alongside more casual clothes for the home that still cost a small fortune. It would be easy to look back and link her need for shopping to the family's hidden secret. Certainly many criminal psychologists have stepped forward to say that her consumer habit at the mall served as some kind of escape for the woman. A chance to momentarily forget about the horror that took place inside the house. This, they argued, explained how she managed to spend way beyond her means, and took to hiding the true nature of her debt from the rest of the family.

'Is this the bathroom?'

The voice took Angelica by surprise. With a gasp, she hurried to replace the lid on the shoebox. Then she twisted around to see Grandpa standing behind her. He was wearing a vest and drawstring pants. For one horrible moment, it looked as if he was about to unbutton himself.

'No it isn't,' she said, rising to her feet. She sounded cornered, perplexed and a little upset. 'It's my closet, Oleg. The bathroom is across the hall. You know that, don't you?'

Grandpa looked even more bemused than Angelica. He took a moment to consider what she'd said, before his eyebrows lifted in surprise.

'Oh, of course! So it is. I'm sorry.'

As he spoke, Angelica's expression shifted from surprise to concern. For decades, Oleg had shown no sign that age was getting the better of him. His wrinkles may have deepened, but this was the first occasion that his mind had let him down. Seeing him like this, as she recovered her composure, just served to make her aware that he wasn't going to live forever. It didn't matter how often Titus joked that Oleg's diet made him immortal, one day nature would take her course. However you conducted yourself through life, whatever path you chose, everyone died in time.

'You've had a senior moment,' she told him gently, before encouraging him to turn and leave the bedroom.

'Have I?' Oleg looked like he had completely forgotten what just happened. Angelica placed a reassuring hand on his shoulder. She could feel his bones and joints at work, as fragile as if fashioned from balsa wood. At the same time, she hoped he wouldn't go wandering downstairs on Saturday in a similar state of undress.

'We have another shoot this weekend,' she told him. 'It's important that we stay out of sight and let them do their job.'

'So the kids told me,' he said. 'But I would've figured it out for myself on account of all the cleaning you've been doing.'

Angelica smiled to herself. It was good to know that Oleg was a long way from living in a complete fog of bemusement. The fact was she had spent much of the day making sure the house was prepared. She had scrubbed and disinfected, dusted and polished and vacuumed every last inch.

'It has to be done,' she said, as he followed her out onto the landing. 'Titus insists.'

'You should just let him pay off your credit card,' said Oleg.

And reveal just how much debt I'm in? Angelica thought to herself. *He'd slay me.*

'Titus has his own concerns,' she said instead, and directed Oleg to the bathroom in case he had forgotten.

'Titus should relax about Sasha,' he said. 'At the moment he's just driving her into the arms of this boy.'

Oleg stopped and looked around at his daughter-in-law. Angelica had been referring to the fact that Titus was preoccupied with work. Even so, Oleg had a point. The last time Titus tried to address the situation with his eldest daughter, Sasha had left the table early.

'Did she tell you that he's invited her over for dinner?' she said. 'A *vegetarian* meal.'

'So, it'll give her wind all evening. Is that the worst thing that can happen? Let the girl learn from the experience.'

Grandpa shuffled into the bathroom. As he turned to close the door, he found Angelica looking at him thoughtfully.

'Titus is just scared that his little girl is growing up.' She gestured at the window overlooking the park and the city beyond. 'It's a big bad world out there.'

'Sometimes it feels as if I can't breathe at home,' complained Sasha later that day. She looked at the ground, which was some way down, and shook her head. 'My dad is such an asshole. It's like, who put him in charge of all the oxygen?'

Sasha Savage was sitting alongside her two closest friends on the back of a ramp at the skate park. Sasha, Maisy and Faria came out here at lunch breaks just to get away from it all. The canteen was always packed with seventh and eighth graders. Even if the girls were starving hungry, the shrieking and the smell of egg, farts and potato chips was enough to persuade them to find some space. It meant Faria could light up while Sasha could air her problems.

'What's he done now?' asked Maisy, a pretty, cheery girl whose manner served her well in her Saturday job as a waitress.

Sasha looked across at her. At that hour, the sun was at

its brightest. She shielded her eyes with her hand before answering.

'It's Jack,' she said. 'Dad hates him.'

'How can anyone hate Jack?' asked Maisy. 'He drives his own car and everything.'

'Anyway, why is your old man so upset?' This was Faria, whose gaze was locked on the school buildings as she took a drag from the cigarette hidden in the palm of her hand.

'It's his new default position.' Sasha checked her bag to see if she had packed her sunglasses. She sighed to herself, but not just because she had forgotten. 'They haven't even met.'

'Typical,' said Maisy. 'Effing dads!'

'Jack's cooking for me this weekend. It's totally romantic. His parents are out, so it's a really good chance for us to get to know each other, only Dad has decided that I'd be placing my life in danger by dining alone with him.'

'Oh, for God's sake,' said Faria. 'It's not like Jack's going to feast on your liver and spleen.'

Sasha returned her attention to the ground, quietly wishing she had some shades to hide behind. Behind them, a couple of boys who'd left school the year before were slamming from one side of the ramp to the other on skate-boards. One worked evenings at the Cheepie Chicken. The other had been rejected by the army. None of the girls paid them any attention whatsoever.

'So, what are you going to do?' asked Maisy.

'I wouldn't want to let Jack down this soon in your relationship,' warned Faria, before sucking on the cigarette like an asthmatic with an inhaler in the midst of an attack.

'There are girls out there who would literally kill for a piece of him,' she finished, on exhaling. 'Let's just say that if you fail to make it to dinner this weekend I don't think he'll be dining alone.' Faria took another hit from her hidden cigarette, seemingly unaware that Sasha was looking at her incredulously.

'Jack wouldn't cheat on me,' she said eventually. 'He wouldn't *dare*.'

7

In her teens, Lulabelle Hart had crossed catwalks from London to Milan. Her height, frame and freckles were perfectly suited for modeling, as was her tumbling red hair that she had learned to flick over her shoulder just as the camera shutter opened. For several years, Lulabelle lived a lifestyle that many would envy. Then the next generation of girls began to attract the attention of designers and magazine editors, and slowly the work took a slide. Now in her mid-twenties, Lulabelle's last fashion shoot featured clothes most people had since passed on to the charity shop. Still, her agent continued to find her work, and though she no longer graced front covers you could still find her advertising sofas and sunrooms in the back pages. Sadly, Lulabelle's A-list days were long gone. What remained was her attitude.

'Explain this to me,' she said, having just swept into the Savage house on the morning of the shoot. She was standing in the front room, where a crew worked hard to set up lights and cameras. The shoot, an ad for a plug-in air fresh-ener, required Lulabelle to play the role of a beautiful but harassed mother who finds escape in the synthetic aroma of a tropical seashore. Lately, Lulabelle had played a lot of beautiful but harassed mothers. Given her dislike of other people's children touching surfaces and door handles, she found it all too depressing for words. 'What is that?'

'What is what?' asked the production manager, a young woman with a clipboard and earpiece. She turned to see what Lulabelle was looking at. 'It's a mirror,' she said, and stood beside the model to admire the framed vintage glass that hung above the fireplace. 'Gorgeous, isn't it? A work of art.'

Lulabelle leaned forward, narrowing her eyes.

'But it's mottled and blotchy.'

'It's antique. That's what happens. The silver backing peels away from the glass over time.'

Puzzled by this, Lulabelle turned to address the production manager directly.

'What's the point of a mirror when you can't see your own reflection?'

Ivan Savage peered through a crack in the door. He watched the model in conversation with the production manager, and wondered who would be first to see the dead vole he had planted in the grate of the fireplace. He had found the creature in the yard that morning, disemboweled and abandoned by next door's cat, and slipped it in just as his mother finished cleaning. Ivan held his breath, waiting for the first one to shriek, only to exhale in disappointment as several crew members placed a large flood lamp right in front of the fireplace. It was a shame because the cat had done a great job in teasing out the vital organs from the mouse, as well as removing its head.

'Ivan! Come away from there.' From the top of the stairs, Angelica Savage was forced to hiss at her son one more time before he closed the door. 'We're not here to disturb them!'

'I'm bored already,' he complained, and made his way back to the landing. 'There's nothing to do.'

'You say that every time.' Angelica ruffled his hair as he passed. 'It's only for the day.'

As Ivan sauntered by, Sasha emerged from her bedroom. She was wearing jeans and a cap sleeve T-shirt, with her hair scraped back in a ponytail. It was clear that she'd made no big effort to dress. That, she hoped, would come later.

'Where's Dad?' she asked, and looked nervously at her mother.

'In his study. Working.'

'But it's a Saturday,' said Sasha.

'He has a lot going on right now.'

'I really need to speak to him about this evening.'

Angelica tipped her head, appraising her daughter.

'This boy, Jack . . . is he important to you?'

Sasha looked a little unsure.

'It's just he's my first,' she said, and looked to the floor-boards for a moment. 'I mean my first, you know . . . boyfriend. I just want to see how it goes for now.'

Angelica met her gaze once more with a smile. Sasha was certainly flowering, but even she could see that her daughter wasn't set to lose her head with this young man. If anything, she sounded as if she was discovering for herself that romance wasn't always a fairy tale.

'Then talk to your father calmly, like a grown-up,' she told her. 'I'm sure he can spare you a moment.'

Downstairs, Lulabelle Hart sat on a stool at the breakfast bar. She wasn't there to eat, despite the offer of a bacon sandwich from the catering manager brought in to feed the cast and crew. Lulabelle didn't really do food at this hour. Ever since she found herself in competition for modeling jobs, meals had become something she felt the need to control. Just then, the smell of eggs in the pan made her mouth moisten. Starting the day with a glass of warm water and a sprig of mint just didn't compare. Still, it meant come lunchtime she would earn the right to make the most of what was on offer. Until then, Lulabelle closed her eyes and tipped her head back so the make-up artist could work.

'Are you sure I can't tempt you?' the catering manager asked one more time, as he loaded the plates on the break-fast bar.

'I'm fine,' said Lulabelle, as a foundation brush whisked over her face. 'Don't torment me.'

Her response was so abrupt it left an awkward silence in the kitchen. It meant when footsteps creaked overhead, everybody heard.

'Someone's on the prowl,' said the make-up artist.

'Who lives here?' asked Lulabelle. 'That mirror is just wrong.'

'Well, they like to cook,' observed the catering manager. 'Kitchens don't come much classier than this.'

Lulabelle eyed the display of knives. They clung to a

magnetic strip above a butcher's block, and ranged in shape and size.

'It's just showing off,' she said, as if to correct him. 'I mean, how many blades do you need?'

'Judging by the grooves in the block,' said the catering manager, who had crossed the floor for a closer inspection. 'I'd say they make full use of them all.'

This was a first for Titus Savage. Normally, the ground floor of the house would be rented out during the working week. It meant he could steer clear all day, forget about the intrusion, and then return from the office to find his wife happy and everything as it should be.

Now he found himself under the same roof as a film crew. Just thinking about them poking about down there made his temples throb. What's more, he had work to do. A lot of it. If the takeover was going to happen, he needed to go through reams of documents to be sure everything was covered. Normally on weekends, Titus liked to close the door and spend time with his family. Instead, he faced a day of hell.

'Dad, can I talk to you?'

Sasha had been sure to knock at the study door first. Even though it was wide open, she wanted to do everything right this time.

'Honey, can it wait?' asked Titus, without looking around from his desk.

'Please? It won't take a moment.'

Titus glanced over his shoulder, sighed to himself and then swiveled around in his chair.

'So long as it doesn't end in slamming doors,' he said. 'I'm too old for tantrums.'

Sasha smiled, embarrassed, and headed across to the window. It looked out over the back garden. From this viewpoint it was striking just how much better the plants and flowers thrived compared to neighboring plots. Mindful of her grandfather's advice, Sasha took a deep breath and hoped for the best.

'I'm thinking it might be good if you met Jack after all,' she said. 'Just so you can see what he's like.'

'There's no need,' replied Titus, sounding disappointed. 'I already have a good idea.'

Sasha reminded herself to stay calm.

'When Ivan first blabbed that I was going out with him,' she said, 'you suggested that I invite him round.'

'That was before,' said Titus gruffly.

'Before you found out he was a vegetarian?' She glanced at her father, found him staring at his desk but nodding at the same time. Sasha had been ready for this response, however.

'What if he was black?' she asked cautiously, facing the window once more. 'South Asian or Chinese? Would you still refuse to let him in the house?'

'Of course not. Honey . . .'

'It's still prejudice, Dad,' she continued, finding her voice now. 'You're judging someone before you've gotten to know them.'

An awkward silence opened out between them. Titus had always considered himself to be a fair man. This accusation, from his own daughter, hurt him deeply.

'Is that all you came to say?' he asked.

'I was also hoping we could talk about this evening,' she began, facing him briefly one more time. 'It would mean so much to me if you let me go.'

The way she phrased this brought a catch to his throat. Letting go at some point was all part of raising children. Not just for a couple of hours, but when they came to leave forever.

'It's difficult,' he began, and rose from his chair. 'We have traditions in this family. It's what makes us strong. To bring a fruit-picker into the fold would risk destroying everything.'

'I don't want to marry Jack,' she said, and turned to face him with both arms spread. 'It's just dinner.'

Titus drew breath, only to respond with what sounded to Sasha like a long sigh of resignation. Just then, Titus realized that he needed to back off. If he didn't, he really could risk losing her.

'I want you back by ten o'clock,' he told her warily. 'Keep your phone with you. If you're worried at any time then call me, understood?'

'Understood,' she said, beaming at her father. 'But you don't have to worry. He's a vegetarian, not a sex offender. There's a difference.'

Before he could reply, Sasha skipped over, planted a kiss on his cheek, and then left him alone in the study. Titus watched her disappear. He gazed at the open door for a moment.

'There may well be a difference,' he muttered to himself, 'but both are inexcusable.'

8

On an empty stomach, Lulabelle Hart could be somewhat fractious. Given her dietary habits, it was a mood that often lasted for much of the day. That morning, fueled by a second glass of warm water (and a grape she had plucked from the fruit bowl in a moment of temptation) her performance was professional but underscored by a very short temper indeed.

'Yes, we can try the lighting in a different way,' she replied to the shoot's director, a diplomatic and gifted helmsman who was simply trying to get the best from his cast. 'Although I had expected to be working with a crew who could get that right first time.'

To be fair to Lulabelle, she could pose as well as she could swagger and strut. She just pushed the boundaries when it came to being civil. Approaching lunchtime, the poor props guy had been forced to empty the air freshener and fill it with a sample from Lulabelle's perfume atomizer, before she 'blew chunks into the camera lens'.

'OK, let's break for lunch,' announced the director, sensing that he might need to turn down the emotional temperature. 'Thirty minutes, everybody!'

While the cast and crew worked on the shoot in the

front room, the catering manager had been busy in the kitchen. When everyone filed through, they found a buffet on the table with dishes appealing to every taste. Lulabelle wasn't the first in line. The transport guys got in before her, but she was close behind. Without word, she began to fill her paper plate until there was no room for anything else. She went for the lime shrimp tacos, the fettuccine with chicken and sun-dried tomatoes, a slice of eggplant and goat cheese tart, a wedge from the pistachio and pork pie, several scoops of beetroot and couscous salad, two bread rolls, four individually wrapped, reduced-fat butter pats and three super-chocolate cupcakes. Nobody liked to comment, of course. Everyone was hungry after such an early start. Still, it didn't go unnoticed when Lulabelle headed to a chair overlooking the garden that her lunch was less of a snack and more of a banquet. It took her the full half-hour to clear the plate. This was partly due to the fact that she spent much of it on a call to her agent.

'The catwalk work,' she was heard to say, still chewing on a Thai fried rice ball. 'It's why I signed with you . . . yes, I realize my career has matured, but there has to be more on offer than . . . well, this.'

As a result of the exchange, most of the crew returned to work fully expecting Lulabelle to be difficult, abrupt and even outright rude. Instead, she performed three further set-ups without complaint. She was also witty and even motivational with the child actress when the afternoon lull set in. On the last take, following a nod from the marketing lady sitting quietly in the corner, the director began a round of applause directed at Lulabelle.

'You were brilliant,' he told her. 'The product will fly.'

With only some close ups of the air freshener left to shoot, Lulabelle asked politely if she could now leave the set. The make-up artist offered to cleanse her face, but by all accounts she was in too much of a hurry. She seemed happy, they said, if a little troubled, like someone who was questioning whether they had left the iron on before setting out for work that day.

Having thanked every crew member, Lulabelle collected her coat and left the front room. She closed the door behind her, but instead of leaving the house she headed straight for the toilet at the far end of the hallway. As she reached for the handle, the sound of the bolt withdrawing on the inside caused her to take a step back. Then the door opened outwards and the lighting man appeared. He seemed surprised to find anyone waiting, and hurried away without making eye contact. Unconcerned, Lulabelle took his place in the toilet, only to come right out again with her face pinched in an expression of utter disgust. *Good grief, what had he been eating?* There was no way she could bear to go in there for at least ten minutes. The way she felt just then, that was ten minutes too long. Which was what persuaded her to take to the stairs and find another bathroom.

Ivan Savage did not enjoy killing time. He liked to keep busy. That morning, having spent an hour battling zombies in his bedroom, the boy grew tired of videogames and turned his mind to other matters.

He had heard Sasha talking to their father in the study. No doubt his sister was hoping to sweeten him up so she could see her new boyfriend. Ivan knew Jack from school. The guy was good at buttering up girls, but that's not how he treated boys in the grades below him. If you didn't step out of his way in the hallway, Jack would just barge through like you didn't exist. It had happened to Ivan on several occasions. If anything, it just reinforced everything his father said about vegetarians. They were just so self-important, strutting around like they had life all worked out. Well, thought Ivan as the day stretched ahead, he would show Jack that sometimes you couldn't simply have everything on a plate.

Even if Sasha talked her way into an evening out, Ivan decided that she should show up at Jack's place with a headache. That would take the edge off any special time they had planned. Not only would it teach Sasha a lesson for making cheap jokes at his expense, he would do it in a way that afterwards everyone would look back and laugh.

At the top of the stairs, Lulabelle Hart decided not to disturb the family. She could hear someone at work in the study, clattering away on a keyboard, while all the bedroom doors on this level were closed. Lulabelle really didn't want to venture up to the next floor and disturb the chatter, gurgling and laughter up there. It sounded like some old guy and a woman playing with a toddler, and left her feeling as if she was trespassing.

So, treading lightly, Lulabelle crossed the landing for the family bathroom. She would be in and out in moments, after all. They would never know.

Lulabelle didn't recognize that she had a problem with

food. She loved to eat, when she allowed herself. It helped her to forget what a slide her career was in. What she loathed was the feeling of guilt that expanded in her stomach soon afterwards. In her business, you just couldn't afford to lose your self-control as she did, which is why she had developed a strategy for indulging herself without piling on the pounds.

'Let's get this done,' she said to herself, on locking the door behind her.

This wasn't something Lulabelle enjoyed. There was some satisfaction to be had from the way it preserved her figure, despite the stomach cramps, but the procedure itself she found to be a bore. She knew just how to trigger the required response, which she prepared to do having knelt in front of the toilet bowl and lifted the lid. Inserting two fingers into her mouth, Lulabelle reached back for her tonsils and prepared for the involuntary gag reflex that would follow.

It was over in moments, as she had predicted. With her partially digested lunch now floating in the toilet, and her eyes watering from the exertion, Lulabelle grabbed some paper to wipe her mouth and then reached up to flush. It was good to do this quickly. It minimized any odor. Wishing fortune would look kindly upon her just once in what was left of her career, Lulabelle pulled the handle down. She would've been unaware that one end of a long length of cotton thread was tied to it. She may have heard a clatter as the iron was jerked from its moorings on the shelf above the door behind her, but it happened too quickly for her to react. With the cord tied to the light fitting overhead, the iron simply swooped across the room before the sharp end penetrated the back of her skull. Such was the impact that Lulabelle Hart was dead before her face dropped into the gurgling water.

9

Vernon English had a habit of nodding off during long surveillance operations. It had happened on several occasions during his time as a serving police officer, and certainly contributed to the suggestion that he retire early or face dismissal. As a private investigator, it still wasn't a quality that served him well, but sometimes his tired old body just called the shots.

As he surfaced from a snooze that afternoon, slouched inside his scuffed white van, Vernon realized that someone had just left the Savage residence. It was the sound of the front door shutting that had woken him. He sat up in his seat, straining to see who it was. He had parked up on the opposite side of the street, some way down from the house. When he saw the daughter emerge on to the pavement, he relaxed visibly. Vernon wasn't here to stake out the wife and kids. Titus Savage was his only figure of interest, and already he had revealed himself to have a sinister side. Photographs Vernon had taken of Titus talking to the man in the back alley revealed a great deal. It turned out that the guy was a mole, an employee of the company Titus was circling. For the time being, Vernon had decided to keep this information to himself. It was just a question of gathering enough evidence so he could truly skewer the predator before he pounced.

'Eyes down,' he muttered to himself as Sasha crossed the street in front of him, before tipping his cap low over his brow. 'That's it, Miss Savage. Walk on by.'

As soon as he heard her pass the van, Vernon opened his eyes and watched her heading down the street. She looked all dressed up, clearly going places. Just then, being a teenager seemed a very long time ago to the private investigator. He didn't want to think about all the screw-ups and the disappointments that littered the landscape of his life from back then until now. Vernon glanced at the time on the dashboard and cursed. He had been asleep for *hours*. Anything could've happened. Fortunately for him, Titus Savage's black 4x4 was still parked in the driveway in front of the house. In all likelihood, the man would be quietly holed up in his study waiting for the commercial shoot crew to pack up and go home. Vernon shifted his buttocks on the seat. It was a relief that he hadn't missed anything. He just hoped that situation would change some time soon.

One by one, the Savages gathered around the body of the model with her head in the toilet bowl. Titus stood with both hands clasped behind him. He was staring at the penetrating wound on the back of her head. The one that had turned the water wine-colored. Grandpa stroked and scratched at his beard, rubbing his gums together at the same time. Angelica stood beside him with the baby on her hip. She closed her eyes and sighed, as if they were simply dealing with a blockage here. Katya was toying with a pacifier in her mouth. She didn't look at all concerned by the discovery of a corpse in the house.

'It was an accident,' said Ivan uncomfortably, loitering by the sink.

Titus turned his attention to the iron. It was still strung up to the light fitting by the flex, twisting gently behind the body of Lulabelle Hart.

'An accident,' he said quietly. 'Right.'

'OK, well, it wasn't aimed at her,' Ivan bowed his head. 'It was a prank meant for Sasha.'

'A joke?' Angelica struggled to stay calm. 'Ivan, you could've *killed* your sister.'

'I assumed she'd see it coming and catch it!' Ivan protested. 'In the nose or her forehead,' he added as if to clarify. 'Nobody warned me someone else would come in here and then kneel in front of the bowl.'

As a defense, even Ivan could tell it wasn't going to fly.

'It's clear you've been creative,' said his mother, searching for some way for him to accept responsibility for what had happened here. 'But there's a difference between being creative and, well, *lethal*.'

'So, blame Jack!' he replied hotly. 'If he hadn't asked Sasha to come over this wouldn't have happened!'

'Darling, you're missing the point.' Angelica shifted Katya into her other arm. 'There's a dead model in our bathroom and the crew is still downstairs.'

'So,' said Grandpa, who continued to size up the corpse. 'What shall we do?'

It was Titus who had found the body. Shortly after

Sasha had popped in to say she was heading out, and promised not to let him down, he left the study to find Ivan outside the bathroom. The boy looked troubled, and reluctant to explain himself after Titus tested the door and discovered it to be locked from the inside. When Angelica, Kat and Grandpa joined them, Titus decided to force an entry. Nobody shrieked or screamed when he succeeded. Instead, the tragic scene that greeted the family was met by sighs and groans, before all eyes turned to Ivan.

'Does this mean I'm grounded?' he asked just then. 'What am I looking at here? A week?'

Titus drew breath to suggest a lot longer when the sound of someone clearing their throat at the foot of the stairs caused them all to start.

'Hello? Anyone there?'

'Hi,' said Angelica, as brightly as she could, while looking thoroughly panicked. 'How can we help you?'

'Just letting you know that we've wrapped.'

'Oh . . . oh, right!' Gathering her wits, Angelica handed baby Kat to Titus and hurried out to the top of the stairs. 'I hope everything went according to plan.'

She found the shoot's director looking up at her from the hallway.

'It went better than expected,' he said. 'Our star did such a fine job that she's already gone home. We're just sweeping the place down to make sure we haven't left anything behind.'

Angelica looked blankly at him for a moment. When she registered what that meant, she brightened visibly.

'So, everything is back as you found it?' she asked. 'Per the terms of your contract with the agency?'

'As good as new,' he assured her. 'You won't know anyone's been here.'

Jack Greenway lived a short walk from the Savage house. To get there, Sasha crossed the park towards the west gate. It was a broad expanse of grassland, tree-lined paths and bushes. Her parents used to take her to the playground near the rose garden or push her in a stroller around the lake. She'd learned to ride a bike here, too. Then, as she grew older, Titus worried that it was no place for a girl like her to be alone.

One day, Sasha thought to herself on reaching Jack's road, her father would recognize that his eldest daughter could take care of herself. Thanks to her family's habits, it wasn't as if she were an innocent in this world.

'Hey,' said Jack, who opened the front door just as she reached for the buzzer. He was wearing a chef's apron with a slim-fit T-shirt underneath. 'Do you like tahini?'

'Oh. I've never tried it, actually.'

Sasha was wearing a shift top, skinny jeans and ballet flats, with her hair pinned as she liked it. Jack checked her up and down, grinned and stepped aside to let her in.

'We're talking food of the gods,' he said, and invited her into the kitchen. 'This evening might even turn you.'

The first thing Sasha noticed was the smell of cooking. What struck her most was the complete absence of any meat aromas. This came as no surprise, but it was still something that failed to connect with her taste buds. She turned and smiled at Jack. He was so handsome it almost hurt her to make eye contact. Sasha still found it difficult to believe that he had just breezed up to her one day and asked her out. That had never happened to her before, though she knew she didn't help herself. Being different from every other human being she had ever met outside her family made it hard to let just anyone into her life. That evening, she was looking forward to getting beyond the good looks to find out what made Jack tick. She saw it as a chance to talk and find out if his personality lived up to his appearance. Just then, what worried her was the possibility that she wouldn't be able to stomach his meal. Aware that he was watching her closely, Sasha inhaled deeply and closed her eyes.

'It smells delicious,' she said. 'I can't wait.'

'You're early.' Jack slipped his arms around her waist. 'I wasn't expecting you for another hour at least, but I know a way to fill the time.'

Seeing where this was going, Sasha smiled and removed his hand from her behind.

'Actually, I thought I could help you cook,' she said, and took a step away.

Jack grinned, nodding to himself as if somehow he'd just been presented with a challenge.

'Everything is under control,' he told her. 'For you, this evening is all about surprises.'

Now it was Sasha's turn to smile.

'Well, being here beats hanging around at home right now,' she said, as Jack pulled out a chair for her. 'It's so boring when the place gets rented out for shoots.'

'Sounds cool to me.' Jack crossed the kitchen floor to inspect a pan on the stove. 'You must've had tons of famous people in your place.'

'Sometimes,' said Sasha. 'But it just means the whole family has to stay upstairs. Nothing interesting ever happens.'

10

The body of Lulabelle Hart lay face up on the bathroom floor. The skin was beginning to take on a mottled texture, much like the mirror over the fireplace downstairs.

As soon as Grandpa and Titus had hauled her out of the toilet, it was clear that she had died with a look of utter surprise on her face. As a mark of respect, and in case it upset the baby, Angelica kneeled beside the corpse and closed her eyelids. At least then it didn't look as if the woman was expecting the roof to fall in on her.

'Do you have any idea what you've done?' Titus asked Ivan, who by now was looking very subdued. He spoke quietly, and not just because of the crew downstairs. In times of anger, Titus never yelled at anyone. Instead, with his eyes pinched at the corners, he would voice his true feelings in a whisper that sounded like a bellow just waiting to break out. 'You can't just go killing people without purpose. How have I raised a boy who thinks this is acceptable? You've let me down very badly here. I'm so disappointed in you.'

The boy shifted uncomfortably from one foot to the other.

'We could always eat her,' he suggested.

Titus closed his eyes for a moment more than a blink.

'Ivan, we have no idea where she's been.'

'But we have to do something,' he said.

Grandpa eased himself down to take a closer look.

'It would be a shame to let her go to waste,' he said, and gently grasped her bicep as if to evaluate the flesh. 'At least that way we know there'll be no evidence left.'

Titus glanced at his wife. Angelica looked down at the body, but Kat was back in her arms and wriggling to be set on the tiles.

'Normally this takes planning,' she said. 'I'm all out of onions, for one thing.'

Joining Grandpa at ground level, Titus reached forward and grasped Lulabelle by the hinges of her jaw. Carefully, he opened her mouth to its full extent before running a finger along the inside of her upper teeth. He stared at the wall as he did so, concentrating hard.

'Eating is out,' he declared, and removed his finger. 'The tooth enamel has been eroded back there. It's caused over time by stomach acids coming back up through vomiting. Whatever caused this poor young lady's problems, she's not a healthy specimen now. We'd be faced with kidney damage, ulcers, even brittle bones.'

Clasping Titus by the shoulder for support, Grandpa rose to his feet.

'That's a shame,' he said. 'For her and for us.'

When Titus stood up, he found Angelica considering him.

'You'll have to drop her off,' she said. 'Tonight.'

Titus had already sensed that this was coming. Even before his wife had made the suggestion, he just knew that his Saturday evening on the sofa would be ruined.

First Course

* * *

Sasha Savage sat alone at the dining-room table. She clasped her napkin nervously. The clock on the wall told her it was approaching half past seven. She could hear Jack in the kitchen, readying what he had called an *amuse-bouche*.

'It's just a something,' he said, on appearing at the door with a little plate in each hand. 'They call it an amusement for the mouth. A palate tickler.'

With great ceremony, Jack Greenway set a plate in front of his guest. Sasha peered down at the offering. It was golden, crispy-looking, and about the size of a kidney.

'Sweet battered courgette flower.'

For a moment, Sasha was lost for words.

'Flowers are edible?' she asked.

'You'd be surprised what you can eat when you forgo meat.'

'Well, I've learned something,' she said, and collected her fork. 'We don't get this at home.'

'Allow me.' Jack took the fork from her, perching on the edge of the table at the same time. Then, giving no chance for Sasha to prepare herself, he jabbed the morsel and offered it for her to bite into. 'Enjoy.'

'I'm sure I will.'

Keen to please him, Sasha took the nugget in her mouth and crunched into it. She wasn't sure what to expect. What she hadn't anticipated was how hot it would be, and instinctively popped it into the palm of her hand.

'Oh,' said Jack, and left the edge of the table. 'After all that.'

'It's not what you think,' said Sasha desperately. 'I just

didn't want to burn my mouth. I'm sure it's fine now.'

In a bid to demonstrate that she didn't hate it, and praying that the temperature would be a little more bearable, she tipped the battered flower back into her mouth and crunched into it.

'So?' said Jack, watching closely. 'Out of ten?'

'Ten,' replied Sasha, and switched it with her tongue from one cheek wall to the other. It didn't taste bad as such; a little bland, maybe, but she sensed that somehow an honest opinion would offend. 'Definitely a ten,' she added instead, and prepared for a trying evening.

As darkness settled, Vernon English wondered whether he should write off the day. He had staked out the Savage house since the camera crew rolled in. Now they had packed up and left, but still Titus remained inside. Vernon figured a financial shark like him wouldn't completely switch off from work for the weekend. Given the questionable methods the private investigator had witnessed him employ, surely he'd use the time to meet up informally and off the record with other players in the looming takeover? No, Vernon couldn't afford to take his eyes off the man for a moment.

At the same time, after nearly ten hours in the van, he was ravenously hungry.

'Come on, Titus, old pal,' he muttered to himself at one point. 'A guy has got to eat.'

Half an hour later, just as Vernon was about to put a call into his favorite Indian restaurant to see if they'd bike him a Tandoori jumbo shrimp and naan bread, his man made an appearance. The private investigator sat up straight in the driver's seat. There at the front door, silhouetted by the light from the hall, Titus Savage kissed his wife on the cheek before turning for his 4x4. He had one of those duffle bags on wheels with him. It looked heavy, judging by the effort Titus put into heaving it onto the back seat. If Titus was about to head out on business, Vernon would be ready.

The private investigator may have neglected to pack a sandwich, but he had an overnight bag on the back seat and a passport in the glove compartment. Living alone, he could fly at a moment's notice. The company that hired him was convinced that Titus operated outside the law. Desperate for evidence, and with time running out, they had instructed Vernon to do whatever was necessary. Checking his key was in the ignition, Vernon waited for Titus to pull out onto the road and hoped they were heading somewhere nice. New York or Barcelona. Any place known for its restaurants and street food.

Vernon kept his distance as they made their way out of the city. He had tailed many people throughout the course of his career, and never been spotted by anyone. Titus wasn't difficult to follow. He was a careful, considered driver. He didn't once break the speed limit, and slowed long before he passed through a speed trap. In a way, it was just too easy. Vernon drove with one hand on the wheel, sighing to himself every now and then as he braked to keep his distance. Without a doubt, Titus was heading for the highway. The private investigator knew this stretch of road well. He was also well aware that they were about to pass a drive-in. His stomach had been rumbling over the sound of the van's radio. Having last eaten at breakfast time, he felt weak with hunger. It would take him no time at all to collect a jumbo bag of chicken nuggets and a strawberry shake. He'd easily catch up with Titus before he reached the motorway. As the neon sign for the drive-in loomed into view, it seemed to him that there could be no other option. Given that his next meal might not come until he was strapped into an airplane seat, it made sense to fuel up now. Leaving Titus to trundle on, Vernon accelerated off the road and screeched to a halt in front of the serving window. It was, without a doubt, the most exciting thing he'd done all day.

'Make it snappy,' he told the youngster serving him. 'Got a flight to catch.'

A minute after placing his order, with the shake lodged between his thighs and a bucket of nuggets riding alongside him, Vernon fishtailed back onto the road and hit the accelerator. By his reckoning, Titus would be back in his sights within thirty seconds at most.

Twenty miles later, cursing at the top of his voice, Vernon English was forced to merge onto the highway with no sign of the man he had set out to follow. He wasn't even sure that Titus had headed in the direction of the airport. All he could do was follow his instinct and drive there anyway. Just then, with the shake finished, the last nugget in the bucket at his side tasted like a very bitter pill indeed.

11

Thankfully for the Savages, Lulabelle Hart had been supple and forgiving when they came to fold her into the duffle bag. From experience, Titus knew that the muscles in a corpse slowly began to stiffen from around the three-hour mark. It took between twelve and twenty-four hours before the body became totally rigid for a while. So long as everything went to plan, as it had on previous occasions, he would be unpacking her with plenty of time to spare. Titus anticipated a little resistance, of course, but he really didn't want to be breaking a sweat trying to straighten the model's limbs before letting her go.

Even with rigor mortis in mind, Titus was in no hurry to reach the coast. Rushing always led to mistakes, which was something he had learned at a very early age. It was his late mother who taught him the importance of patience. *We take our time in the kitchen and look at the results*, she would say. *It's the same when it comes to covering our tracks.*

On the way, Titus considered what to do with his son. Ivan was a complicated boy, but this incident in the bathroom was quite a wake-up call. A cry for help, in many ways, he thought to himself on reflection. It left Titus feeling guilty. As a father, had he let him down? Work took up so much of his time, especially lately with the big takeover he had lined up. Still, that was no excuse. If he'd spent the day with Ivan, instead of shutting himself away in his study, then he wouldn't be driving into the night with a dead diva in the trunk.

By the time he arrived at his destination, which took the shape of an empty headland parking lot, Titus resolved to return a different man. He owed it not just to his son but Sasha, too. He had been a little hard on her about this boy. She had shown maturity in handling the situation, and as her father he needed to acknowledge that. Just then, however, he had a job to do. Titus climbed out of the 4x4, collecting his coat and a scarf from the passenger seat. It was a clear, cool night, with a hint of salt on the breeze. A mothball moon hung over the ocean. The water glittered underneath it, like a silver carpet rolled out from the horizon, but now was not the time to admire the view. Extending the handle to the duffle bag, Titus made his way across the headland towards the cliff edge.

As a scenic overlook, Beachy Head was unbeatable. As a suicide magnet, the towering chalk cliff edge was notorious for drawing the despondent. Given the impact wound to the back of Lulabelle's head, dropping her body onto the rocks way below seemed like the only option available to Titus. She'd pick up many more injuries on her way down, after all, which would cover the real cause of death. At the foot of the cliff, she'd just be another sad statistic. He took no pleasure in considering this. If anything, he felt quite maudlin as he plodded across the grass. Titus was so lost in thought, in fact, dwelling on how he'd failed his son, that for a moment he didn't register the figure sitting with his legs dangling over the edge. When he finally realized what he was facing, he stopped in his tracks and released his grip on the handle of the bag. Then, moving slowly so as not to startle or alarm the young man, Titus stepped wide until he drew alongside him. He guessed the guy was in his early twenties, despite weeping to himself like a lost little boy.

'It's a beautiful night,' said Titus finally, with both hands in his coat pockets. 'It would be a shame if this was your last.'

The young man looked around with a start. Hurriedly, he wiped the tears from his cheeks. Titus nodded in greeting, and then returned his gaze to the horizon line.

'Leave me alone,' he heard him mutter. 'You don't know me.'

'No, but I know why you're here. You're a jumper, right?'

'Don't say that.'

'But it's true.' Titus turned to face him. 'And the fact that you can't even handle hearing the word tells me you don't really want to take your own life. Right now, the idea is more attractive than the reality.'

The young man choked back a sob. Titus noted the bicycle in the grass behind him, and marked him down as a local.

'It's all gone wrong,' he croaked. 'Everything.'

Titus watched him weep for a moment. Then he produced a handkerchief from his pocket.

'Here,' he said, and stepped a little closer. 'Dry your eyes.'

At first the young man refused it, but Titus insisted.

'I loved her,' he said, and blew his nose. 'I know everyone says that breaking up hurts, but I can't go on without her in my life. There's no reason for me to be here any more.'

'I can think of one,' said Titus right away. 'Your family.'

'What do they care?' he sniffed. 'I left home last year.'

'But you never leave their hearts,' said Titus, and tapped his chest. 'Whatever stage you're at in life, you'll always find a place there.'

The young man wiped his nose on the back of his sleeve. Then he screwed up his eyes and attempted to hold back a sob.

'My parents won't care,' he said, and dug his fingernails into the grass as if braced to push himself off.

'Oh, they care all right!' Titus held out his hand, bidding him to halt. At the same time, he was ready if the guy chose to reach out for him. 'Trust me. As a father, it's my role to be there for my kids, even if they turn their backs on me.'

'You think so?' The young man looked like he was listening at least.

'No doubt about it,' Titus assured him. 'Everyone has to tread their own path through life, and make mistakes along the way. I just hope my children know that when they screw up my door is always open.'

The guy was just staring at Titus now. Finally, he blinked as if a spell had broken.

'Anyway, what are *you* doing out here at this time?'

'Well, I've got no plans to throw myself off,' said Titus. 'I'd rather be at home with my wife, in fact. It's where I belong.'

For a moment, the pair looked out across the sea in silence.

'I biked straight here when I read her note,' said the man eventually. 'She'd taken her stuff and everything. Killing myself seemed like the only option.'

'You want to kill the pain,' said Titus, as if to correct him. 'That's understandable, and I imagine just putting it into words right now is helping you to feel a little better.'

This time the man offered a brief smile,

'I guess.'

'So, why don't you take that crappy bike of yours and head back to your folks? Doesn't matter when you last saw them or what was said. Trust me, whenever you're in trouble it's the only place to be.'

The young man just stared at Titus for a second. Then he turned and bowed his head. Titus watched him, close to tears himself, and then smiled when he climbed to his feet and took a step away from the cliff edge.

'Is everything OK?' the man asked next, as he collected his bike from the grass. It was a comment he would go on to share with the investigating officers some months later, for the shaven-headed guardian angel who had just saved his life appeared to be welling up.

'It will be,' said Titus. 'Just as soon as I get home.'

Sasha Savage felt peculiar. After three courses, she'd expected to be bloated and full. Instead, she set down her dessert spoon in the plate she'd just cleared, feeling strangely nourished.

'That was . . . good,' she said.

'You sound surprised.' On the other side of the candle lights, Jack Greenway had been watching his dinner date finish her final mouthful. 'We vegetarians know how to entertain, you know?'

'OK, it was more than good,' said Sasha. 'It was great.'

Jack leaned in a little closer.

'Do you really mean that?'

Following the fried flower episode, things had picked up considerably. Sasha had quite enjoyed the artichoke bruschetta that Jack served for starters. The main dish, a gratin that contained a lot of beans, was certainly edible. What it lacked, in her opinion, was any bite and sinew. Still, this was Jack Greenway cooking for her. Jack *Greenway*. Granted, he had spent much of the meal talking about himself. When he did ask her a question, it was about the food he had cooked for her. Still, it was clear to Sasha that he had made a big effort. Even if the conversation had been a little one-sided, it was only polite that she complimented his culinary efforts. The meal had been much better than she imagined, even if she did wonder if there would be any sliced meat at home for a late-night sandwich.

'I loved it,' she said, and folded her napkin.

'That's great to hear,' said Jack as a grin eased across his face. 'So, after all that, would you?'

Sasha's eyes widened. Having dismissed her father's warnings about dining alone with the guy, she suddenly wondered whether he might have been right after all.

'Would I what?'

'Turn,' said Jack. 'Could you become meat-free for me? I was hoping that this evening has showed you the joy to be had from eating food that didn't once have a mother or a face.'

Sasha screwed up her face.

'Eating meat isn't all that bad.'

'It should be a crime in my opinion,' said Jack. 'Carnivores show no respect for life or the natural order.'

'But a falafel deserves everything it gets?' Sasha said this with such a disarming smile that Jack could find no argument.

'I'm sorry,' he said eventually. 'Sometimes I forget that not everyone shares my views about eating.'

I know the feeling, thought Sasha.

'It's good to believe in something,' she said instead. 'It shows a strong spirit.'

Jack didn't respond for a moment. He just held Sasha's gaze to the point where she had to blink and look away.

'You know I'm thinking about going vegan,' he said eventually. 'Totally plant-based eating. No dairy. Nothing.'

'Wow,' said Sasha, who didn't quite know how to respond to this news. 'Hardcore.'

'I hoped you'd be impressed,' he said. 'And I'm happy this little dinner of mine has given you food for thought.'

'It really has,' said Sasha, and hoped perhaps that things would move from the table to the sofa some time soon. Making out in the front room seemed more appealing to her than this culinary inquisition, though she certainly wasn't the kind of girl to set her sights on the bedroom. Not after such a short time together. Then again, judging by the way Jack remained in his chair with his eyes locked on hers, it didn't look like they were going anywhere.

'So, what do you think about the next seven days?' he asked her eventually. 'Could you go without meat for a week?'

'What?' said Sasha, who struggled to find the right response. 'Seriously?'

Slowly, as a thought took shape in his mind, Jack sat back and lifted his chin by an inch.

'Actually, let's see what you're really made of,' he said. 'Make it a *month*!'

'But, Jack—'

'It would mean so much to me,' he purred. 'I just know there's a vegetarian inside you.'

Ten minutes after her daughter was supposed to return home that evening, Angelica began disinfecting the kitchen surfaces with an antibacterial spray. The commercial people had brought in professional cleaners as the contract dictated. They had left it spotless, and that included removing the eviscerated vole from the fire grate without even a shriek. Angelica hadn't found fault with any of it. They had even sought her approval before leaving. Then again, her reason for going over things one more time had nothing to do with cleanliness. It was simply a distraction as she fretted about Sasha.

Angelica had tried her cell, only for it to go to voicemail. Calling Titus wasn't an option. As a precaution, he had left his phone at home. Taking it with him would only leave a digital footprint, and that was the last thing he needed. All she could do was work the cloth over the countertops and hope that her family would be back under the same roof soon. Angelica struggled not to fear the worst, which was why she gasped when a voice broke the silence behind her.

'*I can't sleep.*'

Spinning around, she found Ivan in his pajamas. He looked paler than ever, and very gloomy.

'My boy,' she said, and opened her arms to offer him a hug. 'I know you've made some mistakes today, but I do still love you so.'

Ivan walked into his mother's arms. He didn't return the squeeze, and just gazed at his reflection in the French windows behind her.

'Dad is really disappointed in me, isn't he?'

'He'll get over it.' Angelica moved her hands to his shoulders, and straightened her arms. She took a long look at Ivan, gazing into his eyes. 'You're his only son,' she said. 'It's important to him that you grow up with his values, just as he grew up with Grandpa's. Killing people for kicks isn't something they would ever consider.'

'I didn't do it on purpose,' he said to remind her.

'I know that,' said Angelica. 'Just don't let it happen again, OK?'

Ivan nodded, and then turned along with his mother at the sound of a key in the front door. Angelica held her breath on hearing footsteps in the hall. When Titus walked into the kitchen, leaving an empty-looking duffle bag behind him, she forced a smile that he saw through immediately.

'What's the problem?' he asked, shrugging off his coat.

Angelica glanced down at Ivan, indicating that the conversation could wait. Titus understood, and considered his son for a moment.

'Ivan,' he said finally. 'I blame myself for what happened. I shouldn't have shut myself away with work all morning. Not over the weekend. That's family time. But we can't go back. It's done now. If you've learned a valuable lesson here, then that woman won't have died in vain.'

The boy nodded, and then agreed with his father that it was time to return to bed. He scuttled off looking much brighter, which drew an admiring smile from Titus. Then he faced Angelica, and breathed out long and hard.

'What a night,' he said, crossing the floor to collect two wine glasses from the rack.

'It isn't over yet,' said Angelica, and paused until she had his full attention. 'Sasha hasn't come home.'

Titus set down the glasses on the counter. He glanced at the clock on the wall, his eyes tightening at the same time. His gaze only shifted at the sound of a car pulling up outside. He looked at Angelica, who stared back, clearly straining to listen just like him. As the vehicle halted, the engine cut out immediately. Even before it came back into life, with barely a squeeze on the pedal, Titus knew for sure that there had to be batteries supporting the motor under the bonnet.

'It's her,' he said. 'The vegetarian drives a hybrid.'

Angelica knew he was talking about those eco-friendly cars, but was in no mood to discuss the advantages and disadvantages.

'Go easy on her,' she said, as if fearful that Titus might

explode. 'And let's keep what happened today to ourselves. The model had an eating disorder, and we shouldn't let our daughter dwell on that. She's at an impressionable age.'

'Which is why we need to know what kind of boy has kept her from home.'

A moment later, Sasha appeared at the kitchen door. She took a breath on finding her parents waiting for her, and pressed a hand to her chest. Judging by the state of her hair, it was also quite clear to Titus and Angelica that their daughter had been thoroughly ravished.

'Oh,' was all she had to say, and looked at the floor tiles between them. 'It isn't as bad as it looks.' She paused there to adjust the neck of her top. 'Well, not *that* bad,' she added, and braved facing her mother and father.

A moment passed before Angelica regained the ability to close her mouth. Titus, however, appeared to see beyond Sasha's late return and disheveled state.

'Hello, honey,' he said, and stepped forward to hug her more tightly than ever before. In his embrace, Sasha looked in shock at her mother, who shared the same expression. 'Everyone is home. Nothing horrible can happen now. We Savages are safe here. Always have been, always will be.' After a moment's silence, Titus pulled back to look his speechless, puzzled daughter in the eyes. 'Hey,' he said, sounding uncomfortably bright, before smoothing her hair with his hand, 'it was nice of Jack to make sure you got back in one piece. You really should've invited him in to say hello.'

'I'm still not sure that's such a good idea just yet.'

'What? Are we embarrassing parents?' Titus touched his fingers to his chest and flashed a grin at Angelica. 'I insist, Sasha. Bring him by so we can meet him. I promise we won't bite.'

SECOND COURSE

12

Ivan Savage had one big regret about the death of the model. Brooding in his bedroom several days later, he wished that he had rigged up a video camera alongside the iron that killed her. Yes, it had hit the wrong target, and he never meant to kill anyone, but surely his father would calm down if he saw what an effective job his son had made of the execution?

'Upstairs is out of bounds,' he grumbled to himself, while combing his hair in the mirror. 'If you come upstairs, you don't go down again.'

What really hurt, though, the thing that really cut and stung, was his father's reaction. Even before he spelled out his disappointment in the boy, Ivan had seen it in his eyes. There was no hint of pride at a clean and imaginative kill. It was all 'you foolish this' and 'stupid that'. He had never felt so small and insignificant in his life. Nor as misunderstood. Yes, his father had cooled down on his return from the drop off, but it was hard for the boy to simply brush off that kind of criticism.

All Ivan ever wanted was some recognition for his efforts. And yet where had his pranks gotten him? Psychiatric assessment with some flashcards of kids crying. Nobody laughed at his efforts. Not once had he been clapped on the back or talked about admiringly, and now this. A clean kill and yet all he'd earned for it was criticism.

There was only one person he blamed for the situation. Sasha's boyfriend, Jack. Why? Because if he hadn't cooked for Sasha that evening, and lured her from home, then she would've been on the receiving end of the iron, not Lulabelle. Of course, Ivan would've found himself in even more trouble had he slaughtered his sister, which came as some comfort. Nevertheless, he held the vegetarian accountable for the fact that he felt so worthless just then. It also left him all the more determined to prove himself to his dad.

The first thing to enter Ivan's head left him staring at his reflection in the mirror. After a moment, he blinked and dismissed the idea out of hand. Depriving Sasha of a boyfriend wasn't exactly going to help him regain some standing in the family. Jack's fate lay in her hands, not his, he decided, before leaving all such thoughts behind to answer the front door.

Before the bell summoned Sasha from her room, she had been lying on her bed, staring at the ceiling. Only one thing occupied her thoughts: just where things were heading with Jack.

In her mind, she had put together a list of all his good points and his bad points. On the upside, he was smoulderingly handsome and passionate about food. He drove his own car, made her packed lunches and had set a challenge that Sasha found herself determined to take on. She wasn't really doing it for him though, as she had come to realize.

Instead, the prospect of turning her back on meat for a month felt like a chance for her to strike out as a Savage in her own right. She was close to her family, and had her parents to thank for that. Even so, going vegetarian felt like a shot at independence that she couldn't refuse.

Then Sasha had begun to compile Jack's bad points. It wasn't a big list, just a problem.

'What am I dating here?' she'd asked herself at one point. 'And why is he dating me?'

When Jack first sprang into her life, it had been a surprise to Sasha and also a relief. Unlike Faria and Maisy, she'd never been able to say that she had a boyfriend. Faria had come home smitten from a summer vacation the year before, and then tortured herself for two months over Skype with flaky Fernando from Barcelona. Maisy had gone out with some boy who was genuinely crazy about her. The trouble with poor Daniel 'Daisy' Duke was his age. He was only a year younger than Maisy, but that was the equivalent of about a decade in school terms. Three weeks in, despite valiantly ignoring all the cougar comments, and the rhymes about 'Maisy 'n' Daisy', poor Daniel's fate was sealed when he showed up for a trip to the movies in shorts, socks and Crocs. Still, at least both girls could claim some experience with relationships. So, when the hottest boy in the junior class turned his attention to Sasha, and showed no sign of stuttering and blushing when he spoke, she really did feel as if her time had come.

In the beginning, Jack had been all over her. It had been flattering and a thrill, but as the weeks passed she wondered if he was as passionate about her as a person. Take the dinner he'd cooked. She couldn't fault the effort he had made. She'd even had a good time afterwards, just making out on the sofa with a movie on pay-per-view. What troubled her was the fact that he hadn't shown nearly the same interest in her mind. Everything they covered seemed to return to the same subject, which was Jack. He had talked in great detail about ethical eating, but didn't once invite Sasha to contribute her own opinions. Of course, she had no intention of sharing how her family justified their chosen path through this topic. The point was he never asked.

Reflecting on this now, Sasha found herself coming to the realization that Jack's personality didn't quite live up to his good looks. In some ways, he reminded her of a fast food burger. He looked delicious, but the content just failed to match the promise. Still, thought Sasha to herself, she was prepared to give Jack a chance. It wasn't as if she had much experience in these matters, after all. In a way, she decided, it was a shame she couldn't be more shallow. That's what Faria and Maisy would advise her. For despite the lack of substance, there was no denying that the boy was a babe.

The weirdest thing about that evening had been the way her dad reacted. Having gotten home late, looking like she'd dragged herself backwards through the hedge to get there, Sasha found him with his arms wide open. He hadn't pressed her for an explanation, and there was no mention of being grounded. If anything, he had seemed overjoyed at the simple fact that she was safely back at home, and equally excited to meet Jack.

'I'm missing something,' she decided, and sat up to place her head in her hands. 'Something bad.'

Sasha sat quite still for a moment, reflecting on things at home and in her love life, and that was when the doorbell sounded.

Angelica Savage was in the garden at that moment. Katya was sitting on a rug on the lawn. She played happily with daisies while her mother worked her way around the roses, deadheading every bloom that showed the first sign of decay. As a result, the garden looked like a patch of paradise. A world away from the reality surrounding them.

'Who is that?' she asked, on hearing the doorbell, and made sure to place the pruning shears out of reach of her youngest daughter.

It was only as she made her way back into the house that she heard Ivan and then Sasha descending the stairs, bickering as they went.

'It won't be for you,' said Sasha, who was anxious to get there first. 'Nobody has come by to see you since the midwife after you were born.'

'Then let's hope it's for you,' Ivan replied, several steps ahead of her. 'It might even be Jack!'

Through the front door's frosted glass pane, Angelica recognized the visitors immediately. Unfortunately, it was too late to stop Ivan and caution him to be careful before he opened up. She stopped, midway along the hall, and quickly checked her composure.

'Hello, kids,' said one of the two police officers. 'I'm sure you know why we're here.'

Angelica watched Sasha turn and look at her. She responded by not blinking, silently imploring her daughter to just stay calm while she handled this. Aware that the officers were awaiting an answer, she then pressed her lips together and nodded.

'The agency called me with the sad news,' said Angelica. 'That poor soul. Had any of us known there was a woman in despair downstairs during the shoot, we would've done everything to talk her out of the fate she chose for herself.'

She saw Sasha glance at her brother now, seeking some explanation still, while Ivan just stared at his shoes.

'May we come in?' asked the other officer, a policewoman who was notably taller than her male colleague.

'Yes, of course.' Angelica gestured for her children to stand aside, her heart rate starting to stir. 'Would you like some tea? Coffee? Juice . . . water?

The male officer responded by pulling out a notebook from his pocket.

'When was the last time you saw Lulabelle Hart?' he asked, and clicked the top of his ballpoint pen. 'It's important that we piece together her final hours before the suicide.'

Angelica noted how Sasha closed her eyes in resignation at this. Her daughter needed no further explanation. That much was clear to her. Fortunately, both officers were waiting for Angelica to answer and didn't catch the look on Sasha's face. Even to an outsider, it betrayed the fact that she knew full well that her family would be involved.

'I'm afraid we didn't see Ms. Hart at all,' Angelica told the officers. 'During a shoot we head upstairs and that's where we stay, don't we, kids?'

Both Sasha and Ivan nodded dutifully when the officer turned briefly in their direction.

'This is just routine,' said the female officer, as if mindful that their presence in this matter might upset the two minors. 'For the report.'

'Did you hear anything untoward downstairs?' asked her colleague, addressing Sasha and Ivan this time.

'Nothing.' Ivan didn't even blink.

'It was just another shoot,' echoed Sasha after a moment and then caught her mother's eye. 'We never laid eyes on her.'

The male officer closed his notebook, having written down what looked like their home address, and nothing more.

'Well, we're grateful for your time,' he said, before drawing Angelica's attention. 'You understand we have to go through the motions,' he said to her quietly. 'Even with a clear-cut suicide.'

'Of course,' said Angelica, well aware that Sasha had just heard every word. 'If there's anything more we can do, you only have to ask.'

Sasha held the door open for the officers, smiling sweetly. It was only once they'd left the house that she turned and ushered her mother and brother into the kitchen.

'Was it Beachy Head?' she asked, straining not to shout in case the police were still outside. 'That's where Dad goes if the kill isn't fit for the table.'

'Honey,' said Angelica, but Sasha hadn't finished.

'I can't believe you'd pick off someone working on a shoot downstairs. That takes fast food to a whole new level! When have we ever taken such a risk?'

'It wasn't like that,' Angelica tried to reason. 'Lulabelle was an accident.'

'Is this why Dad was in such a strange mood when I came home? I fully expected to be grounded for being late. Instead, he hugs me like I've been missing for months.'

'It's just made him aware how precious his family is to him.' Angelica gripped her daughter by the shoulders in a bid to calm her down. 'This wasn't about a feast. It was just a prank that went wrong.'

'A prank.' Without hesitating, Sasha swung around to face Ivan. 'So, *you* killed her.'

'Not on purpose,' he said, shrugging at the same time. 'It was meant for you.'

'Oh, great!' Sasha rolled her eyes and returned her attention to Angelica. 'You know, since meeting Jack I've begun to feel like a normal, average teenager. It's a first for me and I like it. Now, Jack certainly isn't perfect, but he does manage to resist an urge to *murder for the lols*!'

'Now that's enough!' Angelica pulled back and glared at her daughter. 'As a family, we stick together. What happened was unfortunate, but your father has dealt with it. As a result of his efforts, there's no evidence in this house that could link us to the death of Lulabelle Hart. So relax, Sasha. As far as you and Ivan are concerned, you can continue with your lives as normal.'

'But, Mom,' said Sasha. 'We eat people. That's not normal.'

'Tastes good, though,' Ivan pointed out, only to shrink from his mother's attention.

Angelica let a moment pass before beginning again.

'One single aspect of our lives is . . . different, and that difference is because of your dad. He's just trying to give you the best start in life, as it was for him as a boy. Everything else marks us as a typical family, and if we're going to get through this without attracting attention then it's vital that we all carry on just being ourselves.'

'With the exception of Ivan,' Sasha pointed out. 'He's out of control, Mom.'

'Well, yes, your brother really ought to call a halt to the body count,' agreed Angelica, 'and then we all just need to move on. In fact, now would be a great time for your father to meet Jack.'

'Please don't bring him into this,' said Sasha. 'It won't end well.'

'It's perfect,' she insisted. 'An everyday kind of event that happens in households with nothing to hide.'

'Mom.'

'You know he genuinely wants to meet this boy now,' Angelica continued. 'Inviting Jack just shows your father is keen to bring him into the fold.'

'Better in than out, eh?' said Ivan, who seemed very pleased not to be the center of his mother's attention now.

Sasha's eyes opened wide before she blinked.

'But he's vegetarian,' she said, and seemed prepared to spell it out for her if necessary.

'We all have our faults,' said Angelica, who had anticipated her eldest leaping to the wrong conclusion, 'which is one more reason why your dad is keen to find out what you see in him.'

13

As a private investigator, Vernon English mostly picked up a newspaper to hide behind. Reading them didn't interest him much. He liked the TV at the end of a long day, and maybe some talk radio on long stake-outs in the van. On this occasion, sitting at the window of a café that smelled like bacon and bleach, he found himself paying more attention to a small article on the page he'd opened at random than to the figure in the steak house across the street.

'Lulabelle Hart,' he said to himself, on reading of her demise, and then set the paper down for a clear view of the man he was here to observe. 'I wonder what tipped her over the edge?'

Vernon was well aware that the model's last assignment had been at the Savage house. He had retrieved a copy of the call sheet from the bin outside. According to the report in the paper, her behavior that day had been described by some crew members as 'tense' and then 'erratic'. Sadly, nobody present on the shoot had realized quite what turmoil the poor soul was in. According to the police and a source from the coroner's office, this was just a tragic event. Ms. Hart's death was not being treated as suspicious.

Second Course

Having read the article twice, Vernon tightened his gaze on the diner opposite. Titus Savage was just finishing a business lunch. His companion, the mole from the company Titus planned to take over, was doing a lot of talking. This came as no surprise to Vernon, given that Titus had earlier handed him a small fold of cash under the table. The private investigator had been quick to snap a picture, but there was something more going on with Titus Savage, and he was determined to find out what. Take his disappearance on the drive out following the shoot. Vernon still bitterly regretted pulling in for a bite to eat, but just where had Titus been heading? There was no sign of his 4x4 in the airport parking lot, and Vernon didn't need to look at a map to know that a turn off before the highway would've taken him towards the coast. Was Lulabelle's death connected to the Savage family in some way? Now he could take what he knew to the police, or he could find out for himself. The private investigator washed down the last of his coffee, including the dregs, before tearing the article from the newspaper. This was a case he could handle on his own, he decided. Because if he could prove there was a link then not only would it kill the takeover bid, but Vernon English would secure his reputation at last and the offers of work would come flooding in.

Watching Titus ask for the bill, he found himself looking at this case in a different light. Through Vernon's eyes, the man had just become his meal ticket to success.

That lunch break, Sasha joined her friends on the skate park ramp. It was the first time that they'd had a chance to talk since her date with Jack. Naturally, everyone wanted to know details.

'Did you sleep with him?' asked Faria, who was tapping away on her BlackBerry at the same time.

'Obviously that would be a no,' said Sasha, who had just been leaning back on her elbows, enjoying the midday sun on her face. She sat up and rested her arms on the safety rail. 'I'm not saying never. If things work out then maybe.'

'But he tried, right?'

'He isn't like that.' Sasha examined her nails, in case the others caught her eye and saw right through her. 'Not really.'

'Right.' Faria looked up from her BlackBerry, smiling to herself. 'So he went to all that effort cooking just for a kiss on the cheek?'

'It was more than that.'

'How much more?' asked Maisy, who had been listening closely. 'Did you get to see his cucumber?'

'That's none of your business!' Sasha tried hard to sound outraged.

'Does that mean it was more of a zucchini?'

Faria's question was met by silence, but only for a moment.

'Let's just say I had to deal with a lot of vegetables that evening.'

This time, all three girls laughed together.

'So, really, what was dinner like?' Faria asked. 'Apart from light on the chicken.'

'Good,' said Sasha, and then caught her eye. 'Healthy.'

'You mean boring,' said Faria, nodding to herself.

Sasha chuckled and looked to her lap.

'How about the conversation?' asked Maisy.

This time, Sasha failed to muster even a smile. Maisy and Faria glanced at one another and grinned.

'That was boring, too?' asked Faria. 'Don't say that, Sasha. Jack is a babe. You're killing the dream.'

'In your shoes,' said Maisy playfully, 'I wouldn't be that interested in his mind.'

'But I'm not like you,' said Sasha, thinking at the same time what an understatement that was. 'Look, I was flattered by the effort he made to cook for me. Jack is genuinely into his vegetarianism, too. I do admire him for that.'

'You admire him?' Faria paused for a moment. 'Is that the same as lust?'

'No.'

'You're going red,' Maisy pointed out. 'So, if it isn't lust then could it be love?'

Sensing that further protest would be pointless, Sasha told them both to grow up.

'I like him, all right? Yes, he's good looking, and the attention is great, but there has to be more to a boy than a pretty face. It can't last otherwise, but obviously I'm hoping Jack will prove me wrong.'

'When are you next seeing him?' asked Maisy.

'Any time now,' said Sasha, and cast her gaze to the cut-through between the school and the field. 'He's made me a packed lunch.'

'Really?' Faria glanced at Maisy. 'So, now he's your mom?'

Sasha weathered the comment by smiling to herself.

'I figured it would be rude to refuse,' she told them.

'Well, you didn't have a problem saying no to the sex,' said Maisy.

Sighing now, Sasha faced Maisy and Faria in turn before leveling with them both.

'Had I just given in and gone for it,' she said, 'then right now I wouldn't be feeling good about myself. Jack is my chance to prove that when it comes to my life I call all the shots. My dad has already marked him down as someone who could lead me astray. The last thing I want to do is make things difficult by acting like a sheep.'

'You're not a sheep,' agreed Maisy with some certainty.

'You're a wolf,' Faria finished for her. 'A wolf in sheep's clothing.'

Sasha stared at her shoes, nodding to herself.

'As for lunch, here's hoping you like carrot sticks.'

'Listen, I'll give it a try,' said Sasha with a grin. 'It's all part of Jack's challenge to turn me. I'm going veggie for a month.'

For a second, both girls looked lost for words.

'You are kidding us,' said Faria slowly. 'You want his babies. Little vegetarian babies with names like Parsley and Basil.'

'It *must* be love,' Maisy agreed, and drew their attention to the cut-through. There, the young man in question had just appeared bearing a Tupperware box as if it were a bunch of roses.

Jack Greenway had a plan for Sasha. A meal plan. He'd been working on it since their dinner together. The result was now folded inside his jeans pocket as he made his way out of the school to meet her. The hallways were swarming with kids. Ever since he'd started the year as a sophomore, it felt as if he were attending some kind of preschool. On the upside, the sophomore girls looked up to him like he had an A+ in maturity and cool.

'Hey, Matilda . . . What's up, Chrissie? Tess, is that a new ear piercing? What's it called? A tragus! Wow. Looks good on you.'

As for the boys in the years below Jack, they might as well have been invisible. If they got in his way he would simply expect them to move. That lunchtime, it was Ivan who discovered this for himself. He'd just left the canteen, having collected a ham baguette, and was crossing the hallway on his way to chess club. Cutting across the flow of students was never easy, but Jack just made it harder for him.

'Watch out, dumbass!' he snapped, when Ivan walked right into him. 'Do you have any idea what you nearly made me drop just then?'

Ivan looked up at the young man clutching the Tupperware box. He knew full well this was the vegetarian guy dating his sister. Clearly Jack had no idea that he was giving Sasha's kid brother a hard time here. Ivan glanced at the box and took a wild guess at the contents.

'Looks like rabbit food to me.'

Jack Greenway heard him clearly. The kid was confident. He'd give him that. He was also shaping up for a kicking. Not that Jack was a fighter. Violence was something he opposed in every shape or form, from animal testing to any global conflict that resulted in a wrist band he could wear to put his views on display.

'It's got to be better than that crap,' he said, and grabbed the baguette from Ivan's hands. 'What do we have here?'

'Give it back!' the boy demanded.

Calmly, holding it from Ivan's reach, Jack peeled the baguette apart and peered inside. A disapproving look crossed his face, which he shared with Ivan.

'You know this ham is processed, don't you? It contains saturated fat and all kinds of chemicals. In fact, it isn't really ham at all.'

'Well, I like it!' protested Ivan, whose ears and cheeks had turned crimson with anger. 'And you'll be sorry.'

By now, the dispute had drawn a small crowd. Jack glanced around and grinned.

'Kid, I'd be doing you a favor by tossing this. If more people ditched meat completely this world would be a better place.'

Ivan had heard enough. Without warning, he leapt up with his all his might and snatched the baguette back into his possession. Then, before anyone could react, he swung it like a baseball bat directly into Jack's groin. The impact caused the baguette to crumple between his legs and the breath in his lungs to exit in surprise. He looked down, utterly shocked, and then around at the crowd who had just begun to titter and smirk. The assault hadn't really hurt him, but Jack's pride had taken quite a hit. Ivan, meanwhile, appeared completely unrepentant.

'Don't mess with my lunch again,' he said, before taking himself and his battered baguette away through the crowd.

Watching him go, Jack felt more sheepish now than stunned. He looked around, still clutching the Tupperware box, and attempted to dismiss the situation with a smile.

'We're just fooling around,' he said. 'Probably all the additives in that junk he thinks is ham.'

Turning quickly, Jack hurried on his way. He glanced down, just to check the assault hadn't left him with margarine all over his pants, and swore that he would get even with that arrogant little jerk. Just then, however, he wasn't going to let it spoil this moment. For Sasha's first vegetarian lunch, he'd prepared two pots of pineapple and cashew couscous with edamame beans, goat cheese and red pepper. With some fresh grapes to follow, which he was quietly hoping she'd let him hand feed her in his car. The way to a girl's heart was through her stomach, he believed. It had worked wonders on his previous dates. And once he had won them over, everything else would follow.

As soon as he saw Sasha, sitting on the skate ramp with her friends, Jack stopped and waved the lunchbox. He was pleased to see her climb off and make her way across the field. Sasha was his sole interest just then. Her friends were just a pain.

'You're going to love this,' he said, having wrapped his arm around her and led her further from the skate ramp. 'That's if you haven't changed your mind?'

'I'm ready,' she said. 'I can see this is important to you—'

'Not just to me,' Jack cut in. 'Think of the animals.'

'Oh, OK! That, too!'

Smiling, Jack held her gaze for a moment. Sasha was engaging and smart, he thought to himself, and her willingness to give this a shot was flattering. It was just a shame that she hadn't let him go all the way over the weekend. After all the work he had put into that meal, she'd hardly repaid the gesture. In the past, other girls had given in before he'd even served dessert. Jack hoped he wouldn't get bored of her. He'd give it a month, he decided. At most.

'Promise me you won't go back to your old ways over the next four weeks,' he asked Sasha. 'If you do, I'll know.'

'How?' Sasha looked puzzled.

'Your skin,' he said, matter-of-factly. 'A vegetarian diet is so cleansing, as you're about to find out for yourself. Think of it as a detox.'

Sasha touched her fingers to her face. Her complexion had always been clear and trouble-free, which her mother put down to their diet, but Jack certainly sounded like he would recognize any change.

'You don't have to worry,' she said. 'Day one has already begun.'

A lock of hair had come loose from her grip. Jack brushed it behind her ear.

'So, what did you have for breakfast?' he asked.

'A kind of last supper,' said Sasha. 'Muesli. Toast. *Steak.*' She waited for Jack to look truly horrified, before her earnest expression melted away. 'I'm kidding,' she said. 'We carnivores know how to eat a balanced diet.'

Jack presented her with the Tupperware box.

'This is what I call balanced *and* ethically sound,' he said. 'I hope it's going to make a life-changing impression on you.'

'That reminds me,' she said, accepting the box. 'All of a sudden my dad really wants to meet you.'

'Cool,' said Jack. 'I'm sure they want to know who's showing their daughter the light when it comes to meat-free living.'

Sasha peered at the box, wincing slightly at what he'd just said.

'I'm happy you'd like to stop by,' she told him, 'but it might be best to steer clear of the subject of food. My parents have strong views, too, and I really want everyone to get along.'

Jack considered this for a moment, before gently clasping Sasha by the sides of her head and drawing her close to kiss her forehead.

'I promise to be on my best behavior,' he said, and slipped her arm around her waist. 'Now, why don't we go find my car so you can start the transformation?'

'You make it sound so permanent,' said Sasha, as they turned and headed for the junior parking lot. 'I only agreed to go veggie for a month.'

'Let's see how you feel then,' said Jack. 'I'm confident that you won't look back.'

14

That evening, Oleg Fedor Savadski reached the foot of the stairs from the upper floor, and wondered where he was. He looked around, his dressing-gown sash hanging loose around his pajamas.

'Goddammit,' he muttered to himself. 'They must've moved the bathroom again.'

Oleg knew that his mind was beginning to falter. Little things in his daily life had become a test for him, such as the whereabouts of his spectacles or the name of the thing that hung from the ceiling which glowed when he hit the switch. Of course, he knew it was the light bulb. Like the location of the bathroom, it would quickly come back to him. Even so, as he shuffled along the landing, Oleg wished he could do something to restore his wits.

It was the sound of gunfire and explosions that prompted him to stop outside Ivan's bedroom. Despite his forgetfulness, Oleg's memory of the Siege was vivid. Just hearing the crackle of a weapon transported him to the ruins of Leningrad in a blink. Without knocking, he opened the door and looked in on his grandson. Ivan was sitting on the edge of his bed with a videogame controller in his hands. His eyes were locked on the screen across the room.

It showed some frenzied military skirmish, and was the source of all the noise.

'Hi, Grandpa,' he said, without looking around. At the same time, he squeezed a trigger on the controller. The sound of bullets spitting from a clip filled the room for a moment. 'Are you looking for the bathroom again?'

'It can wait,' said Grandpa, watching the action on the screen. 'Good game?'

'*Great* game,' said Ivan, who had yet to blink. 'I love this level. If I can take out every mercenary I'll get a weapons upgrade and then I'm practically unbeatable.'

'Can I play?'

Ivan hit the pause button. The noise gave way to silence. Ivan faced his grandfather, surprised by the request.

'Really?'

'Got to keep my reflexes sharp somehow.' Oleg closed the door behind him. 'Now make room for an old man and pass me the other controller.'

It took a little while for Oleg to get to grips with the game. Thrilled that his grandfather should show an interest, Ivan patiently explained what to do, and even suggested that they fight on the same side.

'I'll be your wingman,' he said. 'Lock and load, Grandpa!'

'The action is a little over the top,' said Oleg, who was leaning forward to focus on the split screen in front of them. 'But it reminds me of the old days, that's for sure.'

For a moment, the pair focused on taking out an incoming wave of mercenaries.

'What was it like?' asked Ivan next. 'During the war?'

'Grim,' said Oleg. 'Like hell on earth, with just a taste of Heaven every now and then.'

'Sniper on the tower,' warned Ivan, and promptly took out the target with a headshot. The body dropped from its position, hitting the floor like all the bones had left its body. 'See ya, sucker!'

'God rest his soul,' said Oleg quietly, but it was enough to draw a glance from his grandson. 'So, what happens to the corpse now?' he asked.

'Nothing,' said Ivan with a shrug.

Oleg looked back at the screen. Smoke drifted across the battleground, which shook as a nearby airstrike hit a building. With a sigh, he set the controller down beside him.

'There is a lot of death in this game,' he said. 'With no respect shown to the fallen.'

Finding himself without a partner, Ivan mashed the controller buttons in a bid to stay alive.

'What do you suggest?' he asked. 'We bury him while the bullets fly?'

'No,' said Oleg. 'We should eat him.'

For the second time since his grandfather joined him, Ivan paused the game.

'This isn't real,' said the boy. 'It's fun.'

Oleg clasped his hands in his lap. He stared at his thumbs, turning them over and over.

'No death should be taken in vain, as we all hope you've learned after what happened last weekend.' He watched the boy press his lips together, nodding at the same time. Then he waited for Ivan to meet his eyes once more. 'Ivan, if a life must come to an end then the body should be treated with ceremony. Your father wasn't unaffected by the disposal of the model. He was forced to take that action for the sake of his son, but it moved him deeply.'

'I know,' said Ivan quietly. 'He hugged us all a lot the next day.'

'It's a shame we weren't able to consume her,' said Oleg, 'In the early history of mankind, a friend or a foe would be feasted upon as a mark of respect. Long before burial and cremation became popular, that's just how things were done.' He stopped there for a moment, seemingly lost in thought. 'Of course, I had no choice but to revive the ritual as a means of survival, but after the Siege it grew to mean so much more to me, and to my family.'

'How was it?' asked Ivan, who had been listening closely. 'The first time?'

Oleg chuckled to himself.

'Awful, torturous, *unbearable*,' he said. 'Your grandmother and I were close to death ourselves. We were gaunt, weak, beyond hope, and struggling to stay alive in a city with more bodies than the living. All the food was gone. There was nothing left we could eat. Nothing but . . .' He paused to reflect for a moment. 'Slowly, it became something that many people considered, but only a few put into practice. Some say it was mostly young mothers desperate to feed their children, but I didn't see that for myself. We had thought about it for some time, of course, but always dismissed it as going beyond the limits of humanity.'

'So what changed your mind?'

'A neighbor,' said Oleg. 'She lived in the apartment next to ours, and had seen every member of her family perish. She was a sweet, quiet soul who had endured just so much misery. The trauma of our existence left her vulnerable. Your grandmother helped her wherever possible, and once even shared a dead pigeon with her that we'd managed to find in the rubble. But, Ivan, her heart was broken. She had no will to survive. Weak beyond reason, it was a small mercy that her heart gave out in her sleep. We couldn't just leave her corpse in the apartment. We had to do something, but at the same time we were desperate people. That morning we had forced down pebbles just to give our bellies something, so you can understand what led us to look at her body in a different light.'

'Was it your idea?' asked Ivan, who had been listening intently. 'Or Granny's?'

'I could read her mind and she could read mine,' answered Oleg, nodding at the same time. 'It was as if an inner voice had awoken in us both, and it spoke so loud and clear that neither of us could ignore it. So, we made a joint decision. Your grandmother folded back the bed sheet and with my pocketknife we peeled off the thinnest layer of flesh from her thigh. Oh, Ivan, the moment moved me to tears. What I was doing felt so wrong and yet so necessary. The sliver wasn't enough to sustain either of us. We halved it, and on the count of three each placed what we had in our mouths. Several times we spat it out, and both of us retched before we finally succeeded in washing it down our gullets with rain water. But once it settled in the stomach we soon went back for more. We were starving to death, Ivan, you have to remember that, so to be nourished at that time was to feel as if God Himself had fed us. I'll never forget it. We were rejuvenated and elated, as if born again! My boy, there is something so special about human flesh that drives a man to devour until nothing more is left. Ever since, I look forward to that feeling each time we sit to feast.'

Ivan toyed with his controller.

'When Granny died,' he said finally. 'Did you?'

'A little.' Oleg nodded. 'Your father was only small at the time, but we both did so in her honor.'

'I was too young to remember my first mouthful,' he said. 'But I wouldn't give it up now.'

'Just be careful,' warned his grandfather. 'One careless kill could mark the end of a family tradition that I hope outlives us all.'

Of all the dinners her mother could've cooked, on what was Sasha's first meat-free day, it had to be pork chops. She could smell them from her bedroom, even with the door shut. Compared to human flesh, this was the next best thing. Her father often reminded them that pigs share ninety-eight per cent of the human genetic make-up, which explained why her mouth was so moist. Still, with exams looming, Sasha had studying to get through. It was a struggle, however. Just thinking about those prime cuts crackling and popping on the griddle wasn't only a distraction. In view of her oath, it was torture.

'When will we be eating?' she asked, having drifted downstairs to the kitchen.

Angelica was at the stove, with little Katya in the high chair at a safe distance from the spitting oil. The toddler looked delighted to see her big sister, and gurgled when Sasha crossed to pet her.

'Any time now,' said Angelica, and flipped a chop with her spatula. 'The mashed potatoes are ready. So, as soon as the peas come to the boil.'

'Do we have any nuts?' asked Sasha. 'Cashews, perhaps. Or almonds?'

Her mother turned, spatula in hand, as if to check she had heard her correctly. 'Nuts. You want nuts to go with the chops?'

'Actually, I was thinking instead of the chops.'

Angelica turned the gas down a notch.

'What's wrong? Are you ill? Something you've eaten?'

'I'm fine,' Sasha insisted, and focused her attention on playing with Katya's curly locks. 'I just thought nuts would be good.'

Angelica looked at how uncomfortable her daughter appeared and knew that there was more to this.

'Sasha,' she said calmly. 'Your father isn't home from work yet. You can talk to me. If there's anything on your mind, I'm here.'

'I know that.' Sasha offered her finger for Katya to chew on. At the same time, the pan of peas on the stove came to the boil. The water frothed over the sides, which drew Angelica's attention for a moment. Once she'd dealt with it, she turned back to Sasha, who knew she'd have to offer her something.

'It's just for a short time,' she said to begin. 'Mom,

don't freak out on me or anything, but I'm skipping meat for a little while. It's for Jack. He asked me. We made a pact.'

Sasha held her mother's gaze for what felt like an age. It only came to an end when Katya bit down on her finger a little too hard.

'Be careful,' Angelica said to her youngest daughter, but kept her eyes pinned on Sasha. 'Your father thinks she's ready, you know? The last of her teeth are coming through. We're thinking soon it'll be time for a welcoming feast.'

Sasha knew full well what she meant. All of a sudden she felt like some kind of traitor to the family.

'This isn't a permanent arrangement. By the time Katya's big day comes, everything will be back to normal.'

'So, how long do you plan to keep this up?' asked Angelica, returning her attention to the pan.

'Four weeks.'

"Four *what*?' Sasha's answer brought her mother round full circle. 'You're seriously thinking of no meat for a month?'

'It isn't like a lifetime. Not really.'

'But why? What does this prove? And what could it do to you? You'll turn anemic or something. It can't be good for your concentration at school.'

'My concentration is fine. School is fine. This isn't me going off the rails or anything.'

'But it isn't making me comfortable,' replied Angelica all the same. 'What ideas has this boy put into your head?'

Sasha examined her finger, which was still stinging. Kat hadn't drawn blood, but she could see her teeth marks.

'This isn't really about Jack,' she said. 'As soon as he laid down the challenge, I began to think it was something I'd genuinely like to try. Just to see if I can, and what difference it would make. Seriously, going veggie for a while isn't a big deal.'

'It will be to your father.'

'Does he have to know?'

Angelica returned to the business of preparing dinner. She reached for the plates and began to lay them out.

'He just called to say he was on his way home from the subway station,' she said. 'By the sound of it, he's had a difficult day.'

'All the more reason not to say anything,' said Sasha, watching her mother as she began to lay out a scoop of mashed potato on each plate, followed by a sprinkling of peas. 'Please, Mom. If he finds out now he'll just put a stop to it without giving me a chance to find out what it's like to do something, well . . . different.'

Angelica didn't reply. Instead, reaching for the spatula, she transferred a pork chop to every plate but one. Sasha smiled in relief, and skipped to the cupboard when Angelica told her that's where she'd find some nuts.

'But you'll have to eat quickly,' she said. 'I'm sure he won't ask questions if he knows you're using the time to study.'

Sasha was already seated at the table when Angelica placed the plate in front of her. She looked up to thank her mother, but Angelica's taut mouth told Sasha enough had been said. Instead, she picked up her knife and fork and began to eat. Without the chop, it just tasted like something was missing, but that was not the point. She could do this, she told herself. However things worked out with Jack, he'd introduced her to something she felt compelled to try. Sasha ate without speaking, keen to be finished before her dad returned home. She fully expected to hear the front door open at any time, so when the bell rang it came as a surprise.

'He's probably forgotten his keys,' muttered Angelica, and made her way to the hall.

It left Sasha to pick up the last of the nuts and shovel them into the pockets of her cheeks as fast as possible. She heard the door open, and crunched on them hurriedly. By the time her mother returned, there was nothing on her plate that would spark a real fight. Then again, the figure that followed Angelica into the kitchen wasn't Titus.

'From the gas company,' said the man with the ID necklace when Sasha looked up from the table. 'Sorry to disturb. I'll just take a reading and be gone.'

Vernon English wasn't exactly a master of disguise. He had a whole bundle of fake identities to call upon. It's just that he looked the same whichever one he chose to wear: a little out of shape, with tangled, receding hair that was just begging to be hidden under his beloved cap. Arriving in the kitchen behind Angelica Savage, he tried hard not to show too much of an interest in his surroundings. The girl looked surprised to see him, but not suspicious, while the toddler in the high chair shrieked in delight and threw out her arms.

'Hello, little one!' Vernon reached out to ruffle her hair,

only to remind himself that this might be deemed inappropriate behavior for a representative of the power company. The last thing he needed was an official complaint, mostly because the ID around his neck was totally fake. 'Cute kid,' he said instead, and turned to find Angelica watching him with her arms folded.

'The meter is over there,' she said, and gestured at a cupboard in a recess beside the French windows.

'As good as done,' said Vernon, and got on with the task at hand.

Some months earlier, the private investigator had picked up a bunch of radio bugs on eBay. This was the first time he'd put one into use. Although highly illegal for the task he had in mind, in his opinion it was a fast track to nailing Titus Savage. Not just for his business dealings but his possible involvement in the death of Lulabelle Hart. The device was the size of a watch battery, and stuck snugly onto the side of the gas meter as he jotted down the numbers on a clipboard he'd brought with him. 'All set,' he said, rising to his feet. He turned to address Angelica once more, only to find the man of the house at the kitchen door.

'Something smells good,' said Titus, as Vernon suddenly pretended to look busy with his clipboard. 'What's for dinner?'

'It's served and ready to go,' said Angelica, before raising one eyebrow at the man in the corner.

'Oh, don't let me stop you.' Vernon kept his head down on making his way to the door. Sometimes making face to face contact with his target was unavoidable, but it couldn't happen more than once. Not without attracting suspicion. 'Bon appetit!'

As he left, both Titus and Angelica exchanged a puzzled look.

'Since when did the gas man ever sound so cheery?' he asked.

'The guy seemed a bit too interested in little Kat,' said Sasha, who by now had cleared her plate. 'Probably a pedophile.'

Titus turned to peer into the hall. By then, the man was gone. He faced back at the three girls in his life, and dismissed their concerns with a chuckle.

'So the gas man is a nice guy. That doesn't make him suspect. Though I have to say it seems like only yesterday that I paid the last bill.' Titus sighed, and then smiled fondly at the little one straining to escape from her high chair so that she could reach her father. Carefully, he lifted her out and held her up. 'And how are you, my little *beauty*!'

'Never better,' said Angelica, and began to bring the plates across to the table. 'She bit Sasha's finger just now. Almost drew blood.'

'Did she?' Titus looked around, still holding the little girl aloft, and then brought her down for a cuddle. 'Then, you know what this means?'

'I do indeed,' said Angelica.

'Who would have thought?' said Titus. 'The last of my children is set to join us in the family ways.'

'It's quite an achievement,' Angelica agreed, as Sasha

took her empty plate to the dishwasher. 'Have you had enough to eat?' she asked her.

'I'm good thanks.' Sasha headed for the door, and willed herself not to look at the plates on the table. No matter how she tried to sell it to herself, mashed potatoes, peas and nuts just didn't feel like a complete meal. 'I'll be in my room,' she said, and glanced at her mother. 'Got to study hard this month.'

'Can you tell Grandpa that I'll blend his dinner as soon as it's cooled. And send Ivan down now. You know how those two like their pork. There's even extra in the pan.'

Sasha reminded herself not to react. Despite the dig from her mother, there was no way that her dad could find out about her pledge. Heading out of the kitchen, she caught his eye, and saw only pride in his expression.

'I admire your commitment,' said Titus, and jiggled his youngest daughter in his arms. 'It's a shame you won't be eating with us, but all the more reason to look forward to a feast. One that none of us will ever forget!'

15

Angelica had never imagined that she would marry a man like Titus. As a young woman, she was fiercely independent, while Titus was clearly looking to settle down and start a family. What seduced Angelica was his sense of chivalry and sensitivity towards her. Looking back, it could be said that Titus waited for her to fall in love with him, before striking with his secret. By then, it was too late. Angelica was smitten. She would do anything for him, knowing that he would do likewise for her.

'We are what we eat,' he once told her. 'That makes you and me so *very* special as a couple.'

With a baby on the way, while Titus forged his career in the city, Angelica quickly found her feet as a homemaker. She surprised herself at how much pride she took in making things look as perfect as possible. The house was run down when they bought it, which presented Angelica with a much-needed challenge.

Back then, the renovation, decoration and furnishing of each room served as a means for her to forget about the one aspect of their lives that should've disgusted her. Having found a way to cope with the horror, Angelica even discovered that she enjoyed the preparation and consumption of human flesh, as well as all the cuts that your average cannibal might discard. It was a waste, they both agreed, and a lost opportunity. Through their eyes, the carcass of a once healthy human being was a banquet waiting to happen. Drawing upon the skills handed down to Titus by his father, she learned to extract the thymus gland from the chest cavity, just below the neck. Raw, it was just a spongy lump. Soaked in vinegar and then flash fried, it became the most glorious of sweetmeats, and the perfect appetizer before the serious business of eating began. And unlike any other food she had tasted in her life, Angelica found that often it was perfectly possible to finish off an entire body between two. At times, in fact, the feasting could transform into a frenzy. It would begin soon after the starters, with the central dishes stuffed away at an unnatural rate, before things finally slowed with dessert, when a profound sense of peace and satisfaction set in.

'It's like a drug,' Titus once explained. 'If everyone knew that feasting on human flesh sent such signals to the brain, we would eat ourselves out of existence!'

It took a decade of married life for Angelica to come to terms with what she had become. In that time, she tried to reason with herself that it wasn't something they did frequently. It was Titus who decided when the time felt right, and that amounted to no more than half a dozen times a year. They weren't like *addicts* or anything. Everything was under control.

Everything, that was, except for Angelica's other consumer habit. At times of self-loathing, she would hit the mall with her credit card. As well as her passion for fashion, she continued to style and dress the house. In her mind, the creation of the perfect family living environment helped to hide the truth about what really bonded them. As for concealing her debts, the situation was fine until the credit crunch. With interest rates rising, Angelica could no longer afford the repayments from the joint account without arousing the suspicions of her husband. It left her with no choice. Following a showdown with Titus, whose offer to write off the debt she refused, Angelica proposed a repayment plan that left him speechless.

'It's time the house paid for itself,' she had told him. 'I've already spoken to an agency.'

'But this isn't just any house,' Titus had reminded her. 'It's the one place where we can be ourselves. The only time we invite strangers inside, they never leave.'

'I need to do this,' Angelica had insisted.

'But what if someone finds evidence?'

'They won't,' she had said, and patted his stomach fondly. 'As you well know, my love.'

Now three years into the arrangement, the Savages had become used to occasionally having large numbers of media people occupy the ground floor. Angelica was happy, having taken responsibility for her spending, while the kids took great delight in spotting their home on billboards and in magazines. As much as he grumbled, she knew that even Titus had come to accept it. Angelica even suspected he got a kick out of the fact that the house was on show to the public, and yet in private hosted scenes that could attract attention for all the wrong reasons. She figured it gave him a sense of control, as it did for her. The incident with the model was regrettable, but Marsha from the agency had assured her that business would come back to the house in time. Angelica hadn't liked the sound of this one bit. Her credit card debt repayment depended on the income it brought her. Then again, she couldn't risk kicking up a fuss because that would just be heartless. A suicide is a tragedy at any time, Marsha had reminded Angelica over the phone later that week. There was nothing anyone could've done. *Apart from not stringing up a booby trap in our bathroom*, Angelica had thought, but kept it to herself. Instead, all she could do was go into denial about the financial implications. She'd done it for years, after all. As for Ivan, he was doing his best to atone for his mistake. He hadn't attempted a single joke that silenced the family, and was spending a great deal of time with his grandfather. It was good to see. He could learn a lot from Oleg, she decided, while Titus had talked about giving his son the chance to prepare the next feast. Combined with what he'd learned from the accident in the bathroom, Angelica hoped that Ivan would come out of this a stronger and more rounded young man. It made the debt issue just that little bit more bearable for her.

As for Sasha, this foolish adventure with fruit and vegetables that Jack had encouraged her to undertake couldn't end soon enough. It had put Angelica in an awkward position. Keeping it a secret from Titus wasn't something she found easy. Then again, she couldn't afford for him to find out. Not now that they were due to meet Sasha's boyfriend for themselves. It was bad enough that he was a vegetarian. If Titus knew that he had invited their eldest daughter to cross over, even for a week, let alone a month, he would skin the boy alive.

Based on what he had heard since planting the bug, Vernon English was sure of one thing: food was important to the Savages.

Parked down the road, within range of the device, he had sat and listened in to all kind of conversations about cooking. Angelica was in charge of the kitchen, so it seemed, but everyone showed an interest in whatever was on the stove, under the grill or in the oven. A feast was planned, he had learned, which was an unusual term for anyone to be using in this day and age. Still, it was hardly evidence that Titus was involved in the death of Lulabelle Hart.

After several days trailing the man home from work and then plugging in his earpiece, Vernon was beginning to think that Titus Savage's worst crime was a weak spot for pickled walnuts straight from the jar. The joke about each one looking like a shrunken brain wasn't funny the first time he had heard it, and yet Titus continued to trot it out. Vernon recorded everything, unaware that it would one day be released to a public hungry for an insight into the family. Just then, the private investigator was half listening to a chat between Angelica and her daughter, Sasha. The pair were preparing tea and cupcakes or some such, he wasn't sure what. Still, he knew it was worth keeping the channel open because Titus was also in the house. To keep himself occupied, and break the boredom, Vernon was munching on a bag of sea salt and malt vinegar flavored potato chips. Having missed what could've been a vital lead, all for the sake of a bucket of chicken nuggets, he wasn't going to let himself go hungry on the job again. Vernon balled the empty packet in one hand and tossed it into the passenger floor well. It landed in among all the other discarded packets, not just for chips but cookies and candy. He eyed them for a moment, wishing he had the willpower to pick up some raisins or bananas instead of the snacks.

'You should watch what you eat,' he told himself, and looked down at his waistline. As a younger man, he'd have described himself as whippet thin. He hadn't grown fat as such. It's just that his gut looked more like a loaf of bread that had failed to rise properly in the oven. He put this down to years of cooking for one after the divorce, which had involved a lot of ready meals. 'We'll bring something next time,' he added, as if to reassure his stomach that he hadn't given up on getting the washboard back.

Vernon surfaced from what was frankly a pipe dream by the sound of a car passing, and then pulling up outside the Savage residence. He sat up in his seat, reaching for his notebook at the same time so that he could take down the registration plate. The young man who climbed out of the driver's side looked strikingly confident to Vernon. He was one of those youths who dressed smartly to counter a carefully waxed and sculpted mop of hair. It was meant to look wind-blown, as if the guy had been brooding on a craggy cliff. Vernon disliked him straight away, whoever he turned out to be.

*   *   *

Sasha had worked hard in the kitchen to prepare for Jack's visit. She'd managed to persuade her parents that a dinner was just too much. It risked idle chat turning into an investigation. Asking Jack to drop by for a cup of tea, before they headed off for an evening out, was surely more than enough to satisfy their curiosity.

'We're only being responsible parents,' Angelica had said, when she found Sasha decorating a batch of cupcakes fresh from the oven.

'I know that,' said Sasha. 'It's the opportunity to embarrass me that I could really do without.'

'Would I do that?'

'It isn't you I'm worried about.'

Angelica didn't need to ask if she was referring to her father.

'These look lovely,' she said after a moment, and inspected the cakes a little closer. It was clear that Sasha had gone to great lengths here, but when she picked one up it left a lot of crumbs behind. Angelica didn't like to criticize, but took a moment too long to reach for a compliment. 'I'm sure Jack will appreciate the effort you've made,' she said eventually.

Sasha finished by scattering a pinch of specially-sourced spinkles over her creations, and figured her mother might as well know.

'It's a vegan recipe,' she told her. 'No eggs or butter.'

All of a sudden, Sasha felt her mother's gaze turn upon her.

'Jack is a vegetarian, no? Eggs and butter won't kill him.'

'He's thinking of cutting out dairy. I just thought this

would give him a taste of what's in store. I used soy milk and vegetable oil as a substitute, but I'm sure they'll taste OK.'

Angelica struggled not to make a face.

'Listen to you,' she said. 'You're a Savage, Sasha. Savages don't go vegetarian, let alone vegan. Exactly *what* is it about this boy that's turned your head?'

Sasha took the cupcakes across to the table, where she'd already laid out plates, cups and saucers.

'This isn't about Jack,' she said, without making eye contact with her mother. 'He's just switched me onto the possibilities when it comes to food.'

'Well, you can eat well and get on with your life,' muttered Angelica, 'or you can put your figure before your happiness.'

'Mom, I promise you this isn't about how I look.' Sasha turned to face her. 'It's about how I feel on the inside.'

Angelica was taken aback by her daughter's force of opinion. Facing her, she looked directly into her eyes and didn't let up as she appealed to her.

'Please don't go vegan. It would be a step too far for your father and me.'

'And for me,' said Sasha, smiling now. 'I wanted just to see how they turned out. It's good to experiment with food!'

'At last, we agree on something,' said Angelica, and some warmth came into her expression. 'Just don't tell your father what's in them.'

'You mean what's *not* in them,' said Sasha.

It was an exchange that served to further soften the mood between them. For the next few minutes, Sasha and

Angelica worked together to clear the kitchen. By the time Ivan joined them, everything was ready for Jack's arrival.

'Mmm, cupcakes!' the boy declared, and grabbed one from the plate. He moved so quickly that it didn't disintegrate until it had reached his mouth.

'Leave that!' snapped Sasha, but it was too late. 'Mom, tell him!'

Angelica was used to intervening in squabbles between the pair. On this occasion, watching Ivan's gleeful expression begin to pinch into distaste, she figured he had just learned not to take food without asking.

'Eww,' he said, having struggled to swallow it down. 'Can I get a drink of water? What's *in* this?'

'Serves you right,' grumbled Sasha, and set about rearranging the plate of cupcakes.

'We have a visitor,' Angelica said, as Ivan hurried to the tap. 'He's picky about what he eats.'

Having filled a cup and taken a swig, Ivan switched his gaze to Sasha.

'The vegetarian is coming here now?'

'Will everyone stop calling him that?' demanded Sasha. 'His name is Jack.'

A trace of a smile crossed Ivan's face.

'I hope he likes cupcakes,' the boy said, as Titus could be heard making his way down the stairs. 'Especially ones that taste like chalk.'

'No stirring up trouble,' warned Angelica, pointing a finger at him, which she then dropped when her husband strode into the kitchen. He was clutching a sheaf of papers, and seemed very pleased with himself.

'Tomorrow is going to be a good day,' declared Titus. 'It looks like the deal is about to be done.'

'The company takeover?' asked Angelica, trying to sound interested.

'According to my sources they've run out of options,' he said, and clapped his son on the shoulder. 'Nobody escapes from the Savages.'

'Dad,' said Sasha, having checked her phone. 'Jack just texted me. He's outside. You will be nice to him, won't you? Promise me you won't tell stories about me when I was younger, or bring up the subject of . . . meat.'

Titus smiled, but said nothing in reply as the sound of the doorbell rang through the house.

16

Jack Greenway had expected Sasha to greet him at the door, not the whole family. It was why he had dropped her a line, hoping she would answer alone so he could make a low-key entry. Instead, even her grandfather could be seen at the top of the stairs, peering down in his dressing gown.

'Sorry,' said Sasha, grimacing. 'He probably doesn't realize it's untied.'

'Now is not the time for apologies,' said Titus, extending his hand from behind his daughter. 'It's great to put a face to the name.'

'Likewise,' said Jack, and did his best to match the strength of the handshake. 'A pleasure to meet you.'

'This is my wife, Angelica.'

'Mrs. Savage,' said Jack, noting that her handshake was in complete contrast. It felt like he had just clasped a dead fish in his palm.

'That's my father upstairs,' said Titus, before pushing his young son forward. 'And here is Ivan.'

For a second, Jack's smile faltered. Ivan, however, grinned at the junior who had tried to humiliate him earlier in the week.

'So, this is your boyfriend?' he said to Sasha. 'You should invite him inside.'

'Well, I would,' said Sasha. 'If everyone can stop being so nice and give him some space.'

'Take Jack into the kitchen,' said Titus, who continued to sound unnervingly welcoming. Angelica hadn't seen him smiling this much since preparations for the last feast. She put this down to the business deal, and hoped that he and Jack would at least get along at some level.

Before the front door closed, Vernon English had already identified the Savages' visitor. A call to an ex-colleague on the police force, which he paid for in pints of beer and a kebab whenever they met for a drink, allowed him to trade the vehicle registration plate for a name and address. Vernon was surprised the car belonged to the kid. Jack Olivier Greenway was in his late teens, perhaps, but the motor was one of those sophisticated types that didn't choke up the environment.

'Spoiled by his parents, no doubt,' he said down the line, before closing the call to his man on the inside.

Placing his cell on the dashboard, Vernon turned up the volume on the bug receiver. By rights, having heard Titus boast of his takeover plans, he should've called the company straight away. Vernon had photographic evidence of all the secret meetings Titus had conducted with their mole. That money had changed hands in exchange for inside informa-tion was a breach of all manner of regulations. It could easily cause trouble for Titus, but Vernon had his sights on nailing the man for a far more serious crime. The longer he spent tailing the head of the Savage household, and learning about his life, the more convinced he became about his involvement in the death of Lulabelle Hart. The police might not have treated her demise as suspicious, but Vernon had carried out his own investigation. He had traveled to the coast and spoken to staff at the train station and the bus company. Lulabelle didn't drive, and yet when he produced a photograph of the woman nobody had any recollection of seeing her on the night in question. It didn't prove anything, of course, but it raised Vernon's suspicions to no end. Unless the model traveled by taxi, at great expense, then her only other likely means of transport involved being zipped inside a duffle bag in the trunk of the Savages' 4x4.

'Come on, Titus,' he said to himself. 'Spill the beans to your friend, Vernon.'

Tweaking the transmitter dial to improve the reception, Vernon settled back in his seat and listened closely as the Savages welcomed their guest into the kitchen. He doubted very much that he would hear a full and frank confession. What interested him just then was how uptight the daughter had sounded about the way Titus might react to her boyfriend. Worrying that your dad might embarrass you was standard issue in households up and down the land. From what Vernon had picked up, however, Sasha made it sound like the man could spring a horrible surprise.

'So, tell us,' said Titus as he crossed the kitchen for the teakettle, 'what is that car of yours like to drive?'

'A dream,' said Jack, and plunged his hands inside his

pockets. 'It's fuel efficient with low carbon emissions.'

'That's good to hear,' said Titus, nodding his approval. 'But what I mean is can you get it out of the slow lane on the highway without the battery dying?'

Sasha, who was standing close to Jack as if to shield him from bullets, felt herself dying on the inside.

'The battery takes its charge from the engine,' she told her father. 'Even I know that. The technology has really progressed.'

'Like the times,' Jack muttered under his breath, and flashed a grin at Sasha.

Titus had his back turned to the boy, filling the kettle with water, but he heard the comment clearly. It was amusing. The kid had quick wits. He didn't like him one bit. If anything, thought Titus, Jack was asking to be tested.

'I hope you like cupcakes,' said Angelica, who had just popped upstairs to collect Katya from her crib. 'Sasha made them herself.'

'I used a special recipe,' said Sasha.

'Cool.' Jack selected one from the plate. 'What's in them?'

'*Ribs!*' cried Kat, just as Jack prepared to take a bite.

'Ignore her,' Angelica assured him. 'It's her only word.'

'*Ribs!*'

Jack looked from the toddler to Sasha and then to the cupcake. 'Right,' he said. 'That's unusual.'

'The cupcake is vegan,' said Sasha, under the sound of the kettle coming to the boil. 'Try it.'

Jack inspected the cake one more time, aware that Ivan was watching him intently. Titus, meanwhile, was staring at the plate as if he couldn't quite believe what was on offer here. Angelica shot him a look, reminding him to be on his best behavior.

'It smells good.' Jack held his palm underneath the cupcake as it began to disintegrate, and quickly grabbed a nibble. 'And it tastes . . . *magnificent*! Isn't anyone else going to try one?'

'Count me in,' said Angelica, who was keen to support her daughter. Setting Katya on the floor, she took a plate and helped herself. 'How about you, Ivan?'

The boy shook his head and looked to his father. Titus turned his attention to the table.

'Anything my daughter has made is good enough for me,' he said, with a hint of a sigh.

Sasha watched her parents eating, and braced herself for the worst. Both of them were clearly struggling, but putting on polite faces for the sake of their visitor. Titus was the first to swallow, just as the kettle boiled.

'Tea,' he croaked. 'I think we need a cup of tea.'

'Do you have any herbal?' Jack turned to Sasha. 'I don't do caffeine.'

Sasha's face fell. It was something she just hadn't considered.

'Actually, we do,' said Angelica, much to the surprise of her husband. 'I thought you may prefer an alternative, so I bought some chamomile this morning. It's in the cupboard above the kettle.'

'I can get that,' offered Ivan, as Titus simply stood and stared at his wife.

Sasha caught her eye and mouthed a 'thank you'.

* * *

It was too good an opportunity for the boy to resist. Despite the incident in the bathroom, Ivan Savage had just one more practical joke to play. It wasn't planned. This was a spur of the moment idea, driven less by a need to amuse and more by a chance to get even.

As his parents found their way into a conversation with Jack, asking him about junior year compared to the rest of high school, Ivan dropped three normal tea bags into the pot, filled it with water from the kettle, and then sought out the box his mother had bought. He found it straight away, covered in floral designs. Extracting a bag as if it was something that had accidently been dropped into the toilet, he set about preparing Jack's cup of herbal tea. Then, glancing over his shoulder to be sure nobody was watching, he reached up into the cupboard once again.

The chicken stock cubes were kept on the shelf above the tea bags. Ivan had no intention of dissolving a whole one in the chamomile. He didn't want to make it undrinkable, just different. With this in mind, he crumbled off a corner into the cup, followed by another corner for good measure. The water darkened straight away, but remained translucent. Leaving the chamomile bag to infuse in the stock a little longer, Ivan transferred the teapot to the table, where his father was clearly itching to take Jack to task about his dietary habits.

'Have you had dinner?' he inquired. 'I'm just wondering whether a young man like you will need a snack to see you through the evening. I imagine you need to be careful about things like that.'

Jack looked a little confused.

'I'm not sure I follow you, Mr. Savage.'

'Your blood sugar levels,' he said simply. 'It's a concern, isn't it?'

'Dad.' Sasha glared at her father. 'Jack's in great shape. We'll be sure to eat, OK?'

Aware that his wife was also frowning at him, Titus shrugged and carefully turned what was left of his cupcake in one hand. Everything from the bland taste to the dry texture had made him want to spit it out, but that would've just been rude. Instead, he poured the tea for everyone, while Ivan returned to the table and set the cup of chamomile before their guest.

'Lovely,' said Jack, and inhaled the steam. 'You can just smell how therapeutic this tea can be.'

Despite sitting across the table from him, Titus's keen sense of smell immediately picked up on the fact that it contained poultry of some form. He glanced at Ivan, who was standing behind Jack looking very pleased with himself. Needling Sasha's boyfriend about his beliefs was one thing, thought Titus, but this was just disrespectful. Even so, there was nothing he could do when Jack picked up the cup with both hands and took a tentative sip. He seemed to hold it on his tongue for a moment, before closing his eyes and tipping his head back by a degree.

'Just what I needed!' he said. 'Do you know what? I haven't tasted tea this good in a *decade*.'

Titus leaned forward on his elbows.

'So, when did you become a vegetarian?'

'Oh, ten years ago,' Jack told him, cradling the cup with

his palms. 'It was the only way forward for me. I just couldn't live with the thought that another living thing had to perish in my name,' he explained, before taking another long sip of the herbal broth. 'People say it doesn't taste as good, but that's a small sacrifice.'

'What about fruit and vegetables?' asked Titus. 'They have feelings.'

'Not again, Dad.'

'Science is leaning that way,' he insisted, wishing his daughter would just let him have this moment. 'Look at the Venus Fly Trap. How do you think it knows when prey has landed in its clutches? And you might not be able to hear a banana scream, but that's what happens when you peel one. You're literally stripping the skin from its body. How can that be humane? It's torture!'

Jack smiled, but clearly didn't feel it was worth entering into an argument. Instead, much to Ivan's delight, he drained the cup before suggesting to Sasha that they should be going.

'We don't want to be late.'

'What do you have planned?' asked Angelica.

Jack looked across at Sasha.

'I thought you might like to go to a talk,' he said. 'At the university. It's open to the public.'

'The university.' Angelica couldn't help but look impressed. 'That beats the back seats at the movies.'

'What is the talk about?' asked Titus.

'It's called "Beyond Vegetarianism",' said Jack, which prompted Sasha to drop her gaze to the floor. 'Why don't you join us?'

Titus took a second to realize that Jack was inviting him.

'I don't think Sasha would appreciate my presence,' he said eventually, and then waited for her to look up. 'But I look forward to hearing all about it.'

The request was met by an uncomfortable silence. Ivan was quick to pick up on it, however. Leaning in beside Jack, he collected his empty cup and said: 'More tea?'

Jack looked back at his girlfriend's kid brother. For someone who had crossed him at school, the boy had been surprisingly forgiving.

'We just don't have the time,' he told him, and toyed with the cup in front of him. 'But that was truly divine.'

17

Amanda Dias didn't look like an impressive speaker. A first-year undergraduate, she was slight in build, with cropped, boyish hair and delicate features arranged around an apparently shy, skewed smile. What silenced her audience was her militant position on the subject of ethical eating, especially those who did not share her views.

'The hunters,' she said at one point, 'should become the hunted.'

Amanda stood with her feet pointed inwards and the microphone clutched in both hands. She turned to address her audience as she spoke, leaving breathy silences between each statement she made.

'Wow,' whispered Jack, who had chosen a middle row alongside Sasha. They were in the university's smaller auditorium, with tables arranged at the sides offering everything from pamphlets to specialized snacks. 'This is intense.'

Sasha had spent most of the time noting Amanda's sense of style. Everything she wore was made from cruelty-free material such as hemp and waxed cotton, as she had mentioned at the beginning as if to establish her credentials. Her navy-blue dress with matching cream cuffs and collar made her look like someone who might've been accused of witchcraft centuries earlier and burned at the stake. This martyr look worked well, thought Sasha, while the bold nature of her talk was clearly making an impression. Sasha struggled to get comfortable on the wooden bench. The girl was too good to be true. Off stage, she decided, Amanda Dias was probably one of those people who jealously guarded her food in the fridge.

'How much of this stuff do you think she got off the internet?' she asked Jack, leaning across so as not to be overheard. 'It's her thesis, isn't it?'

Jack shot Sasha a look that told her he didn't share her outlook.

'We live among murderers,' Amanda continued. 'We share our lives with them. They walk among us. Is this the mark of a civilized society? We must confront the flesh-eaters. Change their way of life, for the sake of our world . . . or stop them from causing further slaughter.'

Amanda was the third person to take to the stage that evening. Sasha had listened closely to the two speakers before her. One was from the university's Animal Rights society, while the other had worked in a hospital cafeteria until his conversion to veganism, refusal to handle meat products, and subsequent dismissal. Until Amanda took the microphone, Sasha had been quietly impressed. It all seemed so grown up, and far removed from sitting on the edge of the skate ramp at school. These were mature individuals with passionate, heartfelt beliefs. This may have been the last place Sasha expected to find herself, but in a way it was beginning to feel like a new kind of home. Having gone without meat for several days, it seemed to her like she had at least earned the credentials to sit here and listen. The Animal Rights speaker made some interesting points, and she admired the stand made by the chef, even if it was pretty clear some drinking issues had contributed to his dismissal. In Sasha's opinion, it was only this militant chick who had failed to strike a chord.

'Amanda,' said one young man in the front row, when she invited questions from the audience. 'Are you saying it's OK to *kill* meat eaters?'

Amanda smiled sweetly, as if she'd just been asked where her dress came from.

'I am simply sharing my thoughts, and hoping to . . . connect, influence, inform and *engage*.'

Jack turned and nodded his approval to Sasha. She waited for him to face the stage once more before shaking her head. It was a shame this girl had been invited to speak. The evening didn't need this pretentious nonsense, from someone who looked incapable of killing an unwanted call let alone a human being. Worst of all, it appeared as if Jack was hanging on every word she uttered.

'There'll be a few minutes before the next talk,' whispered Sasha, when Amanda finally finished to a flutter of applause. 'I'll get us something to eat.'

'You do that,' said Jack, who rose to his feet at the same time as Sasha. 'Just make mine vegan.'

'Really?' Sasha glanced across at the podium, unsure if he had just said that very loudly so somebody else could hear him. Even Jack couldn't resist a quick look, but Amanda was busy collecting her papers from the lectern.

'This is it for me,' he said, when Sasha returned her

attention to him. 'There's no going back now. After listening to Amanda, it seems to me we need to stand up for what we believe in.'

Sasha furrowed her brow. From experience, he just didn't look the sort.

'Jack, you'd never take a life.'

He seemed to think about this for a moment, before looking a little embarrassed.

'I tell you what I could murder, though,' he said, gesturing at a table of food and drink. 'A slice of that chestnut casserole.'

Leaving Jack to clamber over seats to the floor, Sasha made her way towards the end of the row. Most people looked a little older than her, but Sasha didn't feel intimidated. Nor was she starving hungry, as she had been after her first few days of vegetarian eating. She was still surprised by how understanding her mother had been. Rather than simply serve up a dinner minus the meat product, she had created alternatives just for Sasha. The chard and cheddar casserole was nice, even if it had been the first time that Angelica attempted such a creation. It had even proven to be quite filling, which obliged them both to seek out a hidden space at the back of the freezer to keep what was left for another day.

Many people in the auditorium had already headed for the refreshment tables, where a small line was forming. Sasha lined up with her arms folded and looked to her feet. The guy in front of her was wearing scuffed leather shoes, she noticed, which seemed a bit rebellious in this kind of company. She was just mulling over what Amanda Dias would have to say about that when she noticed them rotate to one side a little. She looked up, to find the young man was grinning at her.

'Is it wrong to be disappointed knowing that there's no BLT waiting for me at the front of this line?'

Sasha blinked in surprise, laughed and then touched her fingertips to her lips. The guy wasn't much older than she was. He was as scruffy as his shoes, wearing a hoodie, T-shirt and jeans as well as several days of stubble on a square-set face.

'It would be wrong,' she said eventually, keeping her voice low. 'But I know just what you mean. I feel like I'm lining up to be disappointed here.'

The guy's smile broadened.

'That speaker,' he said, and nodded towards the stage. 'Is she for real?'

'Someone thinks so,' replied Sasha under her breath. 'Between you and me, halfway through I wished I had a bag of bacon-flavored potato chips I could quietly flick at her.'

The guy held her gaze, still beaming broadly.

'I'm Ralph,' he said, and shook her hand. 'It's been eight weeks since I last ate meat, and the whole bacon thing is driving me to distraction.'

'The crack cocaine of the meat industry,' agreed Sasha. 'What turned you?'

'It felt like something I wanted to do,' he said simply. 'But I know what you mean about the whole food fascism thing. Every time I hear someone like Amanda preach that meat is murder I want to go out and buy a burger. I just don't understand why being vegetarian makes you any better than anyone else. What's with the big statements? It's just a choice, in a free society. I think so long as you know where your food's coming from, and you're happy with that, then you should be able to live your life without being judged. How about you?'

Sasha found herself listening so closely to what Ralph had to say that a moment passed before she registered his question.

'Me? Oh, I'm just going without meat for a while. I just want to see what it's like.'

'And how is it going?'

Across the floor, Jack Greenway had finally muscled into a conversation between Amanda Dias and the alcoholic cook. He was nodding furiously, switching his attention from one to the other, but mostly returning to Amanda. Sasha looked back at Ralph. He was next in line to be served.

'I've surprised myself so far,' she said. 'But it's good to know I'm not alone in facing moments of temptation.'

Ralph seemed a little taken aback at this. Then that smile returned, before he turned to face the table. It left Sasha wondering whether she'd just said something, and then realized that she had. Before she could find a way to explain that she hadn't just tried to hit on him, Ralph moved aside for her.

'Some of this stuff looks good,' he said, and then dipped down to find her ear. 'And a lot of it looks like squirrel bait.'

Giggling, and with her cheeks still hot, Sasha decided to say nothing. Instead, she picked up a slice of the casserole for Jack, skipping one for herself, and then collected two plastic cups of cola.

'Are these drinks vegan?' she asked him.

Ralph shrugged.

'Even if they aren't,' he said under his breath. 'It can be our secret if you like.'

Vernon English had slumped so far down in the driving seat that he could no longer see over the dash. He'd done so on purpose, just as soon as Titus Savage strode into view. Waiting for his target to cross the street in front of the vehicle, on his way to the lobby in the building opposite, the private investigator couldn't help noticing that the lower half of the steering wheel was mottled with his greasy fingerprints.

'That's it,' he said to himself. 'No more fries in the van.'

Vernon had been expecting Titus. Having tailed the man for weeks now, and with an ear inside his house, he knew that today would see the takeover completed. It was all over for the company who had hired Vernon. Sure, he could've presented them with some evidence that Titus had engaged in corporate crimes, but what would that achieve? The company would call in the cops, and if the Savage house hid secrets about Lulabelle Hart then Vernon would just be a footnote in the story of his arrest. By staying quiet as Titus broke up the company and sold it off, the private investigator would be sacrificing his full fee. What persuaded him to just keep on the man's tail was the belief that one day soon they would both be making headlines.

While photographers tried to snatch a shot of Titus through the window of a speeding police van, Vernon would be giving lengthy interviews to the broadsheets about how his intuition and persistence had paid off.

'There's blood on your hands,' he said, grunting as he sat up in the seat. Across the street, Titus had entered the lobby. He was there as the company's new boss. The lion had arrived at his new den, and Vernon knew just what would happen next. The man wasn't there to save the business but carve it up and toss out the parts for profit. Vernon had seen it all before. Normally, these guys, the asset strippers, were cold-hearted individuals. Some even got a kick from the misery they caused. Titus was different, however. At home, he made every effort to spend time with Angelica and their children. Through Vernon's eyes, and with his suspicions, there was something about the guy that he was missing. Somewhere, a link existed between the beast in the boardroom and the father who put family first.

The first of the staff to be given immediate notice left about an hour later. Vernon watched them exit, some clutching boxes with their personal effects, others looking shell-shocked and tearful. How could anyone do such a thing, simply to make money? He could just imagine Titus picking off members of the workforce without a trace of emotion. Once he'd got the numbers down to the bone, he'd have them sell off the company bit by little bit. Eventually, there would be nothing but a skeleton plus a fattened bank account, and that's when he'd move on – setting his sights on another corporate kill.

* * *

Towards lunchtime, Vernon was surprised to see Angelica making her way towards the building. She was wearing a pair of large sunglasses, despite the fact that the sky was overcast. A straw tote bag swung from the crook of her arm. Vernon squinted to see what was peeking from the top. A baguette and a bottle of champagne, he realized, before pulling the peak of his cap low in case she happened to glance in his direction.

'So, your husband ruins lives one morning, and you show up with a celebratory *picnic*?'

Vernon shook his head, struggling with the insensitivity of what he was seeing here. Titus and Angelica were one of a kind. Even in the privacy of their home, food came first. It's all he'd heard the pair talk about, but there just had to be more to them than that. Vernon watched Angelica make her way up the steps outside the building, and suddenly realized that he was following the wrong people.

If Vernon English was going to uncover the truth about Lulabelle, then he'd need to find a different way into the family. The private investigator twisted the key in the ignition, and again when the engine failed to start. Titus and Angelica were clearly too wise and experienced at covering themselves, but he felt sure the same couldn't be said for their kids.

Second Course

18

Ivan Savage enjoyed a game of chess. What he loathed was losing. That wasn't why he joined the school club. He was there to prove his sense of strategy and logic was close to perfection. On those occasions when his opponents began to tighten in on his queen, he would turn to rules of his own in a bid to avoid checkmate.

'Prepare for a butt kicking,' crowed Ali Kaar, leaning on his elbows as he studied the board. 'Whenever you want to make your move, I'm ready!'

Ivan watched him closely. He didn't once glance down to consider his position. He barely moved, in fact, but for a tensing in his jaw muscles as he ground his molars together.

'I need to think about this,' he said eventually.

'Take your time.' Ali pushed his chair back and rose to his feet. 'I need to take a leak anyhow.'

They had been playing for several hours. Ivan had opted for an aggressive strategy, but that left him with only one back-up plan when Ali pulled several surprise moves. This took the form of a jug of water and two cups. Ivan always made sure that they were in easy reach before he sat down to play. Then it was his turn to go for something unexpected. This involved refilling his opponent's cup on a regular basis, knowing that he would have to answer the call of nature eventually. As soon as Ali left the table for the toilet, Ivan popped open his schoolbag and carefully fished out a small wooden box. It contained a complete set of both black and white pieces, identical to those used by the school chess club, as well as a thin metal mesh glove. First making sure that everybody else was engrossed in their own games, Ivan slipped the glove on and then set about replacing his opponent's pieces. He'd done this many times over, which meant he had easily completed the maneuver before Ali returned. Finally, when the boy dropped back into his seat, Ivan moved one of his pieces.

'Your turn,' he said, and grasped the corners of the table as if to brace himself for something.

Ali studied the pieces for a moment.

'Is that it?' he asked. 'You've left yourself wide open.'

'We'll see,' said Ivan, who smiled to himself when Ali reached for the pawn he expected him to play. As soon as he grasped it, the boy's face contorted in shock and pain.

'What's the matter?' asked Ivan, as his opponent set the piece back down smartly and shook his hand. A smattering of blood spots hit Ivan's shirt, but he didn't mind one bit. 'Everything OK?'

'Splinter, I think!' Ali examined his finger, where a bead of blood was growing. 'Man, that's really painful.'

'Unlucky,' said Ivan, who gestured at the table. 'Feel free to try again.

For the next few minutes, poor Ali Kaar suffered one assault to his fingers after another as he attempted to make each move. Even when he switched strategies, every time he touched a chess piece it left him gasping. Eventually, with tears streaking his cheeks and his hand shrouded in a bloodstained handkerchief, Ali conceded defeat in order to seek medical help from the school nurse.

'You win,' he sniffed, clutching his hand to his chest. 'I never want to play you again!'

'They all say that,' said Ivan under his breath, and quietly reached for the glove so that he could return the pieces to the box.

It was a satisfying victory. Ivan would've preferred to win without suffering and bloodshed, but sometimes it was necessary to avoid the incomparable pain of defeat. In some ways, he liked to think that substituting the chess pieces for a set with a sprinkling of iron filings glued to them was just another strategy of the game. At the very least, he had thought ahead and used his brain to win.

Ivan left school that afternoon with his bag slung over one shoulder and his hands in his pockets. He headed for home on foot. The school bus only ran after school had finished, but he didn't mind missing it. The afternoon session had made it all worthwhile. It also meant less time fighting with his sister or getting a hard time from his mom about making a mess around the house.

Ivan followed the usual route, heading from school towards the park. It took him by the mall, where he went on to follow the long, curving road towards the pedestrian crossing. It was here, about a minute into the walk, that he became aware of the vehicle. It was a battered white van, not an unusual sight, but it had been parked outside the school when he left the gates. A few minutes later, he had spotted it in a disabled parking spot in front of the charity shop. This time, the van was sitting at an intersection on the other side of the street. Ivan walked on, keeping his head down but listening keenly.

Sure enough, a short time after he had passed the intersection he heard it pull off. The boy glanced over his shoulder. The van was just behind him, moving at a walking pace which increased when the boy picked up his stride. Ivan had heard about moments like this. There were some sick people out there. Back in grade school, a policeman had even come into assembly to talk about stranger danger. It never seemed like such a big deal now that he was older, but suddenly this felt very real and Ivan felt entirely alone. He glanced over his shoulder one more time. Sure enough, there it was. With the sun overhead, reflecting on the van's windscreen, it was impossible to see who was behind the wheel. That's when Ivan's imagination went into overdrive, and a sense of fear caused his skin to prickle.

'Be cool,' he whispered to himself, and reached for his phone. Quickly he found his father's number. It went straight to voicemail, which wasn't unusual, but just then he wished his dad didn't have so many meetings during the day. Hanging up without leaving a message, Ivan turned to check he hadn't been mistaken, and then steered closer to the storefronts as if that might offer him some kind of protection.

* * *

Second Course

The pizzas, when they arrived, looked just as Jack Greenway had imagined. Each one featured a lot of tomato, mushroom, pepper and onions, but with no sign of any cheese.

'Yum,' he made himself say for the benefit of the girl sharing his window table. 'You made a great choice.'

Amanda Dias studied her topping for a moment, declining an invitation from the waiter for a twist of black pepper.

'Food should be pure and simple,' she told Jack, collecting her knife and fork. 'I would sooner gnaw off my own fingers than eat dairy.'

Jack sat across from her with his hands on his knees and just stared.

'Awesome,' he said eventually. 'Just *amazing.*'

He'd contacted Amanda the day after her talk. Friending her on Facebook was out of the question. That would only invite Sasha's suspicions. Instead, he had headed back to the university on his lunch break, where he found her handing out leaflets outside the Union bar. She recognized him right away, and even seemed pleased when he approached. That's when Jack had switched on every charm button in his body and invited her to lunch. He wanted to learn more about veganism, he had told her. From someone who could provide him with guidance, wisdom and inspiration.

The lunch, he had said to finish, would of course be his treat.

Now that Amanda was here, in his company, Jack found himself a little lost for words. It wasn't something that had happened to him before. In fact, he prided himself on being able to talk easily to girls and win them over by showing how much he cared for animals. Sure, Amanda was attractive, but in terms of conversation he felt outclassed. She just seemed so confident. So sure of her outlook on life. Sasha was lovely – beautiful, kind and funny – but she had needed him to lead her into his vegetarian world. Amanda was different. Her views went way beyond anything Jack held, and now he wanted to go there. Having been in the audience when she spoke, he found himself seduced by her hardline veganism.

Unlike Sasha, she also looked like she might go all the way if he cooked for her one night.

'I have a question,' said Amanda, chewing on her second slice of pizza. 'It's hypothetical, of course, but I'm interested.'

'Go ahead,' said Jack, who had yet to start his meal. 'Ask me anything.'

'Let's say we have two dishes on this table. Both of them covered with a lid, but you have to choose one.'

'Sounds good,' he said. 'What's on the menu?'

Amanda pretended to lift an invisible lid from her plate.

'Roast leg of lamb,' she told him, and then repeated the gesture. 'Or braised human heart.'

The way she presented this, with a wicked smile and her eyes penetrating his, left Jack with no air in his lungs.

'Oh,' he croaked finally, and breathed in once again. 'For real?'

Amanda Dias nodded, not releasing him from her gaze for a moment.

'For me, it would come down to ethics,' she said. 'Which animal, the lamb or the human, has caused more misery, murder and suffering in this world?'

'The human,' said Jack, who was beginning to feel the need for some fresh air. 'Naturally.'

'Then there is your answer,' she said, and presented him with the invisible plate he had selected. 'Enjoy!'

For a moment, Jack wondered if she expected him to pretend to eat it. He regarded the empty space where the plate was supposed to be. 'What does braised mean?'

A grin eased across Amanda's face.

'I'm thinking you wouldn't, right?'

Jack sat back, feeling hot and ready for a glass of water.

'I don't . . . I don't know,' he said, faltering once more, and that's when a figure passed the window that commanded his full attention.

'Ivan!' he said out loud, relieved at first that he had found a way out of the conversation. Then Jack considered just how bad this looked from the street, and called out to him more urgently, 'Hey, *wait a minute!*'

Ivan Savage rarely experienced fear. He had seen it in the eyes of many people, of course, and not just the victims of his pranks. His father hated to witness it in those they intended to consume. It was inevitable that they'd freak out when it became apparent why they were in the house and what the family had in mind. Even so, it was important that they kept such suffering to a minimum. It only provoked a rush of adrenalin in their victims, and a hormonal release like that just risked spoiling the flavor of the meat.

It was this thought, no matter how misplaced, that dogged Ivan's thoughts as he hurried past the pizza restaurant. He checked for the van once more. It had pulled in some distance behind, as if the driver were waiting for the moment to snatch him from the streets. Ivan's mouth was dry and his throat felt tight when he swallowed. It was one of the diners on the other side of the glass that caught his eye, but Ivan didn't register that it was Jack until the young man rushed from his table to the door.

'It's not what it seems!' Jack called out to him, with both hands raised as if to calm the boy. 'Amanda is a friend.'

Ivan blinked and glanced back inside at the girl he had left at the table. Then he focused on the van before addressing Jack.

'Help me,' he said, much to Jack's surprise. 'Is your car nearby?'

'Sure,' said Jack, sounding as disarmed as he looked. 'It's parked around the back.'

Ivan gestured at the van.

'There's a man over there. I think he wants to interfere with me.'

'What?' Jack wheeled around, saw the van, and then glanced back, looking a little wary. 'Shouldn't we call the police or something?'

'Take me home, Jack.'

Jack considered the request for a moment. He looked torn.

'But my date . . . my lunch date.'

This time, Ivan's eyes narrowed before returning to the girl, who had just finished her last slice of pizza. Amanda regarded him for less than a second, before helping herself to a slice from Jack's plate.

'Aren't you hungry?' asked Ivan.

'Not anymore,' said Jack, who had just worked out a way to buy the boy's silence. 'Listen, if I drive you home will you forget you saw me here? It never happened, right?'

Ivan didn't even look in Amanda's direction.

'Let's go,' he said.

19

Sasha Savage had returned from school feeling ravenous.

It was a feeling she had become used to in recent weeks. Being vegetarian wasn't easy. Sacrifices had to be made. Not only did she have to plan each meal, and carefully keep it from her father, she found that she needed to eat little and often to make it through each day. And yet despite it all, as the end of her month without meat approached, Sasha was feeling good about herself. Better than ever, in fact. She could see it in her skin, just as Jack had promised. It was supple and elastic, while her eyes were clear and sparkling. What's more, as she hung her coat up in the hallway, she found that she had actually developed a taste for a meat-free diet.

'Hello?' she called up the stairs. 'Is anyone home?'

She waited for a response for a moment, and then smiled to herself. Without a doubt, her grandfather would be in his bedroom, but the house was as good as empty. Not only was he hard of hearing, he hadn't ventured downstairs in ages.

It meant Sasha was free to head for the kitchen and fix herself a tasty snack.

'Let's see,' she said to herself, crouching in front of the

fridge, and began to extract items one by one. 'Tofu is good, cucumber, some mint, yogurt and a pita pouch.'

The tofu block and the pita came from the lowest shelf, hidden at the back behind a ham. It was her mother who placed it all there for her. She had been so kind and understanding about everything. Sasha knew she disapproved, but that hadn't stopped her from helping her daughter keep her food choices a secret from Titus. Laying a chopping board on the surface, Sasha found a knife and pierced the pita bread. Carefully, she drew the blade down, opening up the pouch. It reminded her of those times her father had asked her to help in getting ready for a feast. Over the years, with a corpse laid out on the kitchen table, she had learned to extract everything from top to toe and prepare it accordingly. Using her fingers, Sasha eased the pocket open, just as she would as if preparing to stuff a neck cutlet with herbs, butter and garlic. She had just reached for a teaspoon for the hummus when a shriek from close behind caused her to drop it to the floor.

'What the . . . *Katya*!' Her younger sister was sitting at the doorway. She gurgled happily, before crawling across the kitchen to greet her. 'You startled me,' said Sasha, and plucked her from the floor. 'What are you doing here on your own? Anything could've happened to you! Are you OK?'

'*Ribs!*'

The toddler responded by reaching out for the tofu. Sasha turned, but was too late to stop Kat from grabbing it.

'That's not ribs,' chuckled Sasha, and leaned away to avoid getting smeared. Katya waved the block in the air, before taking a bite from the corner. 'I'm not sure you'll like that . . . oh! So, you *do* like that!'

Turning to more important matters, she carried her little sister into the hallway and called out for her grandfather one more time. Again, Sasha received no answer, but this time she took to the staircase. With nobody on the first floor, she continued around to the second flight. Music floated down from the room at the top. It was a mournful piece, most likely Russian, which she knew reminded him of many things. Sure enough, she found him under the skylight, facing a black and white photograph of old Leningrad, with his head tipped back as he quietly conducted to himself.

'Grandpa,' she said softly, so as not to take him by surprise. When that failed to work, she crossed the room to turn the volume down. As soon as she did so, he dropped his arms and opened his eyes. Sasha tried to look calm and collected for him. 'Grandpa, is Katya supposed to be in your care?'

'Of course, he said, smiling at his youngest grandchild. 'We were just enjoying some music together.'

'She was downstairs,' said Sasha cautiously. 'She must've gotten there all on her own.'

At first, Oleg seemed not to hear her. He stroked Kat's cheek, and watched her gnawing on something in her hand.

'So, maybe she was hungry,' he said eventually. 'Sure looks like she can prepare herself a snack.'

'I gave it to her,' said Sasha. 'Grandpa, she's too young to be left alone on the stairs. Anything could've happened!'

This time, after a moment to register what she'd just told him, Oleg bowed his head and nodded.

'I didn't hear her go,' he said, toying with his beard. 'Your mother asked me to watch her for an hour. Maybe that isn't such a good idea any more.'

Sasha placed her free hand on his shoulder.

'Kat didn't come to any harm,' she said. 'She's happy now.'

Oleg glanced up. As he did so, the toddler waved what was left of the tofu block at him.

'What is that?' he asked, and took it from her. 'Should she be eating this? Should anyone?'

'Let me get rid of that for you,' Sasha said hurriedly, and reached out to take it from him.

Oleg responded by drawing his hand from her reach. He held it close to his nose, before taking a very slight nibble.

'It's a bean curd,' he said, grimacing slightly. 'A meat substitute.'

A sense of unease began to rise in Sasha. She looked at Katya, as if hoping the toddler might provide her with an explanation, and then back at her grandfather. He didn't look upset, however. Just puzzled and even curious. All manner of excuses jumped into Sasha's head, but somehow nothing seemed to fit. It just felt wrong to lie to a man of his years. She only had to look in his eyes to know that he was awaiting the truth. With her heart stirring, Sasha took a breath and heard her own voice break the silence.

'I like the taste,' she said. 'Actually, I like it a lot.'

Jack Greenway held the steering wheel so tightly that his knuckles had turned white. He glanced in the rear view mirror and cursed.

'The van's still with us,' he muttered, and shifted up a gear. 'What would anyone want with a kid like you?'

Ivan sat in the passenger seat, his sightline just higher than the dashboard.

'I'm twelve years old,' he said. 'For some men, that makes me kind of hot.'

Jack glanced at his passenger and frowned.

'So, what do you suggest?' he asked. 'Every turn I take, he's right there behind us. If I take you home, he'll know where you live.'

'How about we go to your place?'

'Then he'll know where *I* live!' Jack swung left without indicating. 'It's you he wants, Ivan. I'm just doing you a favor here.'

'No,' said Ivan to correct him. 'I'm helping you out by keeping quiet about your lunch date.'

Jack grimaced to himself.

'It isn't what you think,' he said.

'What am I thinking?' asked Ivan, staring straight ahead.

'You know. That somehow I'm cheating on your sister by sharing a pizza with a friend.'

'A friend.' Ivan smiled to himself. 'Right.'

Jack checked the rear view mirror once again.

'Do we have to discuss it now?' he asked. 'Isn't it more important that we lose this guy? Let's not forget that I could've just kept my head down when you walked past. Had I ignored you, chances are right now you'd be at the foot of a pit in that man's cellar in the dress he'd ordered you to wear.'

'Let me try my dad again,' said Ivan, and pulled out his cell. 'He makes mincemeat out of creeps like this.'

Jack concentrated on driving while Ivan made the call. Once again, however, the line went to voicemail. Up ahead, a set of traffic lights turned from green to yellow.

'We're not going to make it,' muttered Jack.

'Then put your foot down!' Ivan urged. 'It's our big chance!'

The hybrid could pack a punch. Jack knew that. He was also well aware that running lights could lead to a car wreck, not to mention points on his license and the very real possibility that his father would refuse to pay the increase in insurance. So, rather than floor the accelerator pedal, he coasted to a halt as the lights switched to red. The engine cut out automatically, which left the pair sitting in tense silence.

'The van is three cars back,' Jack whispered, as if fearing he might be overheard. He reached for the mirror, turning it slightly for a better look. 'OK, so now the driver's door has just opened. The guy is getting out.' He stopped there and faced Ivan. The boy looked as terrified as he felt.

'Do something,' said Ivan.

'Like what?' Jack's voice rose in pitch.

'Sacrifice yourself.' Tightening his eyes into a penetrating stare, Ivan held his phone between them. 'Sacrifice yourself or the next call goes to my sister.'

20

Earlier, while waiting for the boy to leave the school grounds, Vernon English had bought himself lunch. Parked on the main street, he'd had lots of choices. A club sandwich had been tempting, along with a granola bar and a bottle of real lemonade, but with a long afternoon ahead he'd opted for something more filling.

The steak and ale pie had just come out of the oven. There was no way Vernon could've eaten the thing until it cooled considerably, so he had placed it on the passenger seat. The van had quickly filled with an aroma that made his mouth water. He reached for the wrapper a couple of times, only to pull away on feeling the volcanic heat through his fingertips.

'I wanted something to eat,' he grumbled at one point. 'Not a sample of the earth's core.'

By the time the private investigator sighted Ivan, and started the engine to trail him, his pie remained untouched. His plan was to stay with the boy just to see where it led him. If the Savage children were involved in the death of the model, he had decided, then surely they would be struggling. Their parents might've been able to play things coolly, as if nothing had happened, but it was different for kids. At that age, you'd have to tell someone. You just couldn't live without that kind of thing in your head. It would spill out at some point. Vernon felt pretty confident as he pulled out after Ivan. The kid was the key to all this, he felt sure. He had been in the house on the day of the shoot, unlike his older sister, which made him Vernon's primary person of interest.

That the boy quickly realized he was being followed came as no surprise to the private investigator.

'You're bound to be paranoid,' said Vernon, who had seen it all before. 'It's what happens when you carry around a guilty secret.'

He made no attempt to back off. In his experience, keeping up the pressure like this simply made it more likely that the kid would crack and confess. On seeing Ivan pass the pizza place, only to wheel around as Sasha's boyfriend bundled out in a state of some animation, Vernon pulled up sharply in the van. Was Jack Greenway in on it, too? What was with the drama? With his eyes fixed on the pair, Vernon reached across for his pie. He found the packet on the seat, and then dropped it again as if he'd just discovered it was wired to the vehicle's battery.

'For crying out loud!' he growled, and flapped his hand until the pain eased. 'You could fuel a power station with this!'

Having his lunch right beside him, seemingly super-heated, was beginning to place Vernon in a foul mood. He was hungry, irritable, and also distracted, he realized, on looking back at the pizza place. Luckily, he caught sight of the pair as they headed for the little parking lot behind the building. He waited for the hybrid to edge out, and then let several cars pass before tailing it. Even if the pair knew they were being followed, he didn't want them to recognize him. Every now and then, he would test the pie on the passenger seat. Each time it felt a little cooler, in that it wouldn't now turn an ocean to steam. Eventually, on reaching a set of traffic lights, Vernon found that he could actually hold it in one hand without having to make a beeline to the hospital's burn unit.

'This had better be worth it,' he muttered, and eased the top of the pie from the packet. With one hand grasping the wheel still, Vernon chewed off a generous corner. His teeth sunk through the pastry crust, which was now bearable. Unfortunately for Vernon, it also insulated what felt to him just then like a filling made from molten lava. Instinctively, he spat it out against the windscreen. The gravy was just as hot, as he discovered a second later as it slopped onto his lap, followed by chunks of steak. 'Get off me!' he cried and tried to swat away what could have been hot coals dropping on him. With his mouth, hands and crotch on fire, or at least that's how it felt to him, the private investigator went into a panic. Despite the fact that the traffic lights were about to turn from red to green, he snapped off his seat belt, threw open the car door and jumped out while attempting to hold the front of his pants away from his skin.

'Are you OK there?' asked a guy on the pavement, holding a Golf Sale sign like a downcast flag bearer.

Vernon English finished brushing himself down with the

cap he had grabbed from his head. He glanced across with flushed cheeks and watering eyes.

'Hot snack,' is all he could bring himself to say at first, just as the cars ahead pulled away at the lights. 'Shouldn't be allowed!'

Sasha Savage felt as if she had just admitted to a murder. For several minutes after telling her grandfather about her developing a taste for vegetarian food, they had sat side by side upon his bed without looking at one another. Oleg simply stared across the room, barely blinking. Sasha was equally lost for words, for her confession had come from the heart. It was rare for her to have been so candid and raw, even with her friends, and it felt both awkward for her and a huge release. Only Katya kept the silence at bay as she gabbled to herself on the floor before them.

'It's just a thing,' Sasha reasoned eventually. 'It doesn't change who I am.'

'A carnivore,' said Oleg, as if to remind her.

'Maybe,' said Sasha, and then dipped down to pull Katya's sleeve away from her mouth. 'Or . . . maybe not any more.'

When she rose up again, she found his attention had returned to the remains of the tofu he had taken from Katya.

'What's the attraction?' he asked, and then shifted his gaze back to Sasha. 'Truthfully?'

Sasha considered the question for a moment. She clasped her hands in her lap, well aware that there was no going back from this.

'To begin with I did it for a boy,' she said, facing little

Kat. 'But now I'm not sure what to think. I've gone without meat for a month, and if I'm brutally honest, I don't miss it that much.'

Oleg nodded, still looking at her sideways.

'How have you kept this from us?' he asked quietly.

Sasha breathed out, focusing on the wall for a moment. It was one thing to admit to her dietary deviation. Revealing that she'd had in-house help was quite another.

'Mom has been good to me,' she said eventually, and grimaced to herself.

Oleg turned his attention to the wall across the room once more. He nodded to himself, shrugging at the same time.

'She doesn't want to lose you,' replied Oleg. 'She's scared.'

'It's not that,' said Sasha. 'She just respects my decision.'

Oleg laughed dismissively.

'Your decision,' he said gruffly. 'You're still a girl, Sasha.'

'But I'm not,' she said, determined not to back down now. 'Grandpa, I'm nearly sixteen.'

'You don't know your own mind yet,' he scoffed.

'But I'm old enough to make my own mistakes and learn from them.'

Her response hung in the air. It left Oleg looking at her searchingly. She knew full well that her grandfather had spent much of his life devoted to a pursuit that he believed brought the family together. He had seen his own son adopt his values, and now here was his granddaughter, turning away from everything he stood for.

'Are you happy?' he asked, in barely a whisper.

'Totally.' Sasha smiled to herself. 'It feels like the right thing to do.'

Oleg placed his palms on his knees. For a moment, he and his eldest grandchild watched his youngest at play.

'This family is bound by a tradition,' he said. 'Feasting is what keeps us tight. It stops us from drifting apart.'

'I know that,' said Sasha. 'But I'm not just a Savage. I'm me.'

Just then, Katya noticed that her grandfather was still holding the tofu. The toddler reached up for it, screeching enthusiastically. At first Oleg seemed reluctant to let her have it. Finally, her persistence paid off. With a resigned sigh, he offered it to her.

'I know how it feels to go without,' he said eventually. 'It takes discipline and willpower.'

'Tell me about it,' replied Sasha. 'The whole bacon thing is killing me.'

Her grandfather glanced around at her.

'I would struggle without human flesh just once in a while, especially tongue. Pan-seared with just a twist of Szechuan pepper.' He stopped there to kiss his thumb and two fingers. 'It's all I ask for in life nowadays. That and the wellbeing of my son, his wife and their children.'

Sasha laughed despite herself.

'So, does this mean you understand?'

'Times change,' he said, as a note of some sadness entered his voice. 'Things that once felt so important can become left behind. If giving up meat makes you truly happy, then so be it. Just so long as you don't give up on family.'

'I'm more concerned that they'll give up on me,' Sasha admitted.

Oleg nodded, knowing just what she meant.

'Your father will find it unthinkable for sure,' he said.

'He believes it is his duty to pass on the family ways from one generation to the next.'

'So, how will I win him over?'

'You can't just tell him as you told me,' her grandfather said. 'To convince him that you'll always be a Savage, no matter what you eat, you'll have to *show* him.'

Sasha found herself nodding as he spoke. She wasn't entirely sure how she might demonstrate her commitment. She figured it would just come to her in time.

'I'll give it my best shot,' she said, before leaning across to kiss her grandfather on the cheek. His beard prickled like crazy but it was a heartfelt gesture. 'Thank you,' she added. 'It means a lot.'

Oleg pressed his fingers to where she had planted her lips.

'Are you hungry now?' he asked. 'I'm hungry.'

'Want something to eat?' Sasha rose from the edge of the bed. 'We're all out of tofu, thanks to Kat, but I know there's some hummus hiding at the back of the fridge. That's if you'd like to try something different.'

'Why not?' said Oleg, who accepted Sasha's hand as he struggled to rise. 'I've done it once before, after all.'

21

Jack Greenway pulled up outside the Savage house. The engine cut out automatically. Ivan looked across at him, releasing his seatbelt at the same time.

'So, you're not going back to finish your pizza?'

'Huh?' Jack looked at him with one hand on the wheel still. Then he realized why the boy thought he hadn't just pulled up to drop him off. 'The car is still running,' he told him. 'It's just being fuel efficient.'

'Right,' said Ivan, with complete disinterest. 'Anyway, thanks for the ride.'

'Is your sister home, do you think?'

Jack's question caused Ivan to pause as he opened the passenger door.

'Most likely.'

'Then maybe I'll come in with you,' he said, and unplugged the car key. As much as he wanted to rush back to the pizza restaurant, Jack needed to check that Ivan wasn't going to break their deal and tell Sasha about the young woman he hoped would still be waiting for him. 'After what we've been through,' he told the boy, 'I could use a cup of that nice tea you made just to calm my nerves.'

The pair had driven around town for twenty minutes

after losing their tail. Jack wanted to be absolutely sure they were no longer being followed. After a short time, turning at random at intersections and roundabouts, he had even questioned whether they were being followed at all. What would anyone want with a kid like Ivan? Even a creepy weirdo would find the boy unsettling, no matter what his intentions.

'It doesn't look like Mom and Dad are in,' said Ivan, gesturing at the empty driveway.

Jack wasn't disappointed to hear this. He found both Mr. and Mrs. Savage kind of intense. That evening he had come round to collect Sasha, he discovered that every time he glanced at one of them they were already looking at him.

'That's a shame,' he said all the same. 'Your parents are sweet.'

Ivan glanced at Jack. He looked like he was going to say something, but then seemed to think better of it.

'They look out for us,' he said instead, and opened up the front door. 'Are you sure you want the same tea as last time?'

'Sure do.' Jack followed him inside. 'So, will you tell your parents about the van?'

'Of course,' said Ivan. 'Whoever it is will be sorry. My dad will make sure of that.'

As the boy led the way through the hallway, voices could be heard from the kitchen. Jack recognized Sasha's laugh, and a shriek from her younger sister. It was a surprise to find her grandfather in their company, looking like he'd traveled from the past to join them. Both he and Sasha were working on something at the kitchen counter. With their backs to the door, it was only Katya who registered that they had company. She sat on the floor behind them, and gurgled as the two boys filed in.

'Hey there,' said Jack. 'What's cooking?'

'*What?*' Sasha spun around, followed by her grandfather. Seeing Ivan with him, they both spread their arms as if attempting to hide something behind them. 'You startled us!'

'Evidently,' said Ivan, who calmly crossed the kitchen for a better look.

'That's close enough!' cried Sasha. 'Seriously, you don't want to see this.'

Ivan stopped in his tracks. He tipped his head, straining to see what was on the counter.

'Is this a feast?' he asked, with just a glance over his shoulder at Jack.

'Back off, my boy,' his grandfather warned, jabbing a finger at the same time. 'It isn't what you think.'

Sasha stood with her eyes wide open. She glanced at Ivan, then Jack, before swinging round to the toddler on the floor.

'Cheese!' cried Kat. '*Cheese!*'

'Did she say cheese?' asked Ivan. 'Ribs is her only word.'

'It's a new one,' said Sasha. 'She's expanded her vocabulary.'

'Well, that's great!' declared Jack. 'Good choice, Katya.'

'Cheese!'

With everyone's attention trained on the toddler, Sasha seized her moment. Without turning, and using one hand, she swept everything behind her into the waste disposal unit.

'What is that?' asked Ivan, who looked up smartly as

Sasha hit the switch and the unit started grinding. 'You're hiding something. What is it?'

'*Cheese!*'

This time, it was Oleg who attempted to regain control of the situation.

'Kat just told you.' Stepping forward, he looked his grandson in the eye. 'It's halloumi, to be precise. We were just about to grill some for a salad.'

'With mint is good,' suggested Jack, only to find himself ignored.

'Halloumi,' repeated Ivan, as if to be sure he'd heard it right. 'And that is what?'

'It's quite salty,' Jack persisted, hoping to be helpful. 'Vegetarians love it, but it's off the menu for me nowadays. I don't do goat cheese or any other dairy product. It's a vegan thing.'

Jack stopped there, anticipating some attention or even respect. Instead, Ivan continued to stare at the pair across the kitchen.

'This salad,' he said eventually. 'Does it contain any meat? Some chicken, perhaps?'

Oleg held his gaze for a moment longer before shaking his head.

'None at all,' he said. 'Sasha hasn't eaten meat for the last month.'

'You can thank me for that,' said Jack, and touched his chest with one hand. 'Didn't I tell you there'd be no going back?'

'Jack,' said Sasha quietly, and flashed him a look of anger. 'Not now.'

This wasn't an expression he had seen in her before. There was something ferocious, even barbarian, behind her eyes. Jack's first thought was that she couldn't be serious.

'That's no way to talk to your boyfriend,' he said. 'Have some respect.'

In response, and without a blink, Sasha reached for the paring knife on the counter. Jack waited for her to go back to slicing the halloumi. Instead, and it took a second for him to comprehend this, she stepped right up to him. Even with the blade just resting casually at her side, Sasha looked completely different to him. She said nothing, didn't even appear to be aware of what she was holding, and yet she possessed this purpose and intensity to her gaze that Jack didn't like one bit.

All of a sudden, the girl he had regarded as a plaything and a project now faced him as a threat.

'But you made it through the month,' he insisted, hoping that by returning to the subject that started all this Sasha would come back to her senses. 'You crossed over,' he added, spreading his hands to reason with her. 'Welcome to my world!'

'No,' said Ivan, in a way that drew Jack's attention right away. Despite the air of calm in his voice, the boy's eyes were hardened just like Sasha's, to the point where they looked like they could turn to flint. 'Welcome to *ours*.'

* * *

The mole stood before Titus Savage looking utterly betrayed. Here was the man who had risked everything to provide inside information on the company's fortunes, and this is how he was being repaid.

'You're firing me?' he asked in disbelief, and pushed his glasses back up his nose. 'But you promised me a job at the end of all this.'

'There aren't any jobs,' said Titus. 'I'm breaking up the business and selling off what's left. It's worth more to me like that.'

'Mr. Savage. This isn't what we agreed.'

Titus was sitting behind the Chief Executive's desk. The office had glass walls. It looked out across an open-plan floor, much of which was in the process of being emptied.

'So, what are you going to do?' he asked finally. 'Complain that I haven't kept my side of a completely illegal agreement with you?'

The mole had no response. He didn't want to go to jail, even if Titus went with him.

'Please,' he said eventually, his voice small and wavering.

Titus didn't look up, focusing instead on signing transportation documents.

'Are you still here?' he asked eventually. 'Don't make me call for security.'

'Security's gone,' said the mole. 'You fired them as well.'

'Did I?' Titus set down his pen. Then he rose to his feet, towering over the man across the desk from him. 'You'll appreciate that if I have to escort you from the building it will involve less than professional methods.'

'But you swore to me that I'd be safe,' said the mole, who took a step backwards. '*Please!* What do I tell my wife? My children? Everything I've done hasn't left me feeling good about myself, but it's all been for them!'

Titus continued to glower at him, but said nothing for

a moment. It was as if this final plea was something he couldn't ignore. Finally, with a sigh, he reached for his inside pocket.

'Are they still good, your kids?' he asked, having produced a checkbook which he slapped onto the desk. 'How old are they now?'

'Eight, twelve and nearly fourteen,' said the mole, clearly sounding as if his mouth had turned bone dry. 'Three girls.'

'Three girls!' Titus looked up, beaming broadly, which took the mole by surprise. It just seemed completely at odds with the level of wilful cruelty the man could display. 'You must be proud of them.'

The mole shifted uncomfortably on his feet.

'I am,' he said, watching Titus scribble out a check. 'But it's my responsibility to support them, and give them the best start in life that I can.'

Titus tore off the check he'd just completed and handed it to him.

'You take good care of those little ladies,' he said, ignoring the man's sudden intake of breath. 'Before you know it they'll be grown up and gone. Now leave the building. You have two minutes. *Disappear!*'

With a sum in his hand that comfortably exceeded any severance package, the mole did exactly as instructed. Titus watched him hurry towards the elevator. Then, leaving the desk, he stood at the door to the office. The floor could support one hundred workers. Right now, just two were at their stations. Both were packing up, shocked into moving in slow motion at such a sudden turn of events. Titus was a ruthless operator. He knew that. It's how he'd made his name in the financial world. Not that it brought him much joy at that moment.

'Is this it?' he asked himself, looking around at the abandoned office. Everything from the desks to the computers, the phone system and the television clusters would be sold off in due course. In his business, this was a great achievement. Just then, Titus felt as empty as the floor itself.

This wasn't like creating a work of art or conquering a mountain. Yes, he'd achieved another goal, but what did it bring him except for money? Seeing his father's mind begin to misfire had prompted him to question what mattered in life. It had come as quite a shock to him, having grown up believing that being at the top of the food chain somehow insured them against death. Titus knew his father wouldn't live forever, of course, but Oleg's moments of confusion brought things closer to home now, as had the demise of Lulabelle Hart.

Ever since he'd deposited the body over the cliff edge, Titus had found himself questioning what was really important in life. Time was precious, so it seemed to him just then. At any moment, everything could just be snatched away without warning. He'd taken no pleasure from what had happened to the model. It had been senseless. A terrible waste. In his view, killing could only ever be justified if it served a useful purpose. So long as it was carried out humanely, and the body brought everybody together at the table, Titus could sleep at night, which was something he'd been struggling with since he had zipped up the empty duffle bag and trudged back to his car. The only occasion when he felt fulfilled and at peace, now he thought about it, was when his family were gathered around him.

Titus remained at the office door for a moment, lost in thought, and then dismissed this quiet crisis with a chuckle. 'There's only way to move on,' he told himself. 'With a feast.'

It was his cell phone that was next to grab his attention. The message came from his eldest daughter, as marked by the special ringtone she had programmed into his phone. Titus collected it from his desk. He stared at the screen for a while, reading it through several times, before deciding with both eyes brimming that it was time to call it a day.

I love you, Dad. Whatever happens x

22

The agency office was a far cry from the interiors they represented. On dropping in after lunch with her husband, Angelica Savage had found it cramped and over-furnished, but Marsha didn't seem to mind. She was more concerned about the welfare of her client's children following the tragedy that had occurred soon after the last shoot.

'We're working through it as a family,' Angelica had assured her, before politely inquiring when the next booking might be. In private, things were getting desperate when it came to the interest on her credit card. It was the stress surrounding the death and disposal of the model that had driven her back to the shops. That's how she had dealt with it, but now she was paying the price. Angelica badly needed the house to keep working for her in order to pay off the installments. Not that she could admit that under such sensitive circumstances. Instead, by suggesting that Lulabelle wouldn't wish the agency to suffer financially for her actions, she had finally persuaded Marsha that it would be better for everyone if they rented out the ground floor sooner rather than later. 'It's what Lulabelle would've wanted,' Angelica had finished, lowering her gaze respectfully when Marsha finally opened her appointment book.

To celebrate, because she had earned it, Angelica returned home with several boutique shopping bags in her grasp. For a short time, a little spending like this would leave her in a shining mood. So, when she opened the front door to find Jack Greenway making his way from the kitchen towards her, she was genuinely pleased to see him.

'What a nice surprise,' she said, only to realize that Jack looked like he was about to throw up. 'Everything all right?'

'Your son,' he snapped without stopping. 'He needs his head examined.'

Angelica stepped aside to let him pass. She watched him grab his coat, just as Sasha rushed after him. Her daughter looked as if she was chasing after an event that had somehow escaped from her control. Angelica noted her leaving a knife behind on the hall table as she followed Jack into the hallway. Judging by her daughter's air of panic, it looked to her as if Sasha wished she'd never picked it up in the first place. Then she called after him, which was when Angelica realized something more immediate had prompted him to hurry out for air.

'Ivan was only joking!' Sasha pleaded. 'He didn't really lace your tea with chicken stock last time you were here. At least I don't think he did. Jack, please!'

When he responded by slamming the front door behind him, Sasha stopped and grimaced in frustration.

'What happened?' asked Angelica. 'Not another practical joke?'

Outside, the sound of Jack's hybrid could be heard starting up and then pulling away with just a hint of a squeal from the wheels.

'Ivan is upset,' said Sasha, before hanging her head. 'He found out that I've gone meat-free. Jack tried to take all the credit, so Ivan turned on him.'

Angelica glanced at the blade on the table.

'How about you?' she asked.

Sasha followed her line of sight. She looked a little sheepish.

'I think Jack finally realizes that I make my own decisions.'

'I see.' Angelica set her bags down under the coat rack. 'Well, at least the month is almost up. You don't need to prove yourself any more.'

Sasha looked away from her mother for a moment.

'I'm not sure I want to go back to my old ways,' she said, and glanced at the front door.

'You're a Savage,' said Angelica sharply. 'Savages don't live on lettuce alone.'

'Mom, you know it's not like that. I've eaten well these last few weeks.'

'No thanks to me. The lengths I've gone to keep this from your father, simply because I thought it was a passing phase. And now you're telling me you want to make it a permanent arrangement?' Angelica spoke quickly, which told Sasha she was upset.

'For now,' she said all the same. 'Grandpa has been very supportive.'

'Oleg knows? Dear God!'

'I was fixing him a halloumi salad when Ivan walked in.' Sasha gestured towards the kitchen. 'Katya was with us. She's hungry, too.'

Angelica grasped her daughter by the wrist and fixed her with a searching gaze.

'Tell me you haven't turned my baby,' she said.

'Kat is fine!' Sasha wriggled in her grip. 'She's been chewing on a chunk of bean curd but it's hardly going to kill her.'

Without word, Angelica hurried to the kitchen. There, Ivan was picking apart the grilled halloumi as if performing a dissection. Oleg had headed to the table, from where he stared through the French windows seemingly lost in thought. On seeing her mother, Katya scrambled across the floor towards her.

'Cheese! Cheese! Ribs, ribs, *cheese*!'

'What have they done to you?' she asked, gathering the toddler in her arms.

'Can you believe people actually eat this?' Ivan turned to face his mother with a carving knife in hand. 'Imagine what Sasha's insides must look like.'

'Now you put the knife down, too,' Angelica said calmly. 'And apologize to your sister for upsetting her boyfriend.'

'I didn't upset him,' said Ivan, still clutching the blade. 'I just pointed out that he wasn't as meat free as he believed.'

'You shouldn't have put stock in his tea,' said Angelica. 'It's important to have respect for people. Sometimes even vegetarians.'

'Your mother is right,' said Oleg, stirring suddenly. 'It doesn't matter what she chooses to eat, Sasha will always be your sister.'

Ivan switched his attention back to Angelica. The boy looked cornered, almost betrayed.

'Wait until I tell Dad,' he said, before dropping the knife in the sink and rushing for the door.

Sasha looked from her grandfather to her mother, and then crossed to the kitchen counter where she had left her phone. Having caused such an upheaval in the home, and dreading how her father would react if he ever found out, she had a sudden urge to assure him that one thing would never change.

Vernon English had parked just in front of a trash can. He opened his car window, balled the chocolate bar wrapper in his fist and took aim.

'Bullseye,' he declared, as the wrapper passed clean through the opening. It was a small achievement, but a first for the day given the disastrous collapse of a piping-hot meat pie in his lap. Vernon celebrated with a small air punch, and then settled back to continue listening in on the conversation taking place in the Savage kitchen.

Having committed himself to investigating a possible link between the family and the discovery of a body at the foot of Beachy Head, it was frustrating to hear yet another heated exchange about food. *What was it with these people?* he thought to himself. Everyone needs to eat but the Savages took it to an extreme. Over recent weeks he'd overheard the eldest daughter and her mother conspiring to smuggle in vegetarian food and hide it in the cupboards and the fridge, but the secrecy just didn't make any sense. So, Sasha was ditching meat from her diet. It wasn't uncommon for a girl her age, but hardly comparable to witchcraft. Vernon had struggled to understand what it was she had to hide. Now her brother and her grandfather were wise to the situation and suddenly the world was coming to an end in there.

'So, what's Titus going to do?' he asked, as if addressing those left in the kitchen after Ivan had walked out. 'Force feed her pork pies?'

'*I'm sorry you had to be involved,*' he heard Angelica say, presumably addressing the old man, Oleg. '*I was hoping Sasha would get it out of her system. It seems I was wrong.*'

'*Don't blame yourself,*' replied Oleg. '*It's Ivan we should be concerned about.*'

'*He's going to tell Dad,*' said Sasha. '*I might as well pack my bags right now.*'

'*Let's not overreact,*' said Angelica. '*So long as he doesn't think the whole family is in on this, he's less likely to explode.*'

'*Cheese! Cheese!*'

Vernon listened to the speaker crackle and pop for several seconds, which marked the abrupt silence that followed Katya's contribution. Yet again, the private investigator was left baffled as to why someone's dietary choice should be the cause of such high drama. As Angelica, Sasha and Oleg went on to discuss the best way to break the news to Titus that his firstborn had forgone meat, Vernon sat back in his seat, closed his eyes and sought to work out just what it was that none of them would put into words.

Titus Savage was not unhappy to find himself caught on a subway during the rush hour. He was a tall man, which allowed him to stand head and shoulders over everyone else. It also meant that he could pick out a passenger and assess their quality at close quarters.

On this occasion, as he headed home from the office, Titus loomed over a lean, middle-aged man with a gray crew cut and matching stubble. The guy was a distance runner, Titus decided, judging by the tanned face and lack of much fat around the midriff. Still, at that age you couldn't help but fatten up. A little padding on lean meat was the perfect combination.

Ultimately, it stopped a cut from drying out in the pan.

It was a short walk home from the station. With some heat and light still left in the day, Titus swung his jacket over his shoulder and wondered what might be for dinner. They hadn't eaten pork in quite a while. As both Ivan and Sasha appreciated a little kick to their meat, he hoped that Angelica would agree that Thai was in order. Approaching his house, Titus decided that even if it meant he had to pop out to the supermarket for a few ingredients, it would be worth the effort. Nothing compared to a feast, of course, but as a midweek meal it would be something they could enjoy as a family. What Titus didn't expect, on passing a rundown van, was to hear the voices of his wife and daughter discussing the contents of the cupboard. He slowed to a halt, just behind the driver's door, and realized that it was coming from a speaker inside the vehicle. He didn't stop to listen in. Instead, he walked on casually, switching his jacket from one shoulder to the next before finding his front door keys.

23

Ivan Savage had been waiting for his father to return home. As soon as he heard the door open, he raced to the bottom of the stairs.

'Dad, there's something you need to know!'

In response, Titus raised his palm and then signaled with a finger to the lips for his son to shut the hell up. Next he found his phone and quickly dashed out a message with his thumbs. As soon as he had finished, Titus showed Ivan the screen.

Our house is under surveillance. Let me do the talking.

'But it's important,' Ivan pleaded, only to fall quiet when his father glowered at him, and then follow sulkily in his footsteps as he hurried into the kitchen. There, Titus showed Angelica and Sasha the screen. Both looked up at him smartly, while Titus did his level best to signal that they should talk as normal. He then crouched before Oleg, whose eyesight wasn't what it once was, and whispered in his ear.

'So,' Angelica began hesitantly. 'How has your day been?'

'Oh, you know,' said Titus, who began to scour the kitchen for the listening device. 'The same as ever. Nothing much to report.' He paused to run his fingers under the cupboards. 'How did it go with the agency?'

Angelica took a moment to compose herself.

'They're as shaken up by the tragedy as all of us,' she said. 'How sad to think that poor woman was in our house all day. If only we'd known what despair she was in, we might've been able to help her.'

Sasha looked from her mother to her father, who continued to scour the kitchen.

'If only,' she echoed, simply to fill the silence, before glowering at her brother.

'Anyway,' said Angelica, eager to move off the subject before someone spoke out of turn. 'The agency's booked the house for another shoot. We'll have to make ourselves scarce in a few weeks from now.'

Titus rolled his eyes, and continued to sweep the room in search of the listening device. Ivan watched him run his hands around the rim of the French windows. It was then his sister crossed over to the cupboard alcove beside him. She did so with a purpose, as if something had sprung to mind that told Sasha exactly where she would find it. Titus stopped in his tracks and watched as she opened the little door. The space contained the gas meter. Sasha inspected it closely, looking underneath it and then at each side in turn. Finally, she stepped away, grinning victoriously at her family. Titus took one look for himself and headed directly for the knife drawer.

'I'll be back in a minute,' he said, and selected his favorite carving knife. 'There's something I need to grab for dinner.'

Ivan looked delighted as his father marched from the

kitchen. He followed close behind, despite Angelica's hushed instruction to stay put. Titus wrenched open the front door. The light from outside immediately cast him in silhouette from behind, but for the glint of the blade in his grasp.

'Do it, Dad!' cried Ivan, who wasn't quite sure what he intended, but found himself completely caught up in the moment. In the street, he heard an engine gun into life. Titus rushed for the road, with his son close behind. Ivan just caught sight of the van's driver as he struggled to find first gear. The guy faced his father looking surprised and a little bit scared. Ivan just stopped in his tracks and pointed at the vehicle as it finally sped away

'It's him again,' he declared. 'He wants me.'

Titus turned to face his son. He looked different to Ivan just then. It was as if inner thunderclouds had gathered behind his eyes, which narrowed when he asked the boy to explain himself. As he did so, Angelica, Sasha and even Oleg had arrived at the front door. Angelica held Katya in her arms, but her attention was focused on Titus.

'Come inside with the carving knife,' she said calmly, and looked around to be sure that the neighbors weren't watching.

Titus switched his attention to Sasha.

'How did you know to look at the gas meter?' he asked.

'I remembered a man came to read it,' she told him. 'He said that Kat was cute.'

'*Cheese!*'

Ivan was alone in taking great delight in the toddler's sudden outburst. Titus looked pained, for a very different reason than Sasha, his wife and grandfather.

'It seems Katya really is finding her voice,' he said slowly.

'Goodness knows where she got that from,' said Angelica, whose smile for the child in her arms looked a little forced to Ivan. 'Cheese and ham, darling. Say *ham*.'

Holding the carving knife loose against his leg, Titus made his way back to the house.

'I believe this means it's time we welcomed Katya into the family ways,' he said, stopping to pet the little girl. 'Now that her teeth are through and she's talking, she needs to know her roots. It'll help her to recognize that we Savages stick together no matter what life throws at us.'

'A feast,' said Oleg, who clearly relished the word, much to Sasha's discomfort.

Titus seemed not to notice. Instead, he drew his only son to his side, glanced down the road to be sure the van had gone, and then clapped him on the shoulder.

'You'll always be safe in my care,' he said, before addressing his whole family. 'And I think we all know who should be on the menu.'

Amanda Dias had been privately amused when Jack bailed from the pizza restaurant. Whatever the kid at the window wanted, it was obvious to her that he was calling all the shots. Jack hadn't even offered an excuse. He'd simply rushed back for his coat, and left her with a series of half-finished apologies and a plea to catch up again very soon. Fortunately, he had told Amanda that he was a regular at the restaurant, given its impeccable vegetarian credentials. Sure enough, after she had finished her pizza, as well as what was left on his plate, the waiter assured her that Jack would settle the bill later.

He was a little young for Amanda, but then she had no time for boyfriends at this moment in her life. There was a cause out there that needed her leadership. So many of her so-called friends had walked away as her views began to harden, but nothing could shake her belief that eating any animal product was fundamentally wrong and punishable. Jack was certainly attractive for his age, but Amanda was more interested in his potent mix of narcissism and enthusiasm for her crusade. As a result, she wasn't flattered but intrigued when he approached her for lunch. Could this be the opportunity, she had thought to herself, to put her militant views into practice? It was something Amanda reflected on afterwards as she stopped by the market to shop for provisions. For too long, defenseless animals had been abused or slaughtered by man and served up on a plate. Cows, pigs, sheep and poultry were sentenced to appease our appetite through no fault of their own. Even the oceans provided no safe haven. In Amanda's view, it left people like her with no choice but to wage war on the predators. Unlike any other species on this planet, humans possessed the intelligence to make choices about what they ate. Food had to come with a conscience, she believed, and if people wouldn't listen they would have to pay the price.

Naturally, Amanda wasn't stupid. She had no intention of actually taking a life. That was down to the foot soldiers. Those who possessed the will, perhaps, but required a little guidance and encouragement to fulfill their true calling. Jack Greenway struck her as an impressionable young man with potential. Clearly, he had designs on sleeping with her, but that was also something she could use to her advantage. Amanda smiled to herself as she pondered her plan on the bus journey back to the university campus. She was well aware that grooming him would require a promise of quite a reward, and then decided on arriving outside her dorm that it had to be worth the investment.

This was largely due to the fact that Jack Greenway was waiting for her at the main doors. Standing beside his hybrid, he looked restless, wired, and a little nervous, all of which seemed to melt away when Amanda beamed at him.

24

Sometimes, Vernon English was thankful that he lived alone. His marriage had crashed long ago, but at least he was free to transform the lounge in his flat into an incident room without being made to take down all the photographs and notes he'd taped to the wall. This wasn't something he'd done before, but the Savage case was beginning to consume him.

'What am I missing?' he asked himself, sitting back on his sofa with his feet on the coffee table. The wall opposite was plastered with long-range snaps of the family, including Oleg and Jack Greenway, as well as magazine ads featuring Lulabelle Hart. He'd penciled arrows between some pictures, and on others added color-coded cards with his thoughts on them. Most made sense at the time. Looking at it all now, the private investigator could be sure of only one thing: he'd need a professional decorator to restore the room once he'd cracked this case.

Leaning forward, with his eyes locked on the wall, Vernon reached for the burrito in the box on the table. It had been cold for some time, but even though he'd been distracted he wasn't going to give up on it. Chewing on his takeout dinner, the private investigator focused his attention on the section of the wall devoted to Titus Savage. The man was behind the death of the model, and he would not rest until he'd uncovered evidence to prove it.

At the same time, Vernon could not ignore the fact that he was a little jealous. Titus was a success in the City, where being ruthless was basically a virtue, while at home he showed a different side entirely and his family clearly adored him for it.

'Some people have it all,' he muttered, and eased himself to his feet. 'Others make do with the leftovers.'

Heading to the window overlooking the dollar store on the main street with the sale going on, Vernon pressed his forehead to the glass and sighed. He kept a handful of pictures in simple wooden frames on the ledge in front of him. All of them were taken during his marriage, from the honeymoon to the last Christmas they'd spent together. In each one, the face of his ex-wife had been carefully obliterated with marker pen. As far as he was concerned, she no longer existed. Even so, he wasn't prepared to deny himself the fact that he had once shared his life with someone special. He picked up one of the frames and studied it. Had things worked out between them, he too could've been a loving father. Whatever Titus hid from the world, Vernon English could only begrudgingly admire his commitment in building a family and keeping it together.

'What is your secret?' Replacing the picture on the ledge, Vernon returned his attention to the wall. His eyes darted from one image to another, following pencil trails and then imagining fresh alternatives. Yet again, it just looked like a tangled mess. Vernon turned away, his thoughts switching to the possibility that there might be some hot sauce in the kitchen cupboard, and then came around full circle. 'There it is,' he said, and took a step back to gain some perspective. This time, he didn't focus on individual surveillance shots or his scribbled hunches. He just stared at the little gap at the very heart of it all. All of a sudden, it looked like the eye of the storm. Vernon grabbed a pen from the top of the TV and scribbled one word in the space. He underlined it with a slash before standing back once again. Everything he had discovered about the family was tied to it in some way. What he'd missed until now was that it had to include the death of Lulabelle Hart.

'Food,' declared Vernon, reading it out loud as if that might help bring him clarity. It didn't prove anything, but just then there was something in it that the private investigator pledged to pick apart. 'Food is the key,' he said with some confidence, and glanced at a shot of Titus once more, 'or I'll eat my words.'

A cheer broke out from the boys who had gathered on one side of the skateboard ramp. One of their number had just pulled a frontside five-forty turn. It was an impressive trick, but went completely ignored by the girls opposite. Sasha Savage, Maisy and Faria sat across from them with their backs turned, elbows flat on the safety rail and their feet dangling over the drop. They were on lunch break, talking about everything and nothing in particular.

'You're quiet,' Faria said to Sasha. 'Everything all right?'

'I'm good,' Sasha replied. 'Just hungry.'

Faria offered her a cigarette.

'It'll kill your appetite,' she said. 'And then some.'

Sasha smiled but declined the offer.

'She's waiting for Jack,' said Maisy, and flashed them both a look. 'It would be rude to eat now if he's planning on sharing his lunchbox with you.'

Everyone giggled at this, including Sasha.

'Seriously, he's been good like that,' said Faria. 'Why can't he do the same thing for us two?'

'Because we eat meat,' Maisy said, as if to remind her. 'Plus he's not that into us.'

'How do you know?'

'When was the last time you saw the inside of his car? Sasha's the only one who gets a ride in there.'

'Maisy!' Sasha pretended to look scandalized, only for Faria to adopt a charitable expression. Sasha picked up on it straight away. 'What's wrong?' she asked.

'Nothing,' Faria replied quickly, but found she couldn't escape Sasha's gaze. 'Probably nothing, anyway.'

'What nothing?' asked Sasha.

Faria sighed to herself.

'My sister saw him last weekend,' she said. 'He was up at the university campus. Dropping off some girl.'

Faria stopped there and turned to Sasha as if perhaps she could provide an explanation.

'Jack was upset with me the last time I saw him,' she said, thinking back to that moment in the house, 'but he wouldn't do that.'

'It was his hybrid,' insisted Faria. 'For sure.'

Sasha held Faria's searching gaze for a moment more, and then broke off with a shrug.

'You don't seem too concerned,' said Maisy.

'It's probably something to do with his new vegan regime,' said Sasha. 'Jack is taking things much further with his food than I'm prepared to go, but I'm sure he'll have an explanation. I'll ask when I see him.'

'Why was he upset with you?' asked Faria.

'Not me as such,' said Sasha. 'My brother confessed to a practical joke he'd played on him.'

Both Faria and Maisy sucked the air between their teeth.

'Did Jack suffer any injuries?' Faria enquired.

'He'll survive,' said Sasha, and winced to herself at the memory of the knife she'd pulled without thinking.

'Whatever the case, he's late,' said Maisy, checking the time on her phone. 'He's usually here for you by now.'

Leaving straight after morning classes, Jack Greenway's journey from school to the university took twenty minutes. The journey was unplanned, but he felt compelled to catch up with the young woman who had moved into his thoughts. Amanda Dias wasn't hard for him to track down. He found her handing out leaflets at the main entrance to campus.

'Do you drink milk?' she asked Jack when he trotted up to greet her.

'Sometimes,' he said hesitantly. 'I should stop that, too, shouldn't I?'

'It would be kinder on cattle to drink their blood,' she said. 'Did you know that in some industrial dairies calves are *forcibly* removed from their mothers so they don't drink from the udder. It might mean a higher volume of milk for the farmers, but how would you like to be taken from the teat?'

'Me? Oh . . .' Jack wasn't sure if this was a direct question. He had planned a conversation on the way to campus, but mostly it involved what nice weather they were having. 'I don't know,' he said hesitantly. 'Thirsty?'

Amanda thrust a leaflet into his hands.

'You'll find all the facts here.'

Jack looked down at the leaflet, his focus swimming.

'Give me a handful,' he said. 'I'll hand them out at school.'

Finally, Amanda offered him a smile.

'It's good to see you,' she said. 'I enjoy our chats.'

For several days now, Jack had sought out Amanda and treated her to everything from coffee to lunch and dinner. Every time they visited a café, bar or restaurant of her choosing. Jack spent much of the time just listening to her views on man's crimes against the natural world. He made all the right noises as she laid out her vision for a vegan society, in which compassion towards animals replaced their suffering. He even kept up the enthusiasm when she talked about how to achieve her dream. Privately, all the stuff about waging war against the worst offenders Jack took with a pinch of salt. It was the force of her convictions he found entrancing, plus the fact that up close Amanda Dias was hot as hell.

'I couldn't wait until this evening,' he said just then. 'I needed to see you.'

Amanda handed a leaflet to a passing student. The guy tried to avoid it, but she was insistent.

'I thought lunchtimes were reserved for your girlfriend,' she said.

'My girlfriend?' Jack tried to look as baffled as possible. 'Oh! You mean Sasha? She's not really my girlfriend as such—'

'Really? You looked like a couple at the lecture.'

'We're just, y'know . . .'

'Friends?'

Jack grinned. After the episode in the Savages' kitchen, he wasn't even sure he could bring himself to speak to Sasha again. Her brother's prank with the tea still made him feel queasy, and the kid would get a pounding for it at a later date, but above all he'd struggled to shake off the memory of that look she had given him. Jack couldn't put his finger on it, and although he would never admit this Sasha had left him feeling a little bit frightened. The knife in her hand hadn't helped, but he felt sure that wasn't meant as a threat. After he'd left, she'd probably gone back to core an apple or something. Maybe chop some celery for that salad she'd been making.

'I've been helping her to give up meat,' he told Amanda, with some pride in his voice. Then he looked to the pavement and adopted a face as if what he had to say next was difficult. 'We were good for a while, but . . . her family.'

He stopped there and twisted a finger against the side of his head. Now he had Amanda's complete attention.

'So, they didn't like losing a carnivore?'

'Exactly that, I guess,' said Jack. 'Her dad in particular had a real problem with it. He's one of those old-school meat eaters. Can't accept that there's a better way of living.'

'Would you kill him?'

The way she asked him this, in public and out of nowhere, took Jack's breath away. He looked at Amanda, aghast for a moment, before checking he had heard her right.

'Do you mean . . . for real?'

'Absolutely.' Amanda stepped closer so she could murmur in his ear. 'It would bring me closer to you.'

Jack moved back to find her gaze once more. This fruit loop wasn't joking, he thought to himself. The girl had it all worked out. She batted her eyelids at him, like the wings of a butterfly at rest.

'I'll do it,' he said, despite having no intention of carrying out such a crime. 'For you.'

Amanda brushed Jack's cheek with her lips.

'For the environment,' she said to correct him. 'For a better world.'

25

As a hunter, Titus Savage had learned everything from his father. Over the decades, Oleg taught him how to trap his quarry and finish it off both quickly and humanely. From an early age, Titus learned that a noble cannibal showed respect towards a victim. You didn't eat them alive. That kind of thing was the stuff of myth and legend. A modern-day flesh eater carried out careful preparations with a view to serving up a dish to die for.

When it came to the kill, Titus considered himself a natural. As a boy, he'd taken to the pursuit with a perfectionist's eye. It was something he had begun to pass on to his own son. In fact, as the family made plans for Katya's celebratory feast, he intended to stand back and let Ivan do the honors. In a way, Titus decided, it would allow him to close the book on the accidental death of the model in the bathroom.

Firstly, however, Titus had to identify the person they intended for the plate.

'This man,' he said to Ivan and Sasha at breakfast time that week. 'Can you describe him to me?'

Sasha thought back to the time he had entered the house disguised as a meter reader from the gas company.

'Middle-aged,' she said. 'Tired-looking with quite a heavy-set face.'

'He reminded me of a bloodhound,' added Ivan. 'Also he was wearing a hat when I saw him. Not a flat cap. Something funkier. A funky bloodhound.'

Titus looked across at Angelica.

'Sound familiar?' he asked.

'Nobody we know,' she said. 'So how do we find him?'

Titus was at the French windows. He turned his back on his family for a moment, half wondering whether he should head upstairs and consult his father. Back in the day, Oleg would leave the house at sundown and work under cover of darkness. In the morning, his wife would find a body laid out on the table, naked, washed and shaved from head to toe. Always the romantic, Oleg would pin a note to the chest of the corpse using the tip of a knife, dedicating the coming feast to her. Nowadays, of course, it simply wasn't necessary to go stalking back alleys for the drunks and the dispossessed. With access to the internet, it was perfectly possible for Titus to source someone of better quality who met their requirements perfectly. In particular, the social networks provided Titus with everything he needed to know about their health, wellbeing and background. He could work out their move-ments and, of course, assess friendships. Anyone too popular was off the menu. You didn't want their disap-pearance to spark headlines, campaigns and vigils, just an entry in the missing persons register that would gather dust over time.

'There's only one thing we know for sure about this

guy,' said Ivan, who drew his father's attention once more. 'He's sexually attracted to me.'

Titus sighed to himself.

'I suspect that I'm his main person of interest,' he said, before addressing Angelica once more. 'This is business, I think.'

'But Ivan may be on to something,' she said. 'Even if this does have something to do with your work, the fact is he followed our son.'

'Because he's the weakest link,' suggested Sasha, who promptly received a kick under the table from her brother.

'At least someone is into me,' he fumed. 'When was the last time you saw your boyfriend? Even I've heard it's finished, and nobody speaks to me at school!'

'Mom,' complained Sasha. 'Tell him to stick to swapping chess pieces.'

'Face it,' grinned Ivan. 'He's over you.'

'Lacing Jack's tea hardly helped,' she snapped at him.

Ivan sat back in his chair, considering his sister.

'But if he has dumped you,' he said next with a sly glance at their father, 'does that mean you'll give up with the sausage dodging?'

'*Mom!*'

This time, Angelica responded by glaring at her son so fiercely that he visibly shrank in his seat. She had already spoken to Ivan about staying out of Sasha's personal issues, and made it quite clear that there would be consequences if he breathed a word to his father. Angelica glanced across at Titus, who continued to be the only family member who wasn't wise to Sasha's newfound vegetarianism. Much to her relief, he seemed so lost in thought that he clearly hadn't heard a word. It was only when Titus noticed that everyone was looking at him that he blinked back into the room.

'Our boy can be the bait,' he said after a moment, and then nodded to himself as if he had just road-tested the idea to see how it sounded.

'What?' All of a sudden, Ivan didn't look so confident.

'Like a goat tethered to a stake,' suggested Sasha, but their father was on a roll.

'You don't have to worry,' he assured the boy. 'When our man comes prowling, we'll be waiting for him. And that's when he'll learn how it feels to be preyed upon.'

Vernon English no longer needed an inside ear in the Savage household. The bug had served him well. Titus had probably destroyed it now, but not before the private investigator had heard enough to know that this was a family with one very strange obsession with food.

Given all the hushed conversations he had heard between Angelica and Sasha, it seemed they lived in fear of Titus finding out that his eldest daughter had turned her back on meat. At times, they made out the man was some kind of dietary dictator. Then there was the coroner's report that Vernon had obtained. It was only a side note, but of major interest to the private investigator, for Lulabelle Hart had been secretly struggling with an acute, long-term eating disorder. Had the model crossed Titus because she didn't conform to his views, and paid the ultimate price? It was a far-out theory, but not one that Vernon English could easily dismiss.

Once again, the private investigator was alone in the van with his thoughts. There was no way now that he could return to the Savage residence. That Titus had bundled out with what looked like a carving knife only strengthened Vernon's suspicions that he was dealing with a dangerous man. Besides, Vernon was off duty at that moment. He'd just finished his weekly supermarket shopping. The bags he'd loaded onto the passenger seat contained a range of microwavable dinners that fueled his work. He'd gone in with good intentions, but ultimately there was nothing in the fresh produce section that appealed. Leaning across, Vernon buckled the bags against the seat for the journey back to the apartment. Just then, however, it simply reminded him that he had nothing for company but a bunch of ready-made meals.

'I wonder what Titus would make of my diet?' he asked, addressing the shopping as he started up the engine. 'Not that I have plans to invite him over to eat. You're all mine, so rest easy.'

It was only as he pulled out of the parking lot that he realised he had forgotten to buy any ketchup. Unwilling to turn around, Vernon told himself that he would just have to nip out again later. For some time, he'd been meaning to do his shopping online. Only recently, while staking out the Savages, he'd watched a delivery van unloading a week's groceries for the family. It looked like such a quick and easy way of getting a supermarket shop directly into the house, he reflected, and promptly hit the brakes hard as a plan of action sprang to mind. Several horns sounded behind him, but Vernon paid them no attention whatsoever.

'Oh, man, you're good,' he told himself. With the horns still blaring, Vernon found first gear and moved off again. 'It's high time I saw what's on the menu.'

Jack Greenway had thought long and hard about Amanda's proposition. Murdering a man was nuts, of course. Still, he had another motive for meeting her in a coffee shop to go through the plan in more detail.

'That's an interesting bracelet,' he said, looking for a way to make her feel special.

Amanda didn't even glance at her wrist.

'What you're about to do takes courage,' she said quietly, while stirring a vegan gingerbread latte. 'Naturally, people will be horrified that you've taken someone's life because of what they eat, but if it means they rise up against us then what we'll have on our hands is a *war*!'

'Right,' said Jack, who was content to go along with Amanda just to see where it would take him. 'Is that a good thing?'

'We vegans are morally superior,' she told him. 'In a battle for hearts and minds, victory is ours for the taking, and it'll all be thanks to the provocative actions of one brave soul . . .' Amanda stopped there and held his gaze. 'You're about to change lives, Jack. Your place in history awaits you.'

Jack stirred his latte as he listened. Amanda had recommended the gingerbread drink, but frankly it didn't look all that appealing. Still, that wasn't why he was here. 'What about afterwards?' he asked hopefully. 'Do I hide out in your dorm?'

Amanda smiled seductively. At least that's how Jack tried to read it. In truth he wasn't really sure.

'Once the deed is done we'll go online anonymously, claim responsibility, and then sit back and watch the flames rise.'

'I see.' Jack hoped the sitting back park would take place in her bedroom. 'Flames.'

'Anyway,' she continued, 'you really don't look like the sort of person with previous criminal convictions. Why should the police suspect you?'

Jack collected his cup in both hands, mindful of his outstanding library fine. Taking a sip, he reminded himself that he had no intention whatsoever of slaying Sasha's father. He didn't really think that Amanda was being serious. It was, without a doubt, the talk of a fantasist. Privately, he hoped she was the sort of person who got turned on by indulging in this kind of role play, and that was fine by him. The way Jack saw things, it would be perfectly possible for him to leave the Savage house claiming he had carried out the kill. Even if Amanda was being serious, he thought to himself, that would give him time to reap the rewards before she learned that somehow Titus had survived the attack. The girl was nuts, but just so sexy that it had to be worth playing along with her. The latte sloshed down his esophagus, leaving an aftertaste of warm cardboard in his mouth.

'Count me in,' said Jack. 'I'd be honored to go into battle with you.'

'Good boy,' said Amanda, and found his ankle under the table with her foot. 'When can you do it?'

'Give me a little time,' said Jack, thinking she would at least need to see him entering the Savage house. That meant he'd have to stop freezing out Sasha and pretend that all was still good between them. 'As soon as I'm ready,' he added, 'you'll be first to know.'

26

Angelica Savage began working on the menu with Katya in mind. This feast was in her honor, after all, so it was important that the choices on offer appealed to her. Sasha found her mother at the kitchen table, with a notepad and pen in hand. She peered over her shoulder, reading the list with interest.

'Liver pâté biscuit bites,' she said hungrily. 'Mom, don't tempt me!'

Angelica looked around.

'It would put an end to a lot of problems,' she said. 'At some point before this feast, we're going to have to tell your father why you won't be joining us.'

Sasha sighed and took the seat beside her. She placed her phone on the table and set it to one side. Katya was in her high chair opposite. She was clutching a wooden spoon, which she dropped to reach across the table for her older sister's hands.

'I've tried to find the right moment,' said Sasha, collecting the spoon from the floor, 'but every time he's been grumpy about work.'

'No matter what you say he'll go crazy,' replied Angelica. 'What's important is that he doesn't lose sight of the fact that you're his daughter first and foremost, no matter what you choose to eat.'

Sasha watched her mother writing on the pad.

'Liver and pistachio pâté?' Sasha grinned at Katya. 'You're going to love this, but it isn't making it any easier for me.'

'How about that thing I do with the loin?' Angelica set down her pen. 'The carpaccio?'

'With plenty of basil and garlic?' Sasha closed her eyes, as if the suggestion triggered memories of the taste. 'Mom, you know how much I loved that when I was little!'

Angelica returned her attention to the list.

'Maybe I should add it anyway,' she said to herself, with just a glance back at her daughter. 'Now, what would everyone else enjoy?'

For half an hour, both mother and daughter explored all the different dishes they could create from one human body. It was a time marked by a great deal of discussion and laughter, which came easily with little Katya sharing the table. Slowly, the list began to grow, as did a sense of warmth between the pair. It felt good to Sasha, just to be involved at this level, and she could see that Angelica felt the same way. When Sasha's phone rang, just as they were planning dessert, her first thought was to ignore it. Then she glanced at the caller name, and snatched it into her hands.

'I need to go out,' she said after a brief and hushed exchange. A hint of disappointment came into her mother's expression. 'I'll be back shortly,' Sasha added, before rushing from the room. 'I promise!'

*   *   *

One week. That's how long Titus Savage had asked his son to walk to and from school unaccompanied. Ivan didn't usually mind traveling alone. With no friends, he was used to sitting on the bus or trudging along the pavement with his thoughts, but this was different. Some creep was out there stalking him.

'It's not you he's interested in,' his father kept assuring him. 'I'm his man.'

'But what if you're wrong?'

'I'll be watching every step you make,' said Titus. 'All you have to do is trust me.'

Ivan had every faith in his father. He'd never let him down before. Even so, the boy took steps to protect himself. He didn't like feeling threatened and though Titus swore he was close by, just waiting for their man, the boy still felt vulnerable. Such lack of control left him tense and edgy. Not once did he see the van in question, but that just made him more anxious. Back home, Ivan would fire up his war videogame and attempt to regain some sense of control by going on a virtual rampage. Even that didn't stop the bad dreams. Slowly, his stalker invaded every aspect of his existence. On the final day of that week, when a figure stepped out from behind some bushes in the park, Ivan immediately moved to defend himself.

'It's me,' said Titus, and promptly threw himself to one side as a dart-like electrode whizzed past his shoulder. 'Hold your fire, Ivan! Put the Taser away!'

The boy had pulled the weapon without warning. It belonged to his father, who had only ever used it once to disable a victim before bundling him into the boot of the car. The Taser was effective at delivering a soul-sapping electric shock. Titus had picked it up from a security outfit he had stripped down and sold off. He had kept it hoping to keep up with the times, only to find he preferred a more traditional means of incapacitation.

'You scared me,' said Ivan, who began to reel in the dart by the wire that attached it to the weapon.

Titus looked one way and then other. They were in view of the playground. Fortunately, none of the parents and their children had noticed.

'What were you thinking?' he hissed, and retrieved the dart for him. 'The hatch in the shed floor is sealed for good reason. We only break it before a feast.'

'I'm sorry.' Ivan had crouched to finish winding in the wire. He looked up at his father and blinked back tears. 'I don't want to be bait any more.'

Titus considered his son for a moment. Then he offered the boy his hand to help him back onto his feet.

'We'll find him,' he promised. 'Now put the Taser back in your bag and let's go home.'

'Good idea,' said Ivan, and wiped his eyes with the sleeve of his school jacket. 'Will there be anything to eat when we get back?'

Titus smiled.

'I'm hungry, too,' he said. 'It's always that way before a feast. Your grandfather believes our body metabolism has learned to accelerate beforehand. He's convinced we burn off excessive fat storage to make room for the flesh that follows.'

'I feel it.' Ivan placed a hand on his belly. 'It's an ache that won't go away. A cramp sometimes, too.'

Together, Titus and Ivan continued along the path. Titus placed his arm between his son's shoulder blades, both to steer him in the right direction and offer him a sense of protection. They chatted as they walked. Titus talked about spending more time together. He was tiring of the takeover business, so he said. There was nothing wrong with hard work, but if it ceased to be rewarding then it was time to seek out fresh challenges. As they made their way to the park gates, and then up the street towards home, Titus had convinced himself that it was something to discuss with Angelica. He was also well aware that the next feast couldn't come soon enough. As ever, it would revive his spirits and help him to forge a way forward that put the family first. Seeing the grocery delivery van outside the house, however, left Titus with mixed feelings. His dear wife always worked so hard to put on a memorable spread, but by now he'd hoped to have taken care of the central ingredient.

'The perishables have arrived,' observed Titus, just a moment before a figure emerged from the driveway and climbed in through the side of the van.

At once, and without further word, both father and son stopped in their tracks.

Vernon English had waited several days for this moment. Loitering in the park, with the Savage house in view, he had tried his best not to invite suspicion. He pretended to read the paper on several benches, or simply pressed his phone to his ear and had a long conversation with the imaginary person on the other end. Vernon was feeding the ducks when the grocery van trundled into view. Emptying his pockets of the remaining bread, he placed one hand on his cap to stop it from blowing free and broke into a brisk trot. It was only as he approached the vehicle that he slowed right down. He could hear the driver in the back, sorting out the delivery. Looking around to be sure he wasn't being watched, Vernon side-stepped into a neighboring drive and stood quietly beside a trash can. He only wanted a moment inside the van. He knew exactly where to look to find the delivery checklist, having observed several drop-offs outside his own block that week.

'Come on, fella,' he muttered. 'Do your thing.'

Vernon levered down a branch in the bush that hid him from view. He could see the driver at work, pulling the family's order from cold-store compartments. Finally, the guy stepped down onto the pavement and stacked three baskets onto a cart Vernon braced himself to make his move. As soon as the man set off for the house, he headed straight for the van and jumped in without using the step.

The clipboard was hanging from a hook by a loop of string. The Savage address was printed in the upper corner of the top sheet. Vernon snatched it free and scanned the list underneath.

'OK, what have we got?' It was just a hunch after years in the profession, but something told the private investigator that the key to unlocking the secret about the Savages had to be right here. His eyes dropped from one food item on the list to the next, and again on the other side of the sheet. Finally, he looked up and searched his mind. There was enough stuff here for a banquet, some kind of roast that would befit a royal, but one thing was missing. It was a glaring omission. Without it, this blow-out would be incomplete. Vernon looked up with just one question on his mind. 'Where's the meat?'

The response, as such, came in the shape of a dart to Vernon's left buttock. He barely felt it puncture his pants and skin, largely on account of the fifty-thousand volt shock it delivered to every fiber of his body. Vernon didn't make a sound, having momentarily swallowed his tongue. He simply snapped upright in pain, his eyes bulging, and then sheer surprise when the convulsions stopped and a hand appeared from behind him clasping a silk neckerchief. It was doused in a sweet-smelling chemical, he realized, on finding it clamped to his mouth. A second later, overcome by chloroform fumes, the private investigator slumped back into the arms of his assailant.

THIRD COURSE

27

Sasha Savage paused outside the café. She was nervous about the conversation that was about to take place. It wasn't something she had expected, but as soon as she heard his voice on the phone it felt like the right thing to do. Taking a breath, she pushed open the door. There he was, rising from the table on seeing her.

'Hi,' said Ralph, and gestured at the seat opposite. 'What can I get you?'

Sasha lit up at the young man she had spoken to briefly at the university talk. He was as scruffy as she remembered, with a heartfelt smile and a crinkle beside each eye that told her how much he liked to laugh.

'Whatever you're having is good,' she said. 'As long as it isn't vegan.'

Sasha had given Ralph her number during the break. It had been good for her to meet someone who was also embarking on a trial without meat at the same time. Ralph shared the same hopes, doubts and weaknesses as she did, and so when he asked to keep in touch she didn't look for an excuse. As he tapped the digits into his phone, he had jokingly promised not to stalk her. Sasha had been too shy to ask for his number in return. It didn't seem right, given that she was supposedly with her boyfriend. It was only afterwards, on the drive home, that she began to hold out hope that he would call. Jack had just not stopped talking about Amanda. It wasn't only her crazy beliefs that he admired. He even praised her sense of style and the courage he felt it would've taken for her to stand up and share her views. Then, on dropping off Sasha at her house, he'd had the nerve to put the moves on her again. Sasha had responded to his wandering hands by climbing out of the hybrid. That evening, she had gone to bed hoping Jack would wake up and realize how insensitive he'd been. Instead, he'd gone quiet on her. More immediately, to Sasha's surprise, she found she wasn't greatly upset about it.

Jack had opened her eyes to many things, and that included the growing realization that she just wasn't that into him. He'd certainly swept her off her feet in the beginning, and seduced her with his views on food, but beyond that he only seemed to be interested in bedding her. Sasha had been prepared to see how things panned out, to give him a chance to show he had a deeper side, but seeing him flounce from the house over the prank with the tea just convinced her it was over. She hadn't felt too bad about it. That Jack hadn't been in touch himself made her think the feeling was mutual.

'Jack and I want different things,' she told Ralph over coffee. 'But I don't have any regrets. They say you should always try something before you decide whether or not you like it.'

Ralph smiled, clasping his mug with both hands.

'I didn't know if I should call you,' he said after a moment. 'I hope it's OK.'

Sasha was pleased that he had. Ralph really seemed like a genuine guy. At the same time, after everything that had happened with Jack, she realized just then that what she needed here was friendship. As someone else setting out on the same path as her, she could see in Ralph's eyes that he felt the same way.

'So, how are you doing with the whole vegetarian thing?'

Ralph set his mug down on the table.

'Well, it's tough!' he said. 'I'm definitely a veggie at heart. I just can't speak for my stomach sometimes.'

'Any bacon moments?'

'Oh, constantly.'

'Me, too.' Sasha grinned, her eyes locked on his. Ralph held her gaze with ease.

'I need to tell you something,' he said finally. 'It's confession time.'

'Go on.'

Ralph toyed with the sugar packet.

'Once or twice over the last couple of days,' he told her, 'I've given in to temptation.'

'No!' Sasha pretended to look shocked, but laughed despite herself. 'Actually, I wouldn't be surprised if I did the same thing.'

'Really?'

Sasha considered what she had to say next.

'OK, it's my turn,' she began. 'Sometimes, I crave something so unspeakable I can't even put it into words.'

'More unspeakable than bacon?'

'Oh, *so* unspeakable.'

'Want to try me?'

'No,' said Sasha, 'but it feels good just telling you that. Like a weight off my shoulders.'

Ralph held her gaze for a moment, and then chuckled.

'So, why not give in to temptation?' he suggested. 'It won't kill you.'

Sasha thought about this for a moment.

'I suppose there are no rules to say that I can't.'

'Exactly,' said Ralph. 'All these people beating themselves up about not eating this or only eating that. I'm beginning to think sometimes it's best to just go with what feels good.'

Finding herself nodding before he had even finished, Sasha smiled and wagged a finger at him playfully.

'You're a bad influence,' she told him. 'Just when I've been doing so well.'

'Hey, don't let me influence your eating habits.' Ralph held up his hands, grinning still. 'I'm not here to judge you.'

'Glad to hear it,' said Sasha. 'And I'm not here to give you a hard time about bacon. A treat is good for the soul every now and then.'

'So it is,' said Ralph. 'Especially on white bread with ketchup.'

'We all have our favorites,' agreed Sasha.

'I'm glad I'm not alone.'

Sasha glanced at the table, as if summoning the courage to speak from the heart.

'You're not alone,' she said quietly.

Ralph nodded, still playing with the packet.

'Likewise.'

For a second they said nothing. There was no need. The silence was only broken when Sasha's mobile phone began to ring. She glanced at the name on the screen and immediately rejected the call.

'That's the first time Jack's tried to reach me since he slammed our front door in my face,' said Sasha. 'I wonder what he wants now?'

'You should speak to him.'

Sasha pocketed her phone.

'I will,' she promised. 'It's important that one of us does the right thing.'

Vernon English came to his senses over the course of an hour. At first, as he surfaced from the anesthetic properties of the drug vapor he'd inhaled, he struggled to register anything more than the fact that he was still alive. His whole body felt like a dead weight, not least his head, which throbbed like crazy. As for his surroundings, Vernon's clouded brain initially told him that he must be in the hold of a ship at sea, for all he could hear was the creaking of timber and ropes. Eventually, he summoned the presence of mind to open his eyes. Thanks to a solitary light bulb, he realized that he was in fact in a concrete-lined room, with no windows or door. It contained one plastic chair and a tall, wall-mounted steel cabinet. Both appeared to be upside down, he noted as his vision continued to recover. A moment later, the private investigator realized the furnishings just looked like that because he was strung up by his ankles from an oak beam overhead.

'Hnngghh!' he croaked, though his appeal for help was muffled by the gag in his mouth. Vernon twisted and bucked against his restraints, which wasn't easy as his hands were also tied behind his back. His nostrils flared as he breathed in and out, both eyes wide with fear. A closed hatch in the ceiling corner offered the only way in and out, with iron rungs fixed to the wall that served as a ladder. Vernon followed the rungs with his eyes. At the bottom, beside a drain, he spotted his cap. Not only had it come adrift from his head, which always left him feeling exposed, it looked badly trampled. '*Hnngghh!*'

It wasn't until some hours later, when he gave up hope of raising the alarm, that Vernon found himself in company. His temples felt as if they might burst. This wasn't just down to the blood sloshing around in his skull. At one point, he had tried to raise the alarm by swinging himself against the wall. After a couple of minutes of banging his head against the rock hard surface, he had succeeded only in temporarily knocking himself out. Since then, he'd just dangled there and sobbed quietly. Tears streaked his forehead, and though he occasionally pulled and tugged at the ropes that bound him, Vernon English was a defeated man. Even when the hatch pulled away, a second passed before he glanced up. Two faces peered down at him. Despite the gloom, he immediately recognized the bald dome of Titus Savage and his son's intense stare.

'Is he ready?' asked the boy.

Titus climbed down into the space. He stood back from the trussed man hanging upside down before him and then produced a wallet from his back pocket. Immediately, Vernon recognized it as his own.

'Vernon Ray English. Forty-four-year-old Caucasian male. A private eye, which is no surprise. He's divorced and lives alone.'

'That's good,' said Ivan, climbing down beside his father. 'Isn't that good?'

'It means he's less likely to be missed,' said Titus, who was now sizing Vernon up and down. He stepped closer to his terror-struck captive, whose muffled gasped marked the moment Titus began to gently press his sides and stomach. 'The liver is a little enlarged, which is often due to alcohol, but the kidneys are in good shape.'

'He looks healthy enough,' observed Ivan. 'In a tired sort of way.'

Titus slapped Vernon's left thigh, before taking a step back.

'He'll need stripping down and washing,' he said next. 'And shaving, of course.'

Vernon responded to each instruction with a squeak and a whimper.

'I can do all that,' said Ivan eagerly, before facing up to his father. 'I can do . . . everything.'

Titus thought about this for a moment.

'Very well,' he said, only to caution him by extending a finger. 'Just be nice, OK? I'm letting you do this alone because I trust you to have respect for this gentleman.'

'I won't let you down, Dad. I promise.'

Ivan held his father's gaze, who nodded to himself after a moment.

'My boy,' said Titus eventually, and ruffled his hair. 'It's time to make a man of you.'

By now, Vernon was making an almighty noise. Seized by panic, he began thrashing like an escapologist over flames. Titus and Ivan observed him calmly, as if they'd seen it all before. Finally, Titus grasped the man by one arm, and waited for him to fall still. Then he crouched and yanked the gag from his mouth.

'Let me go!' Vernon begged him, gasping for air at the same time. 'Whatever you want with me, we can pretend it never happened.'

'We could do that,' agreed Titus, 'but I have to think of my family.'

Vernon struggled to keep his composure from cracking.

'What kind of family are you?' he asked, sobbing at the same time.

'A private one,' Titus told him. 'A family that doesn't take kindly to people bugging their kitchen.'

'I know you had something to do with the death of Lulabelle Hart,' spat Vernon. 'You're not just a crooked businessman. I should've gone to the police with my suspicions!'

Ivan looked up at his father.

'Lulabelle was an accident,' said Titus, as if speaking for his son.

'But we didn't eat her,' added Ivan, who seemed surprised when Vernon responded with a harrowing scream.

28

Jack Greenway was not used to being ignored. Three times he had tried to reach Sasha by phone. On each occasion, it had rung off before her voicemail kicked in. Finally, he had texted her, a simple 'WTF?' but that too had failed to draw a response.

Jack also knew that he only had himself to blame. Ever since the thing with the tea and the knife, he'd done his level best to avoid Sasha. Amanda had become his top priority, but now there was a problem. In order to fulfill her fantasy, which he hoped would earn him a very special reward, he needed to get back into Sasha's good books so as to gain access to her house. Finally, Jack went looking for her one lunch break. As he'd failed to show up with his Tupperware container at the skate ramp all week, he learned from Faria and Maisy that Sasha had gone to the nearby express supermarket to buy a sandwich. When Faria cheekily invited him to sit with them and share the box, it was clear he felt his efforts had gone to waste.

'Another time,' he said with a sigh. 'It isn't the same without Sasha.'

Later, after classes had finished for the day, Jack was

spotted in the junior parking lot. He was sitting in his hybrid, picking at the contents of his container with his fingers, clearly brooding. He was just dropping a pinch of bulgur wheat with pomegranate seeds into his mouth when a knock at the driver's side window caused him to sprinkle it down his shirt.

'*Sasha!*' Hurriedly, Jack wound down the window. 'I've been trying to get a hold of you.'

'Is now good?' she asked.

'Perfect!' said Jack, stowing the box and brushing himself down. 'Where shall we go?'

Sasha looked at him uncomfortably.

'I haven't got long,' she told him. 'I promised Mom I'd be back to help out in the kitchen. We have a big meal planned for the weekend.'

'Then let me drive you home,' said Jack, thinking at the same time that this would be just the opportunity he needed to talk her into inviting him round.

'I'm not sure,' replied Sasha hesitantly. 'There's just something I need you to know.'

Jack pressed the ignition button.

'Tell me on the way,' he said, and gestured at the passenger seat. 'In this car we'll barely leave a carbon footprint.'

For the first few minutes of the journey, the pair exchanged small talk. Jack reported that the vegan life was like finding his spiritual home, and while Sasha complimented him on the commitment her voice lacked enthusiasm. Jack wondered whether she had relapsed as a carnivore, but reminded himself that his goal here was to make sure

Sasha felt that things were good again between them. It wouldn't be difficult, he thought to himself. She was crazy about him.

'I like your mascara,' he said, without taking his eyes off the road. 'It really suits you.'

'I'm not wearing any.' Sasha wound down the window by an inch to get some air. 'Jack, this thing we have—'

'It's going places,' he cut in, and shifted up a gear. 'I'm sorry I haven't been around much lately, but I really do feel we're heading in the right direction.'

'It's over.'

'What?' Jack glanced across at her, and pulled back into the lower gear. 'It can't be.'

'I'm sorry,' said Sasha. 'I thought that's what you wanted.'

'But you can't,' Jack replied, his voice tight with panic, and found himself torn between looking at Sasha and the road. 'I need to see you. This weekend.'

'We're finished,' she said as if to spell it out. 'You've introduced me to some things, and I'm grateful for that. I've just come to realize that I'm not comfortable sharing my life with someone quite as intimately as you'd hoped. I had to give it a shot to realize this, and I just hope we can be friends. That's all I want in my life right now, Jack. Family and friends.'

For the last few minutes of the drive, Jack pleaded with Sasha for a second chance. At the same time, all he could think about was the very real possibility that his opportunity to bed Amanda could vanish.

'Is there someone else?' he asked at one point. 'Is it that

guy from the talk? The one who looked like he needed a bath and a shave? I saw you chatting to him in line. Don't think I'm completely stupid.'

Sasha looked at the floorwell.

'It's not what you think,' she said. 'Ralph and I just have a lot in common at the moment.'

Jack's grip on the steering wheel tightened. Sasha was beginning to annoy him now. No girl had ever broken off a relationship with him. It just didn't work like that in his world.

'Does he drive?' he grumbled.

Sasha sighed to herself.

'He doesn't drive,' she said, pinching the bridge of her nose. 'Nor is he a vegan. He's trying hard not to eat meat but struggling with the whole hardline thing. To be honest, I know just how he feels.'

As they approached the Savage house, Jack felt utterly defeated. He pulled up outside. The engine cut out automatically. The silence inside the car was clearly as painful for Sasha as it was for him.

'So, that's it?' he said.

Sasha dropped her gaze, but offered him a smile all the same.

'It's for the best,' she said, before reaching for her school bag. 'I'll see you around.'

Jack drew breath to ask if the weekend would be good, but already Sasha was climbing out of the car. As she did so, he noticed that she'd left something behind on the seat. An earring, he realized, on picking it up.

'Wait!' he said, just as Sasha closed the door. Returning

his attention to the earring, Jack held it up for a closer inspection. He didn't know much about jewelry, but this was one of those dangling kinds with a silver clasp. It held a little bauble that could've been carved from bone. His first thought was to hurry after Sasha and hand it back. Then an idea crept into his mind. One that caused him to curl his fist victoriously around the earring. Jack looked at Sasha one last time, who didn't turn as she opened up the door to the house. He smiled to himself, before slipping what would be his golden ticket inside his shirt pocket. 'You can have this back on Saturday,' he said. 'I'll drop it off. Really. It'll be my pleasure.'

Dangling by his ankles in the pit beneath the shed, there was a moment when Vernon English's sense of terror exceeded anything he had ever known. It came when Titus prepared to leave him alone in Ivan's company.

'You can't!' Vernon pleaded. 'Don't abandon me down here. Not with . . . him!'

'He's my son,' said Titus, seemingly irritated by the man's lack of respect. 'He might well make mistakes the first time, but you know how it is.'

'*How?*' Vernon roared, and then broke into a sob. 'I don't eat people. I don't even have kids!'

'You don't?' If Titus was preparing to leave, this stopped him in his tracks. He considered the man trussed up before him. After a moment, his irritation appeared to have been eclipsed by pity. 'They drive you crazy sometimes, but every now and then they make you so proud your heart could burst.'

'I don't want to die,' croaked Vernon. 'I'd still like to start a family one day.'

Titus watched Vernon sobbing for a moment. Then he looked to the floor, ran the palm of his hand over his shaved dome and sighed.

'You know too much for me to let you go now,' he said, and gestured at their surroundings. 'I'm sorry you missed out, Mr. English. Building a family is one thing. Keeping it together is where sacrifices have to be made.'

Without further word, Titus turned and took to the rungs.

'Please!' cried Vernon. 'I'd make a good dad. I'm sure I would!'

Once he'd climbed out of the space, Titus responded by lowering the hatch into place. Vernon looked back at Ivan, and found his gaze tight upon him.

'It won't hurt,' said the boy. 'Not this part.' Ivan turned to the cabinet behind him. He unlocked the door with a key his father had handed him and swung it open. First he fished out a butcher's apron. It was striped blue and white, but mostly stained with deep red splatters, and way too big for him. With his eyes locked on the cabinet still, Vernon screamed again, much to the boy's annoyance. 'Could you, like, shut up? They're just tools.'

He stepped aside, offering Vernon a clear view. Knives, hooks and saws with jagged teeth hung from the upper rail in the cabinet. Some larger equipment was stored underneath. Much of it looked industrial.

'This is a joke,' breathed Vernon, his teeth chattering with fear. 'A sick joke.'

Ivan returned to the cabinet. First he hauled out a pressure washer. Then he found a barber's clipper which he placed on the plastic chair. Finally, after some rummaging, the boy returned with what looked like a short-handled hammer in one hand. As he twisted it in his grip, Vernon noticed that one side sported some nasty triangular studs.

'Relax,' said Ivan. 'It's just a tenderizer.'

'*What?*'

'You know?' he said, and patted the instrument in the palm of his hand. 'It softens the fibers. Makes the meat easier to chew.'

Vernon English struggled to take in what the boy was saying here. Gripped by panic, still hanging upside down from the beam, he began to tremble, twitch and gasp for breath.

'Your dad said nothing about a tenderizer!' he said in desperation. 'A wash and a shave is all he asked you to do.'

'It's my first time,' said Ivan with a shrug. 'I want to do things properly.'

'But you told me it wouldn't hurt!' he wailed.

'It won't.' Ivan placed the tenderizer on the chair and turned for the cabinet once more. When he came back around, Vernon saw to his horror that he had just collected a bolt pistol. 'You'll be dead by then,' he said, and pulled the bolt back on the spring. It locked into position with a click. Ivan caught his eye and smiled. 'On the bright side, if I accidentally nick you with the clipper in a minute from now you won't feel a thing!'

'*Don't do this,*' whispered Vernon, as Ivan placed the bolt head to his temple and found the trigger with his finger.

THE SAVAGES

He drew breath to plead with the boy once more, only for a thunderous bang to mark the moment that his world went black.

29

For Titus Savage, a feast was always preceded by a day of preparation. Like his father, he considered it to be a kind of ritual that involved the whole family. There were tasks for everyone. Throughout the next morning, Sasha helped her mother assemble the side dishes, while Titus visited the market for those last-minute items. In the afternoon, having set out the place mats at the table, he found the mahogany box that contained the special cutlery and took it upstairs to his father's room. Oleg liked to play a part, and polishing the silverware was something he had done for decades.

'I hope you're hungry,' said Titus, as his father pushed his spectacles into place. He waited for the old man to find a cloth in his drawer before outlining what was on the menu. 'We could've opted for something leaner, and less tearful about his lost opportunities in life,' he pointed out, 'but what else could I do?'

'I hear that Ivan is in charge.' Oleg shuffled across to the table under the skylight, where Titus had just placed the box. 'I remember your first time as a little boy. It was a proud moment.'

The pair exchanged a smile.

'Ivan tells me everything went according to plan,' said

245

Titus. 'He stayed up until the early hours to get the job done. He hasn't even surfaced yet.'

Oleg picked a dessert spoon from the box.

'I wonder if this is something Ivan will pass on to his children?'

'Of course,' said Titus without hesitation. 'He's a Savage. Tradition is in our blood.'

Oleg focused on polishing the spoon for a moment.

'Will Sasha be joining us?' he asked.

'She's in the kitchen with Angelica right now.' Titus narrowed his eyes, unsure why he would even check his granddaughter would be present. 'Is something troubling you?'

'Me? No!' Oleg rubbed the spoon handle vigorously. Then he stopped and sighed. 'We're all Savages, Titus. We always will be in name at least, no matter how many of us gather around the table in the future.'

Titus looked baffled. He was standing over his father, who next selected a fork to polish.

'Well, every one of us shall be eating this evening as we welcome little Kat to the fold,' he said, and clapped Oleg on the shoulder as if that might reassure him. 'You don't need to worry about your grandchildren. It's my duty to make sure they understand the importance of dining like this on a regular basis.' Titus turned to leave the room. At the door, he stopped and addressed his father one more time. 'You know, it's true what they say that the family that eats together, sticks together.'

'Maybe not the family that eats *people* together,' muttered Oleg.

'I'm sorry?'

The old man looked up and around. He seemed startled to find Titus was still there.

'Oh, nothing,' he said quickly and held the fork up to the light.

Angelica hadn't stopped all day. The menu, which she'd written out by hand, was stuck to the fridge using painted magnets from a local art fair. With Sasha's help, the potatoes were peeled, the vegetables chopped and herbs picked from the garden. The only thing missing, in fact, was the meat. Still, Angelica had everything under control, with help from her eldest daughter. Sasha was at the stove, stirring a pepper and port wine sauce, while little Kat was on the floor by the French windows, her hands pressed to the glass, babbling at the birds on the feeder.

'It's going to be a late night for her,' Sasha said.

'You know how it is,' said Angelica. 'We don't sleep until everyone is full.'

By now, the sauce was beginning to simmer. Sasha turned the heat down by a notch.

'Ivan says there's a lot to share out this time.'

Angelica had just finished refilling the salt cellar. She stopped and faced her daughter.

'There'll be even more to go around if you don't join in,' she said.

Sasha focused on the sauce, which was still bubbling even on the lower temperature.

'Will Grandpa be eating down here or in his room?' she asked, in a bid to change the subject.

Angelica wasn't surprised, but persisted anyway.

'This feast might be all about Katya,' she said, 'but I want it to be a celebration for you both. A welcoming to one daughter and a farewell to the other.'

Sasha stirred the sauce a little quicker.

'Mom, I really appreciate how supportive you've been to me these last few weeks. I'll be at the table with you all. Nothing changes there.'

'Everything changes,' said Angelica to correct her. 'A vegetarian will be eating among us.'

'I'm not sure about the whole label thing,' Sasha replied, as the sauce finally began to thicken. 'It can feel a bit suffocating.'

'Which is why we never call ourselves cannibals,' said Angelica, prompting her daughter to catch her breath.

'Mom!'

Sasha looked scandalized. Like Angelica, she then scrambled to look as busy as possible when Titus appeared in the kitchen.

'Did I just hear the "C" word?' he asked, and inspected several dishes. Sasha stirred the sauce wildly. Angelica tightened the top of the salt cellar, well aware that Titus was gazing directly at her. Just then, Ivan appeared at the doorway in his dressing gown. He yawned, stretched, and then dropped his arms on realizing he had just walked in on something. Normally, his mother would scold him for lying in bed throughout so much of the day. Instead, Angelica shot him a look that told him he needed to be elsewhere.

'I just wanted something to eat,' the boy grumbled, and headed for the back door. 'I'm starving.'

As soon as he was outside, Titus addressed Angelica and Sasha once more.

'We're not cannibals,' he said as if to remind them. 'Cannibals boil people alive in cauldrons. I prefer to think of us as evolved eaters. As a family, we're at the forefront of fine dining. Human flesh is an acquired taste, and I've worked hard to give you all the chance to appreciate it for yourselves. It's what keeps us tight, am I right?'

Angelica glanced at Sasha, who looked back at the sauce, sighed to herself and then nodded.

'Let's all take a seat,' said Angelica, and gestured at the kitchen table. 'Sasha has something to share.'

Vernon Savage saw a bright light. Having been dangling from the beam for so long, and in total darkness, the opening of the hatch caused him to blink and wince.

It was the sight of the crazy kid, Ivan, easing his way down the rungs that persuaded him to stay still and silent. Vernon knew he was supposed to be dead. If he started shouting and screaming, Ivan might have another go with the bolt gun. Fortunately for the private investigator, the boy's lack of practice meant the weapon had recoiled when he pulled the trigger. Instead of punching through his temple and into his brain, the bolt had simply knocked him out. Vernon considered this to be a small mercy given the indignity and horror of what had evidently followed. When he resumed consciousness, he found he had been stripped of his clothing, washed and shaved from head to toe with the barber's clippers. Finally, he realized he'd been swaddled in what felt like a diaper made from kitchen foil. It crinkled every time he moved, which he tried to keep to a minimum on account of the pain he was in. Even without being able to see anything, Vernon knew that Ivan had hit him with the tenderizer at least a few times, but not enough to have much effect on his flesh. It left him wondering whether the boy was incapable of carrying out the job properly. If so, thought Vernon in his traumatized mind, Ivan's inexperience might just save his life.

It was for this reason that he played dead before Ivan hit the light switch. He then held his breath as the boy circled him. Whatever happened next, Vernon hoped this young psychopath would continue his hapless streak. With his head just above the ground, Vernon dared to glance up to see that Ivan, wearing his dressing gown, was clutching a short blade in one hand. He stifled a gasp. This wasn't looking good, but what option did he have?

'Oh yeah,' said Ivan, as if he'd suddenly remembered something, and turned for the cabinet behind him. 'A bucket for the bleed out.'

On hearing this, Vernon's heart began to hammer so forcefully he could almost hear it with his own ears. He let his eyes go glassy as Ivan came back and slid a rubber trough underneath him. On feeling the cold edge of the blade against his jugular, however, the man could take no more.

'No!' yelled Vernon angrily, and blinked back into focus. 'Get away from me!'

This time it was Ivan's turn to cry out. He scrambled backwards, knife in hand, but not before scratching Vernon's throat with the tip. It was enough to produce a bead of blood that swelled and dropped into the trough.

'Ouch!' said Vernon with a grimace. 'Will you leave me alone?'

Ivan looked aghast.

'But I killed you,' he said. 'You're dead.'

'And so are you when I'm free,' growled Vernon, the foil crinkling wildly as he writhed and bucked against his bindings. 'Help!' he cried out, filling his lungs. '*Help me!*'

Panic-stricken, Ivan looked to the open hatch and back again at his captive.

'Shut up,' he said. 'Shut your mouth or I'll get my dad!'

'*Help! Someone, please help!*'

It was all too much for the boy. Dropping the knife, he raced for the rungs as Vernon continued to raise the alarm. Even with the hatch back in place, and the pit returned to darkness, the stricken private investigator continued to bellow while the trough below him collected his blood drip by little drip.

30

Titus Savage sat in grave silence. Across the kitchen table, his wife and eldest daughter looked on uncomfortably. Only Katya remained her sunny self. At that moment, however, nobody paid her any attention.

'Who is responsible for this?' asked Titus eventually, his voice on the verge of cracking.

Angelica and Sasha exchanged a glance.

'The boy I was seeing,' said Sasha. 'But it's over now.'

'I see.' Titus furrowed his brow. 'Couldn't he have left you with something more traditional like a broken heart, maybe, or herpes?'

'Titus!' Angelica shot him a look. 'Be civil. This isn't easy for Sasha.'

'It's OK,' Sasha cut in, and held her hands out to calm them both. 'It was my decision to go vegetarian. Jack just introduced me to the idea, but this isn't a question of who is to blame. It's about understanding.' She paused there and looked away for a moment. 'Understanding and respect.'

'What about respect for the family?' Titus asked, and slammed his palm on the table. 'You're turning your back on a tradition that unites us in a shared secret. It grounds every one of us, so we can each make the most of our lives!'

'And I'd still willingly take my place each time you sit down to feast,' said Sasha. 'I'll just stick to the vegetables,' she added quietly.

Titus scoffed dismissively.

'My daughter, the grazer.'

'There you go again,' said Angelica with a sigh.

'Belittling me won't change my mind,' said Sasha, in such a way that commanded her father's attention. 'This is who I am now, and I just feel better for it.'

Titus sat back in his chair, considering her.

'What about the feast we had before Christmas two years ago?' he asked. 'You begged me to do the honors, and a very clean kill it was, too, but how does that sit with you, Sasha? Now that you're better than us?'

'Dad, I'm just trying to be true to myself. Isn't that what you want for all your children?'

Just then, the back door crashed open. Nobody at the table looked around.

'Help me out, Sasha,' said Titus, sounding a little calmer. 'I'm struggling here.'

It was Angelica who was first to look around as her son appeared before them. He looked wild-eyed and a little breathless.

'Dad, I need your help.'

'Not now.' Titus kept his gaze locked on his eldest daughter.

'But, Dad—'

'I *said* not *now*!'

It was a sudden outburst, delivered with such force that everyone present shrank into themselves. The silence that followed was only broken when Katya started bawling.

'Now look what you've done,' muttered Titus, and rose to collect her from the floor. 'Go to your room, Ivan. And just stay out of trouble!'

'I just really think you need to—' Ivan stopped short as his father turned and glowered at him. 'Fine, then!' he grumbled before heading for the stairs. 'Don't blame me if dinner is ruined!'

Soothing Katya in his arms, Titus stood by the French windows, overlooking the garden and the shed at the back.

'It's not too late to change your mind,' he told Sasha. 'You need to think long and hard about what this means for your family.'

Sasha waited for her father to face her before she replied.

'Would you say the same thing if I had just come out as gay?'

'Is that your next bombshell?' asked Titus, and turned to Angelica.

'Just answer the question,' she said, folding her arms.

With Katya calm, Titus set her back down on the floor. He crouched there for a moment, offering one of her plastic bricks to play with. Finally, when he was sure of his composure, and that his voice wouldn't crack, he rose up once again.

'Of course I wouldn't say the same thing. That would be different.'

'So, would you rather I'd stayed quiet about going veggie?'

said Sasha. 'This last month has been really tough. If it wasn't for Mom's support, I'd never be here now, being open about who I am.'

'A month?' Titus looked in astonishment at his wife.

'Sasha needed time to work things out.'

'I'm still a Savage, Dad,' she said. 'The only difference now is that I'm really happy being me.'

By now, there was nothing Titus could do to stop a tear from tracking down his cheek.

'Then I'm happy for you,' said Titus, and wiped it away with his shirt sleeve. From across the table, Angelica mouthed the words 'thank you' at him. 'It seems I have a lot to learn from this,' he added. 'Perhaps I should follow your example.'

'By giving up meat?' asked Sasha, her mouth falling open.

'Don't push it,' said Titus, and recovered with a grin. 'I mean by being honest with myself.'

Angelica was still watching her husband closely.

'Is there something you want to tell us?'

'Oh, it's nothing,' said Titus, batting away the question. 'I'm just feeling a little restless at work lately. Maybe I've been in the business for too long, but I'm starting to wonder if I should move on to new horizons. A challenge, perhaps.'

'Like what?' asked Angelica. 'You're a natural at what you do.'

'I'll think of something,' said Titus, who turned just then to inspect the dishes on the counter behind him. 'For now, whatever anyone chooses to pile on their plates, let's focus on making this feast one of the best we've ever had!'

* * *

Without blinking, Ivan hammered at the trigger button on his handset. On the videogame in front of him, he was an effective killer. It helped him to block out what a mess he'd made of things in real life.

'I'll finish you,' he muttered to himself, and not just to the women and children fleeing from the crosshairs of his gun. 'You'll see.'

A knock at the door drew his attention from the screen.

'Are you looking for the bathroom again?' he asked his grandfather.

'I don't need directions,' said Oleg, and showed him the box of cutlery he'd finished polishing. 'Look at that. All ready for the feast.'

'Whatever.' Ivan returned his attention to the screen.

Oleg watched him turn his sights on a fleeing crowd for a moment.

'So, your father let you do the honors last night. Congratulations.'

Ivan unleashed a storm of bullets, cutting down dozens at a time.

'The kill is still alive,' he said simply. 'And he won't shut up.'

Oleg's expression changed from concern to surprise.

'But a kill is supposed to hang for twenty-four hours after death to improve the flavor.' He checked his wristwatch. 'We'll be cooking shortly.'

'I thought I'd finished him,' complained Ivan. 'Somehow he survived and now he's making a big fuss.'

'Does your father know?'

Ivan shrugged and shook his head.

'He's busy with Sasha. I think she's finally come out to him.'

Oleg considered this for a moment.

'I'm sure we won't let her share go to waste,' he said, only for his shoulders to sag as he sighed. 'That's if there's meat to eat.'

On the screen, Ivan appeared to run out of bullets. He pressed the trigger button a couple of times, but by then it was game over. Tossing the controller to one side, he faced his grandfather directly.

'Will you help me?' he asked. 'Please?'

Even as the words came out, Ivan doubted his grandfather would agree. At his age, what could he do? Sure enough, Oleg looked to the floor with a sigh. When he glanced back again, however, Ivan saw a gleam in his eye that for a moment made him look like a younger man.

'It'll be just like old times,' he said, and stepped aside so his grandson could lead the way.

Titus could still be heard in the kitchen as they crept downstairs. His conversation with Sasha and Angelica sounded just as intense, but with some laughter now. Even so, Ivan had no intention of interrupting him again. With his grandfather's assistance, he figured his dad need never know there had been a problem with the kill. Only Angelica noted him creeping towards the back door with Oleg shuffling close behind. Ivan pressed his finger to his lips, glancing warily at Titus at the same time. She frowned, but returned her attention to her husband as he talked about how proud he had been at Sasha's first feast. Ivan clicked open the door, before turning to check on his grandfather.

'Can you make it quick and clean?' he asked as they stepped out into the yard.

Oleg squinted in the light, even though it was beginning to fade. His skin looked strikingly waxy to Ivan, who was reminded that this was the first time he had seen his grandfather outside since he moved in with the family.

'I'm not quick anymore, my boy,' he said, and used his cane to walk, 'but I'm always clean. It's a skill. Something you'll pick up over time.'

The garden path was carefully concealed by overhanging branches and foliage from the borders. This was thanks to Titus, who liked to make sure that it couldn't be overseen by the neighbors. As Ivan approached the shed, it struck him that the rungs into the pit might present a problem. He quickened his pace, anxious to work out a way to assist his grandfather so that he could get the job done. The plastic chair, he thought to himself, would give him something to stand on to help the old man descend. Lifting away the hatch, the boy turned and scrambled down to the concrete floor. He looked up, just as Oleg's face appeared.

'You can do this, Grandpa,' said Ivan, and slid the chair into place. Oleg looked down into the pit. He seemed confused to the boy, which wasn't unusual. Ivan reached up with his hand, ready to steer the old man's foot onto the top rung. 'Come on. Let's finish this!'

'But it looks like we're too late,' said Oleg.

Ivan glanced over his shoulder. With a gasp, he then turned round so quickly that the chair tipped underneath him. The boy crashed to the floor, but he barely seemed to notice. He picked himself up and reached for the stub of rope that dangled from the beam. The rubber trough on the floor contained a couple of inches of blood at most, but the captive from which it had come was nowhere to be seen.

31

Vernon English was in a sorry state. He had lost just enough blood to bring him close to fainting, while his body, shaved and lightly tenderized by Ivan, made him look like a badly plucked chicken in a silver foil diaper. On top of everything, his escape bid had almost knocked him senseless.

It was his junior captor who was also responsible for this bid for freedom. As soon as Ivan had dropped the knife and fled, the private investigator had made every effort to work his wrists free from the rope bindings. Desperation drove him, fueled by a fear that failure would see him meet a gruesome end. It had taken a while, and left him with a badly skinned right hand, but eventually he had done it. Vernon's next challenge had been to swing and stretch until his fingertips brushed the knife handle ever closer across the floor. Laughing deliriously to himself once he had grabbed it, he reached up with all his might and attempted to cut the rope. Success sent him crashing head first to the floor. He had narrowly missed the trough, hitting the concrete instead. As a result, he went on to haul himself from the pit in a traumatized daze. Too weak to speak, Vernon had blinked in the late light and tottered towards the house. He had heard the back door opening, but that wasn't what persuaded him to stumble sideways in the direction of the French windows.

It was the sight of the little angel watching him from behind the glass.

This blue-eyed girl with blonde ringlets had beamed at Vernon, entrancing him. Having been through hell, it was a glimpse of heaven that drew him closer. At the window he sank to his knees, and pressed his palms to the glass where she had pressed hers.

'Save me,' he croaked, and mustered a smile as she giggled and chattered at him. Just then, the vision before Vernon represented everything that was good with the world, and all that he had missed. If he survived this ordeal, he thought to himself, he would change. Work had already cost him one marriage and the chance to start a family. That couldn't be allowed to happen again. Life was too precious, as this sweet baby kept saying in his head, over and over again. Dimly, Vernon was aware of some people at the table behind her, but in his mindset this apparition was all that mattered. She practically glowed, which was mostly due to the fact that Vernon's blood pressure was all over the place and it had left him with tunnel vision. 'Take me home,' he added, and promptly began to weep. 'Show me the way. *I'm ready!*'

In response, the little girl patted at the window with both hands. The private investigator let his head slump against the glass. By now, his tears were falling freely. At the same time, he heard startled voices from inside the kitchen, along with the scraping of chairs. He was also aware of activity spilling out of the shed but nothing could move him from that moment. Vernon English lifted his eyes, found the little girl looking over him, and just then it felt like a blessing.

Titus Savage was as surprised as everyone else to see the central ingredient at the window. As soon as Vernon came to his attention, he kicked back his chair and rose to his feet.

'Ivan,' he muttered under his breath, before repeating his name at full volume.

'What's he done now?' asked Sasha, who turned to face the French windows. 'Oh.'

Angelica was quick to pluck her youngest daughter away, as if the man on the other side of the glass might harm her.

'Unless Ivan's planning on a surprise barbecue,' she hissed at her husband, 'you really need to get that man indoors.'

Titus didn't need to be told. He hauled open the French windows, slipped his hands under Vernon's arms and then dragged him over the threshold. At the same time, Ivan rushed breathlessly onto the patio behind him.

'Is this a feast?' asked Titus angrily. 'Or a fiasco?'

Ivan glared at the man his father was now supporting.

'He'd better taste good,' the boy muttered. 'All the trouble he's caused.'

Vernon turned to Titus, who was practically holding him upright.

'I eat a lot of junk food,' he said, sounding faintly delirious now. 'That can't be good for you.'

'You'll be fine as a one-off,' said Titus, sounding clipped. 'So long as you're part of a balanced diet.'

As he spoke, Oleg shuffled in from the patio. It had taken him all this time to join his family. Sasha was quick to find her grandfather a chair, which he accepted gratefully.

'So,' he said, and turned his attention to Titus. 'We got a live one, eh?'

'Not for much longer,' growled Ivan, and crossed the kitchen for the knife rack. 'I won't let you down this time, Dad,' he said, and reached for the largest blade.

Vernon squeaked like a cornered mouse, and fainted backwards. Titus caught him as he fell, and glowered at his son.

'At least he won't see it coming,' he said as Ivan approached with the knife raised in both hands. 'Just get it right this time. I've been working up an appetite all day.'

Outside the Savage residence, as stars began to prick the sky, Jack Greenway pressed the doorbell and then took a step back. He glanced over his shoulder. Across the street, standing in the park, the young woman he had come here to impress watched intently.

Man, he thought to himself, Amanda was sex on legs. It was a shame she had a screw loose, but he could live with that. All he had to do was spend a few minutes inside the house. So long as he left in a hurry, it would be easy to convince her that he had murdered a meat eater. Just to be sure, he had picked up a vial of fake blood from the joke section of the local toy store. On leaving, he'd dip behind Mr. Savage's 4x4 and flick it over his chinos or something. It would be enough to convince Amanda that he had carried out her wishes. He'd also have to ditch his pants, which Jack hoped would happen in her company.

'See you on the other side,' he said quietly, and offered her a wave.

Amanda responded with a scowl, having ordered him not to draw attention to her, and faced the other way. Jack turned back to the door. The Savages were definitely at home. He'd heard some activity inside before ringing, only now it had gone silent. He reached for the doorbell again. Before he could press it, however, the front door opened up.

'You again?' It was Ivan. Sasha's kid brother. Immediately Jack remembered the stunt the boy had pulled with the chamomile tea and reminded himself that he wasn't here for payback. He forced a cheery smile. Ivan responded by flattening his lips. 'We're busy,' he said, and moved to close the door.

Jack responded by placing his foot in the boy's way.

'I have something for Sasha,' he said, and produced her earring. 'She left it in my car the other day.'

For a second time, Ivan tried to close the door. He did so with such force that Jack was moved to push back to stop his foot from being crushed. At the same time, he heard urgent whispers from the kitchen.

'She isn't here,' said Ivan, glaring at him. 'I'm home alone.'

All of a sudden, Jack began to worry that his simple plan was falling apart. He only needed a very short time inside the house, only now he couldn't get beyond the threshold.

Mindful that Amanda would be watching from a distance, Jack took it upon himself to barge past Ivan and into the hallway.

'Look, I know you have a special meal happening this evening,' said Jack pleadingly, and clicked the door shut. 'This will only take a moment.'

'But you can't—'

Before Ivan could protest further, Jack turned and hurried into the kitchen. There, he found Sasha helping her mother at the counter while her grandfather played with little Katya in the high chair.

'Jack!' Sasha sounded a little tense as she turned to greet him. 'What a surprise.'

'I hope I'm not interrupting,' he said, and opened his palm to show her the earring. 'I just wanted to return this.'

'Oh, thanks.' Sasha snatched it from his hand. She looked at him expectantly. 'Bye, then.'

So far, Jack calculated that he had been inside the house for all of thirty seconds. It wouldn't be enough to convince Amanda. He needed several more minutes at least.

'So,' he said. 'You're entertaining?'

'Any time now,' she told him, nodding.

Jack looked over Sasha's shoulder. He found her mother and grandfather looking at him nervously.

'Impressive spread,' he said, and nodded at the side dishes on the counter. 'What's on the menu?'

Sasha looked lost for words, which Jack found curious. She turned to Oleg, as if seeking some kind of prompt, who in turn faced Angelica.

'It's a surprise,' she said weakly.

Her explanation hung in the air. Jack looked back at Sasha, and wondered if she was about to be sick. It was then that she glanced around him, just for a moment, but with such tension in her manner that Jack couldn't resist turning to look for himself.

It wasn't the fact that Titus Savage was hiding behind the kitchen door that persuaded Jack to yelp in shock and horror. It was the bald and battered figure swaddled in kitchen foil. The one Titus was struggling to restrain with one hand clamped across the man's mouth.

'Well, hello again, young man!' said Titus, as if this was just a regular get-together, only to grimace in pain as the bald guy chomped into his fingers. With a roar, he released his grip to nurse his hand.

'Don't let them eat me!' cried Vernon, and threw himself upon Jack. All of a sudden, the stunned young man found himself smothered and pinned to the butcher's block. 'I don't want to be dinner!'

'Get off me!' cried Jack, and tried in vain to push him away. 'You're freaks! All of you!'

'Hey!' growled Ivan, who had been watching from the hallway. 'This is our house. Have some respect!'

From underneath Vernon, who had him in a desperate bear hug, Jack glared at Sasha. 'I always thought there was something weird about you and your family!' he snarled, his face contorted with shock and anger. 'Now I know I was right!'

Sasha had been trying in vain to haul Vernon off her ex-boyfriend. When she heard this, however, she let go and took a step away.

'I really thought I'd lucked out when you first showed an interest in me, Jack. You're at the top of every girl's list. You're good looking—'

'Thanks,' Jack said through gritted teeth, still fighting to push the man off him.

Sasha glared at him for interrupting, amazed at the same time that he would even acknowledge her under the circumstances, and then continued with what she had to say.

'Above all, I admired the fact that you called all the shots about the food you eat. That really sold you to me, but then the whole preaching thing kicked in. It might leave you with a clear conscience, Jack, but no meat-free diet can disguise the fact that you're full of crap.'

'Go to hell,' snarled Jack, still pinned to the block. 'And take this lunatic with you!'

Sasha turned to her father.

'Jack dumped me for a vegan,' she told him. 'Only he never had the courage to be upfront about it.'

'Is that true?' Titus focused on Jack, seemingly unconcerned by the gibbering weight on top of him. By now, Vernon had clamped his hands around Jack's wrists. Nose to nose, he was pleading with him incomprehensibly. 'You ditched my daughter for a . . . for a *herbivore?*'

'Someone has to think of their figure!' Once again, Jack attempted to push the sobbing madman away. It was then he remembered that the girl who had seduced him into coming here was watching from the park. 'Amanda, call the police!' he bellowed at the top of his voice, hoping she'd be within earshot. Immediately, Angelica rushed to close the French windows to seal in the noise. 'Call the police, Amanda!'

With one almighty heave, Jack finally succeeded in pushing Vernon aside. The private investigator stumbled backwards, regained his footing and looked around as if expecting another assault. For a moment, nobody moved. Then a noise built in Vernon's throat. At first, it sounded like a whimper, but slowly grew into a growl and finally a battle cry. Then, without further warning, he scrambled over the kitchen table and charged for the French windows. He was out on the patio before the first shard hit the floor, only to stumble and crash onto his belly. With a thud, the crown of Vernon's shaved head hit a pottery plant pot.

'Let him go,' muttered Titus. 'The man deserves some breaks in life.'

Hearing this, Angelica faced her husband. He nodded in response, as if some unspoken exchange between them had just determined the fate of the family. It was then that all eyes turned to Jack. This time, every single member of the Savage household, including baby Kat, stared at him balefully.

'What?' he asked, shrinking from their gaze. 'Sasha, tell them to back off! Even if you're mad at me because I didn't tell you we were finished, this is outright intimid-ation.' Jack took a step away, only to find himself backed against the butcher's block.

'Your comment just then,' said Sasha quietly. 'Are you suggesting I'm fat?'

'I never said that!' Jack looked around, but found no support from her family. He held out his hands. 'You're not fat, Sasha . . . not yet.'

'Here we go again,' said Ivan with a sigh. 'Another attack on meat eaters.'

'You're all crazy,' Jack spat back, frantic now, and glowered at Sasha once more. 'I should've dumped you after our dinner date!'

To his surprise, Sasha smiled to herself and nodded.

'You might have helped me see the light as a vegetarian,' she said, sounding strikingly calm. 'But right now what I need is comfort food.'

'Look, just let me go and you can all get back to your dinner.'

'That won't be possible,' said Titus calmly, and nodded at Ivan. 'If you leave now,' he added, as the boy produced the knife once again, 'we'll have no main course.'

'Jack has been trying to turn vegan,' Ivan pointed out, like this might be a problem. 'And there's no time to properly prepare him.'

Titus didn't once let his gaze slip. If anything, his eyes slowly narrowed. Such was the overwhelming menace in his glare that Jack just froze and whimpered.

'Think of him as corn fed,' he said, and stood aside for his son. 'Corn fed and rustic.'

Amanda Dias heard the cry for help. She had been sitting on the park bench at the time. At first, she chose to ignore it. If Jack Greenway had attempted to carry out a killing, she wanted no part of it if something had gone wrong. Instead, she clasped her hands and focused on the ducks settling in the twilight.

There was something delicious about this moment, she thought to herself. That somebody would commit the ultimate crime for a cause she believed in passionately left her feeling so powerful. Amanda was beyond the law here. Untouchable. The cops would catch up with Jack, of course, and he could protest all he liked that she had set him up to force food ethics onto the agenda. It would never wash in court. There was no evidence beyond his word. Amanda had been sure to check it out, hypothetically, of course, which proved simple as Daddy was a lawyer.

A moment later, Amanda heard the sound of tinkling glass. It came from the direction of the house. Her first thought was to walk away. The noise caused several dogs in the neighborhood to start barking, but after a moment the hum of the city spread out below the park returned a sense of normalcy. She folded her coat against the evening chill, glanced at her watch and waited. From what Jack had told her of the Savage family, they didn't care what meat went into their mouths. If he truly shared her belief that a slaying of this nature would ultimately force people to think about the food that they ate, then the head of the household was a legitimate target. Titus Savage wouldn't be able to defend himself from such a surprise attack. Not like the hunters of old. Those who depended on flesh for their survival.

So, when Jack failed to emerge, her curiosity began to rise. In the back of her mind, Amanda wondered whether he had made up with his ex-girlfriend. He was certainly taking his time in leaving. Of course, she couldn't care less about that, she told herself, though the thought that a boy would choose someone else over her finally prompted her to rise from the bench and find out for herself. She knew it would be safe to take a look. Jack certainly couldn't have stuck a knife in the guy, as he'd promised he would. Had he done so, the alarm would've been raised and the place swarming with police. Whatever was going on in there he'd let her down badly, Amanda decided. She'd been wasting her time.

'Once a vegetarian,' she muttered bitterly, 'always a vegetarian.'

Amanda walked past the house three times before she dared to venture onto the drive. The lights were on, and she could clearly hear activity inside. There was certainly some cooking going on because the stove fan was blowing at full tilt. Immediately, she figured they had invited Jack for a bite to eat. Given how easily he had abandoned his pledge to kill a man, no doubt he had thrown away everything and was enjoying some beef, pork or chicken. Feeling let down, betrayed and angry, Amanda headed for the passage around the side of the house. All she wanted to do was peek inside. Just to confirm that she'd been dealing with a creep.

It was the sight of the flabby-looking man face down and bleeding on the patio that caused her to freeze. At first she thought he was drunk, judging by the way he was groaning, but the silver foil underwear just baffled her. Was this some kind of bachelor party, she thought to herself, and then dared to peer around the corner of the house. She could hear a lot of noise from the kitchen, like dogs competing to wolf down the last few kibbles from a bowl. Crouching at the drainpipe, she saw the broken glass from the French windows. Then, very slowly, she turned to focus on the interior.

'Oh . . . wow,' she whispered to herself after a moment. Her eyes began to widen, her face illuminated from the kitchen as she emerged from her hiding place. Without a doubt, this was an atrocity she was witnessing, but in her mind it took things even further than she had ever imagined. In a stroke, she had stumbled on the only way to eat meat with a clear conscience. The realization hit her so suddenly that it felt as if her life's work had been leading to this moment. Amanda smiled, rising to her feet to face the diners inside. For she had arrived, as darkness closed in, to witness humans turn upon their own kind. A woman stood at the stove, flash frying thin steaks that had come straight from the source thanks to the bald-headed figure carving expertly in the background. As for what was left of Jack, splayed out over the butcher's block, he looked as if he might have died of fright. Still, no animals had suffered for their dinner here. Not the innocent kind. The flesh on the plates was fair game. It was, she realized, on drawing ever closer to the broken window, the *ultimate* in ethical eating.

Just then, one of the family members picked up on her presence. It was the girl that had accompanied Jack to the talk. She seemed different in this light, thought Amanda, and not in a bad way. In fact, the whole family looked to be the sort of people she wanted to know better.

'What is it like?' she asked them.

Such was Amanda's expression of wonder that nobody looked at all threatened by her presence. If anything, they looked transported to another dimension by the food they were eating here.

'Bacon,' said the girl between mouthfuls. 'The best you ever tasted.'

'May I join you?' Amanda Dias waited for her response, entranced by what she had discovered, before carefully making her way across the glass shards that covered the threshold.

DIGESTIF

To the neighbors and nearby residents, it felt like ages before the media moved on. For weeks after Vernon English found the strength to stumble into the road to raise the alarm, the house was under siege from camera crews, journalists, photographers and the plain curious. The police cordon held them back while the house was practically pulled apart. When the investigation finally finished, building contractors moved in to board up the doors and windows. From that day on, the house set about a slow decay. Weeds sprung from every crack and crevice in the brickwork, while dead leaves gathered in the porch as if seeking shelter from the wind.

Once, at the skate park, Maisy and Faria overheard Liam Parker boast that he had managed to climb into the Savages' back garden at night. Together with his cousin Tyler, they claimed to have broken in through the back door and then taken a tour by flashlight.

'What was it like inside?' asked Maisy, who turned to pay him attention for what felt like the first time in her life.

'The place is stripped bare,' said Tyler, a heavy-set kid whose stripy T-shirt and tight jeans made him look like a badly squeezed tube of toothpaste. 'Looks like it hasn't been lived in for one hundred years. There's dust and cobwebs everywhere.'

'Were you scared?' asked Faria.

Liam punched the end of his skateboard with one foot. He aimed to flip it into his hand, but instead it just slapped him in the groin.

'The Savages aren't coming back,' he croaked, and collected the board to hide the fact that his face was knotted with pain. When he straightened up, he found both girls waiting for more. 'They're gone,' he said with some certainty. 'But it's frightening to think that they're out there somewhere.'

Vernon English's physical injuries didn't take long to heal. It was the mental scars that ran deep. He had been picked up by a squad car, following reports at first light that a man in a silver foil loincloth was staggering about attempting to flag down motorists near the park. Initially, his claim that he'd been kidnapped by cannibals was met with disbelief. The man was disturbed, the arresting officer assumed, and had most probably inflicted the injuries on himself. When a doctor was called to the station, largely because Vernon was so agitated, it was quickly recognized that he couldn't have shaved his own back, and so two officers were dispatched as a precaution to the address he kept repeating.

What they found didn't match the description of sheer horror that Vernon had described. There was no evidence that a freshly slain human body had been disemboweled, cut up, cooked and consumed. The kitchen was sparkling, though they couldn't ignore the smell of fresh bleach in the sink and the waste disposal unit. What raised their suspicions further was the French window. Despite the absence of any broken glass, the pane was missing on one side. With no sign of anyone at home, they decided to radio in some concerns.

The Detective Inspector, when he finally arrived, had a keen eye for what was missing from a potential crime scene. In this case, once he'd conducted a search of every room, he concluded that the Savage family should be located as a matter of urgency. They weren't suspected of any wrongdoing, so he stressed at the time, but it certainly seemed as if they had packed and left for a long vacation. Something wasn't right, specifically in the kitchen. The fridge and the freezer had been stripped and cleaned, and the oven washed down with some kind of industrial scouring agent. As it was highly unlikely that thieves had broken in to clean the house from top to bottom, the decision was taken to call in forensics.

From that moment on, slide by slide under the microscope, the secret that the Savages had strived to keep to themselves began to seep out.

It started with a shred of grilled meat trapped between the seat and the back rest of a toddler's high chair. As soon as that was proven to be of human origin, a full-scale inquiry was launched. Within the space of a day, the house was cloaked in scaffolding and tarpaulin, and crawling with specialists in white biohazard suits.

The investigation was intense, but it was only following

a visit from Vernon that things began to piece together. Still barely speaking following his ordeal, he led them to the white police tent that covered the shed, hauled back an old piece of carpet and pointed to the concrete floor. It had proven to be surprisingly easy to break through, as if only recently set, and horribly upsetting when the first investigator pointed a flashlight into the pit. Not only had they uncovered some kind of underground slaughterhouse, several trash bags had been dropped in containing clothing, along with the bones of an adolescent male. Following tests, it was concluded that the human remains had reached a high temperature, not in some failed bid to incinerate the evidence but as if roasted in a domestic oven.

Everyone knew it was Jack Greenway before the police confirmed it at the press conference. He had gone missing at exactly the same time as the Savages. During their witness interviews, Faria and Maisy reported that Sasha and Jack had been experiencing issues in their relationship, but stressed that nobody expected her to break off with him like this. For a while, in private, the pair talked about what they knew in total disbelief. Surely their friend wasn't capable of some of the things they were hearing? Slowly, however, as the story began to sink in, they looked back at their time with Sasha and began to see her in a different light. Food was important to her, as Vernon kept stressing during questioning, and so was family. Despite all the friction with her father, there was a bond that seemed to strengthen whenever they sat down to eat. That was when they talked. It was the glue that held them together. Maisy and Faria's testimonies also backed this up. At school, they even found themselves defending their friend at times. Not for the flesh-eating. That was gross and always would be. Sasha might've had a taste for human heart, but despite it all, they maintained, hers was in the right place.

For the Savage family, it was to be their last supper in that house. Maybe Titus had already decided that it was time to move on, or perhaps he let his appetite get the better of him. Whether it was an oversight or deliberately planted so there was no going back, one tiny sliver of what turned out to be Jack's bicep, trapped down the back of the high chair, was all it took to make headlines. Whatever the case, Titus knew how to vanish with his loved ones. Everything was shut down overnight, from his company to Facebook profiles, email and bank accounts, but not before he settled his wife's outstanding debt and notified the locations agency that their services were no longer required. Titus had everything covered so well that in effect the family consumed themselves.

Despite an international manhunt, no trace of Titus, Angelica, Sasha, Ivan, little Katya and their grandfather was ever discovered. Nor did the authorities ever learn what fate befell the vegan extremist, Amanda Dias. Before the alleged atrocity took place, CCTV cameras picked her up in the park, looking tense and restless. Some minutes later, she had taken off in the direction of the Savages. Inside the house, her fingerprints were found on a fork, but that was where the trail ended. Her father argued that she must've grabbed it in self-defense. Others quietly believed she had crossed over to a side that was generally believed to be unthinkable. It provoked no war between food factions, just a lot of discussion.

As for Vernon English, the private investigator at the center of the saga, he worked hard to profit from the situation before taking early retirement. His book, a memoir about the experience, and how he solved the mysterious case of Lulabelle Hart, went on to become a huge Christmas bestseller. Combined with the criminal injuries payout, he now lives happily on the south coast with his publicist and partner. The couple are expecting their first child.

Faria and Maisy didn't receive as much attention from the media. This was mostly down to their parents, who agreed between themselves that it was in the girls' best interest to be sheltered from the storm. They had their exams, after all, which they took in a packed hall with one spare desk set aside for the student on unauthorized leave of absence. Both are now in their junior year, but no longer hang out on the skate ramp. As Maisy has just learned to drive, they prefer to head into town at lunch break.

Once, when the pair opted for the sandwich shop, they spotted a guy with a hoodie and an early-stage beard who was also interviewed during the investigation, and came out with his reputation intact. Neither knew what Ralph had meant to Sasha, but they could appreciate what she saw in him. Watching him select a hummus, arugula and chickpea on whole wheat, only to switch it for a bacon, lettuce and tomato on white, Maisy joked that he'd probably opted for the meat in memory of what was missing from his life. Faria wondered out loud, a little too noisily for Maisy's liking, whether Sasha might secretly be in touch, but the pair weren't brave enough to approach Ralph and ask. Instead, they figured that even if he was in possession of that kind of information, he didn't look the sort who would betray her. Both Maisy and Faria treated the encounter as a bit of a giggle, and indeed it's clear the two friends are determined not to let the Savage saga overshadow their future. Still, you only have to look at the sheer number of people who follow the pair on Twitter to recognize how hard this will be for them. As the majority are strangers, it's clear their lives have been opened up to the world forever by Sasha and her infamous family.

From time to time, when curiosity gets the better of them, the girls scroll through their followers, and wonder which one their friend has created as cover. It's just a feeling, they say, and joke that's how it must be for antelope on the plains. Then the laughter trails away, for both remain convinced that Sasha and her siblings, as well as her parents and grandfather, aren't just watching but working up an appetite. At any time and place, so they believe, and possibly with new recruits to their cause, the Savages will return from the wild.

ACKNOWLEDGEMENTS

I was serving tea to my children when I came up with the idea for this novel. We were tightening our belts on the budget front, and I'd worked out that it would be cheaper to cut the meat from their diets. Knowing there would be protests – not least on the morality of making this decision on their behalf – I decided to stay quiet. Instead, I bought a vegetarian cookbook, and made a big effort to serve up tasty, nutritious and flesh-free suppers. The result? Rare compliments about my cooking and second helpings all round. It only lasted for a fortnight or so before someone asked out loud when we'd last had bangers and mash, but as a culinary experiment it gave me a great deal of food for thought.

As well as the kids in their role as guinea pigs, I should like to thank my wife, Emma, for her help and support as I cooked up the story. For managing me in different ways, I'm indebted to my literary agent, Philippa Milnes-Smith, her assistant, Holly, all at LAW, as well as Franca Bernatavicius and everyone at ILA. The historian, Roger Moorhouse, graciously helped me with the finer details regarding the Siege of Leningrad, while our sausage dog, Hercules, did little to assist the peace as I worked by barking at every squirrel outside my window.

Finally, I should like to thank my original publishers for this opportunity to bring you *The Savages*. Hot Key Books are new kids on the block, but quickly becoming the coolest. I've worked elsewhere with my editor, Emily Thomas, but she really wasn't expecting this. Even so, she showed great resolve when I first pitched it, and her enthusiasm for the story has been second to none. It's been great fun working with the whole team, and my wholehearted thanks go out to Sarah Odedina, Georgia Murray, Megan Farr, Kate Manning, Becca Langton, Naomi Colthurst, Jet Purdie, Sara O'Connor, Amy Orringer, Sarah Benton, Cait Davies, Olivia Mead, Ruth Logan, Jan Bielecki, Tristan Hanks and Dominic Saraceno. I'm also grateful to the wonderful and enthusiastic team at The Overlook Press in New York for bringing you this edition of the book.

MATT WHYMAN

Matt Whyman is a distinctive contemporary voice in cutting edge teen fiction. His books include the acclaimed *Boy Kills Man* and the Carl Hobbes thrillers, as well as the comic memoir *Oink! My Life with Minipigs*.

Find out more about Matt at www.mattwhyman.com and on Twitter: @mattwhyman